MURDER
2014 FIRST WINNER
MYSTERY/SUSPENSE
Kindle Book Promo/LuckyCinda International Contest

MURDER IN ONE TAKE

This perfectly crafted Hollywood murder peels back the curtain on not one, but two worlds, giving the reader a glimpse into the glamour of show business and the slow grind of down-and-dirty police work, blending the two domains in clever metatextual ways. Plenty of snappy banter and clenched-jaw exposition...all the intrigue of Hollywood's big-budget blockbusters.

— *Kirkus Reviews*

MURDER: TAKE TWO

Kelly and Lyons return to their distinctive brand of mystery starring the LA-based duo (Maureen O'Brien and Blake Ervansky) who combine traditional investigation with the Hollywood perspective. Darker than its predecessor, this installment doesn't sacrifice the humor or turns of phrase that were the hallmarks of the first. Tight and sharp-witted.

— *Kirkus Reviews*

MURDER: TAKE THREE
2014 SHAMUS AWARD FINALIST
Best Indie P.I. Novel

Also by Marsha Lyons and April Kelly

Murder: Take Two

Murder: Take Three

Also by April Kelly

Winged

To Margaret! Enjoy!

MURDER IN ONE TAKE

by

April Kelly & Marsha Lyons

MURDER IN ONE TAKE
is a work of fiction. No resemblance between the characters in this novel and any person, living or dead, is implied or intended.

Published April 2012

ISBN: 978-0615645339

Library of Congress: TXu 1-784-886

For additional information about this or any other Flight Risk Books fiction, or to contact one of our authors, please go to http://www.flightriskbooks.com

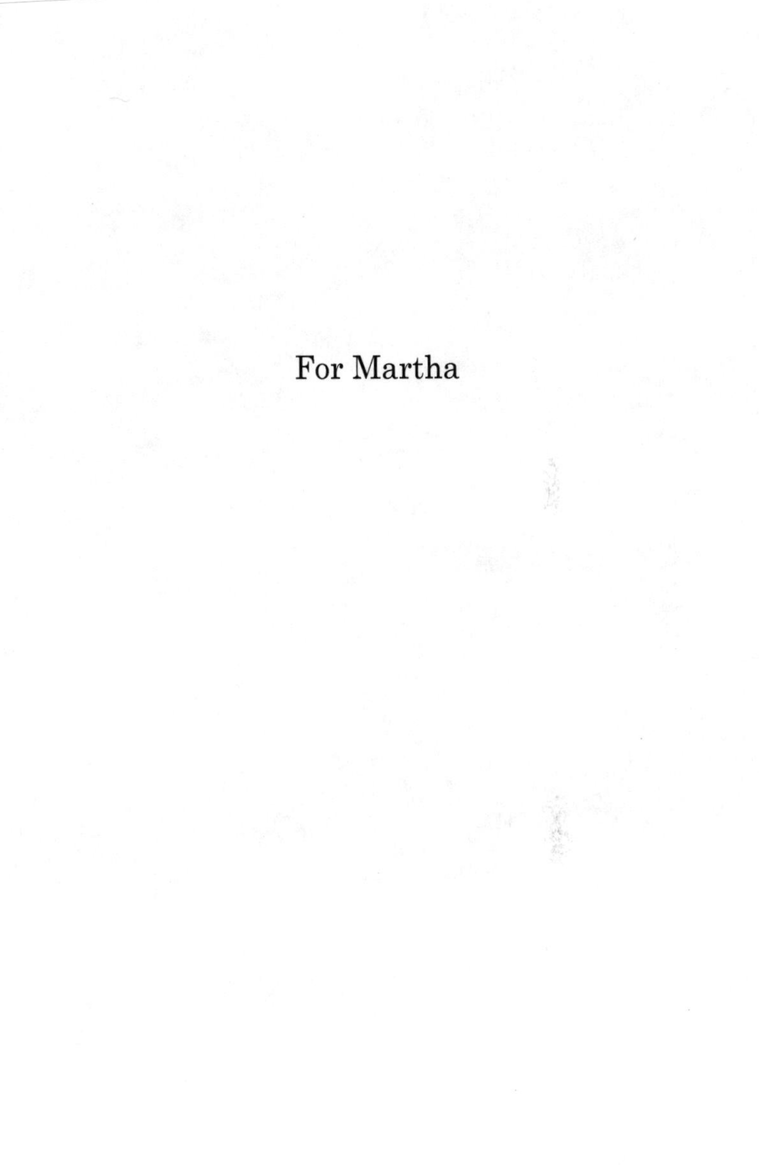

For Martha

If I don't die in the next two minutes, Blake thought, I have a pretty good chance of being alive at the end of the day. As a police detective, he was well aware of the risk involved when interacting with the armed and dangerous criminal element of the ironically named City of Angels, but he was pragmatic enough to admit the most harrowing part of his workday was backing out of his carport onto that snaky ribbon of asphalt that was Lookout Mountain Avenue.

When Blake bought the house three years earlier he had considered only two things, the just-shy-of-Olympics-sized swimming pool in the sunken back yard, and the record-low interest rates that meant his mortgage payment would be lower than monthly rent on the elfin-sized West Hollywood apartment he shared with an actor-waiter hyphenate.

The realtor had sucked the naiveté out of him the way a hyena does marrow, using words like "lush, tree-shaded seclusion" rather than the less salable "brush fire hazard," and reframing the house's seediness as rusticity. She confided that an über producer had lived there before massive success propelled him out of hippy-dippy Laurel Canyon and into the more rarefied atmosphere of Bel-Air. Her proof was the image of the computer-generated dragon that had been the star of the producer's first blockbuster movie, painted on the underside of the toilet lid in the master bath.

Having foolishly bragged about his new home's pedigree at the station, Blake quickly learned there wasn't a bungalow, hotel room, house or apartment in LA that didn't claim at least a tenuous link to Hollywood legend, past or present. He didn't care; he loved his home and had spent the last thirty-six months on do-it-yourself projects to soften its flaws and inch it back toward its glory days, circa 1978.

The only problem Blake hadn't been able to solve was the poorly designed carport. There were no sidewalks up in the canyon, and the impossibly short concrete ped went right to the road's edge without an inch of driveway. The carport was barely wide enough for two vehicles to be nosed in—as long as you didn't try to open your doors all the way. Because the cramped space wouldn't allow even the smallest of wheel bases to negotiate a three-pointer, and since the house was situated below the hairiest of the many hairpin turns on Lookout, every morning Blake backed out blindly and hoped for the best.

Today the man he had decided was an agent did not come hurtling down the mountain in his Hummer, cell phone in one hand, cigarette in the other, and Lord-only-knows-what steering that land yacht. No agitated soccer mom in her suburban assault vehicle careened around the hairpin, yelling at the kids in the back seat while trying to keep her coffee in its cup as the SUV tilted against the centrifugal force of the turn. And mercifully, not one of the future Indy 500 drivers attending Hollywood High was qualifying this morning.

Hey, thought Blake, as he headed down the mountain, a quarter past five and no one has tried to kill me so far. He drove the tree-lined corkscrew down to the light at Laurel, where the lack of gridlock finally made him realize why this morning was different; he was leaving two hours earlier than usual, so the hookers, junkies and club zombies had already gone night-night, while the worker bees, tourists and people of leisure hadn't gotten up yet.

Say what you will about the mass-death horror of a postapocalyptic hellscape, Blake mused, but the driving's going to be sweet.

Det. Blake Ervansky was on his way to pick up Sgt. O'Brien, his partner of less than twenty-four hours. Yesterday had been the last day for Artie Lassiter, his previous partner, and it was during the cake, coffee and gag-gift send-off party that the lieutenant had brought O'Brien in to be introduced.

The not-so-subtle hiss that accompanied O'Brien's entrance had been the sound of a man sucking in his gut, multiplied by a factor of every male cop in the room. In a city where the bar for beauty was set almost impossibly high, Sgt. O'Brien was a stunner.

"Ervansky, I'd like you to meet your new compadre, Sgt. Maureen O'Brien."

"Hey," Blake said, extending his hand and

getting a handshake that was firmer than expected. "Good to meet you."

"And this is Artie Lassiter," continued the lieutenant. "He chose early retirement rather than spend another week riding in a car with Ervansky."

Hoots from the crowd as Artie also shook hands with the new member of the squad. "You know, boss, I'm rethinking this whole retirement thing. Maybe Blake should go and I'll ride with O'Brien."

Sgt. O'Brien smiled good-naturedly as she shrugged and said, "Fine by me," eliciting a few more responses from the entertained audience.

The lieutenant glanced over at the two female detectives who watched with amusement as all the boys preened and posed. "I'm counting on you two to make sure none of these guys gives Sgt. O'Brien a reason to discharge her firearm into his person. Ervansky, can I have a word?"

"Sure."

Artie began making the intros all around while Blake followed Lt. Rhee into his office.

"Go ahead and shut the door," Rhee said, settling into the chair behind his desk.

"What's up?"

"Two things. First, you're not going to be in on the Pico takedown tonight."

"Screw *that*. I've been working the case for three months."

"Yeah, we've *all* been working it," Rhee admonished. "So nobody gets to be a superstar tonight. Between our guys, SWAT, the K-9 unit and those two from the DEA, I'm pretty sure we can do this without you."

"Who'd I piss off this time?"

"All of the regulars, but that's not why you're sitting it out." He took a sheet of paper from his desk and handed it to Blake. "We finally have a fix on Randall Vayne." As Blake scanned the page, an incredulous look on his face, the lieutenant continued. "A year we've been searching for that douchebag and it turns out he's working five blocks from here."

"Sometimes you can't see the felons for the trees."

"He's a nervy bastard, all right. Scored himself a stock clerk job, although how a high-end store like Carrera's didn't see through his phony resume is beyond me."

"I'm assuming he leaves off all that grand larceny and incarceration stuff," Blake said.

"Yeah, well, before he backs up a U-Haul and makes off with a few million bucks' worth of designer suits, I want you and O'Brien to grab him in the morning when he shows up to work at seven."

"Why don't we do it now?"

"By the time I got that e-mail, he had left for the day, and we still don't know where he's holed up. Our best bet is the store, and we've got to do it before regular shopping hours."

"Ah, the manager doesn't want his rich clientele watching a street creep get cuffed on the cravat aisle."

"You have the gist."

"Okay," Blake sighed, laying the sheet of paper back on Rhee's desk. "I'll do it. But you owe me a violent drug bust."

"Put it on my tab."

Blake walked toward the door, then right before his hand grabbed the knob, the lieutenant spoke again. "Blake?"

"Yeah?"

"You remember the job I sent you and Artie out on *your* first day?"

"The rabbit smuggler?"

"Yes. While you two were busting an old Asian man for sneaking meat bunnies over the border, the rest of us went into a warehouse full of cocaine with guns blazing."

"And the moral of that story is what? You didn't think I was up to the task?"

"The moral is I don't like any of my people getting shot at on their first day." He reached for the phone and punched in a number. "Call it a quirk."

When Blake got back to the squad room, everyone had gone but Artie and Sgt. O'Brien. It was only a little after four, but all the deets had gone home to rest up before their midnight rendezvous back at the station.

"There he is," boomed Artie. "I'm getting O'Brien wired into the system." He glanced down at the sergeant, who tapped away at the computer on his old desk. "Got your password set?"

"Yep. I was torn between *password* and *booger*, so I went with the less obvious." She hit a final key, looked up and smiled. "Done."

Artie slung his bear-like arm around Blake's shoulders and gave a quick crunch. "You take care of my partner, Sarge. He's like a brother to me."

"A taller, better-looking and much-younger brother," Blake added, then winced as Artie's second crunch did some damage.

"Blake, I'll see you tomorrow night at

Roy's. And you are welcome to join us," Artie said to O'Brien. "Your new partner's buying."

"Thanks. I may take you up on that."

Artie turned to leave, raising his right hand in a combination salute and wave.

Sgt. O'Brien looked up at Blake. "Roy's?"

"Roy's Ranchero on West Olympic. So-so Tex-Mex and a full bar."

"What's the occasion?"

"Artie's *real* going-away party. Cake and coffee here in the house is a bit of kabuki theater for the brass. No member of this squad retires without consuming his body weight in beer, tequila and enchiladas."

"I'll see if I can still squeeze into my quinceañera gown."

As Blake sat at his own desk, he smiled at the mental picture of this very Irish redhead wearing a flouncy wedding cake of a dress for the Hispanic equivalent of a bat mitzvah.

"So, while you were confabbing with the lieutenant, I heard some buzz about a raid tonight."

"Sadly, he rescinded our invitation to the shootout."

"Damn. I've got on a Kevlar cami today."

Blake barely contained the urge to drop his gaze to her chest, maintaining eye contact as she grinned. He had the distinct impression she knew exactly what he was desperately trying not to do. "No, you and I have an early morning date to pick up one of America's Ten-Least-Wanted criminals. He won't be armed, but he is slippery. Not to mention fast."

"I'll wear running shoes, Detective."

"Blake."

"Blake it is. And I'm Maureen."

"Do people call you Mo?"

"Only once."

"Got it. Sorry I had to leave you to the wolves earlier, but I'm guessing Artie gave you the tour."

"He seems like a terrific guy. They were all really nice. Actually, all but one."

Blake dropped his chin to his chest and squeezed his eyes shut with aggravation. "Willis?"

"Does he get *all* his material from the *Hustler* magazine pick-up manual?"

"Let me give you a blanket apology for anything and everything Willis says to you in the coming months."

"Oh, I've handled worse," Maureen said, amused.

"You could do us all a service by goading him into making a sexist remark in front of witnesses. One more flag in his file and he'll be busted down to uniform."

"I can do that. But first I'd like to bat him around like a ball of yarn for a few weeks."

The smile she flashed Blake was dazzling. Evil, but still dazzling.

As Blake turned left off Franklin Avenue and headed up into Nichols Canyon, he went over his first impressions of Sgt. O'Brien. She was obviously aware of how attractive she was, and yet she had that self-effacing sense of humor usually found in women who need to rely more on their personality than looks. Maureen was sensitive enough to know Artie was a harmless teddy bear and that his comment about riding with her was a humorous icebreaker for the squad, but she had pegged Willis immediately and was too smart to take his bait.

Her clothes had been simple and tasteful, dark brown slacks, tailored shirt in a cream color, and a tan blazer. No accessories and no jewelry other than small diamond studs which he only noticed because a loose ponytail pulled back her red hair. And not that God-awful orangey color sported by rock stars and Carrot Top. More of a reddish gold.

His overall impression was that Maureen O'Brien was one of only a few women in Los Angeles trying to play down her looks rather than emphasizing them. In the ten years since he moved here to go to UCLA, he had learned that with the right hair stylist, makeup artist, fitness trainer and plastic surgeon, any plain girl could become a real cutie, a cute girl could aspire to being pretty, and the pretty ones could be transformed into absolute beauties. He couldn't imagine what impact O'Brien would have on people if she bothered to darken the lashes around her electric blue eyes, dusted a little blush on those cheekbones, wore something a little girlier than slacks and a blazer, and let those red-gold waves fly loose.

Blake jolted out of his reverie, realizing his thoughts had strayed way beyond a new-partner evaluation and were heading towards something he didn't want or need to be thinking about. She had told him Acacia was a tiny cul-de-sac halfway up the canyon, so he engaged his mind in locating the turnoff.

When he found Acacia and made the left, he saw there were only three houses, the two on either side that were set back from the street far enough to be nearly obscured by trees, and the two-story Spanish dead ahead. Even before he drove onto the wide circular driveway and pulled up in front of the impressive porte cochere, Blake could tell the house was in the two-million-plus range. O'Brien must rent the guest house, he thought, as the arched wooden front door swung open and she came out. The palette was black, white and gray today, but the understatement was the same.

"You're early," she said, sliding into the shotgun seat.

"I sacrificed a goat to the traffic gods."

She pulled the seat belt across and clicked it into place as Blake slowly rounded the curve of the drive. Right before he rolled back out onto the street, he hooked his thumb over his shoulder and said, "That's some house."

"Isn't it beautiful? I really love it."

All the unasked questions hung in the air when she didn't elaborate, so Blake decided a little joke might prod her into an explanation. "Don't tell me; you live with a rich old guy who buys you everything your heart desires."

He expected a laugh and an admission that she was house-sitting for some celebrity who was vacationing in Europe, but what he got was a surprised—maybe even disappointed—look. Then she stared straight ahead and said, "He's *older,* yes. But I don't think he'd appreciate being called *old.*"

Oh Jesus, Blake thought, I've stepped in it now. But before he could verbalize a back-pedaling apology, Maureen, still staring out the front windshield, continued. "And he *does* buy me some pretty lavish gifts. Jewelry, techie gadgets, even the car I drive. Anything else you need to know before we work together?"

Blake realized whatever he said would only make the situation more uncomfortable, so he shook his head and minded the road. After a few hour-long minutes went by, Maureen asked, "You talk to anybody about the raid?"

"No," he replied, thankful for neutral turf. "I checked in at 4:30, but no one was back at the station yet. Was anything on TV?" He knew there hadn't been, but he was desperate to keep a safe conversation going.

"Nothing on the national news."

"Yeah, the locals are probably only getting it about now."

Silence again in the car, but without the static charge of a few minutes earlier. Maureen appeared to be fine, but Blake knew she had to think she was being judged by him. Here the lieutenant had gone out of his way to give them a safe and sane first ride together so they could do the usual bio-swap and begin that unique cop bonding that eventually makes you dead certain your partner has your back, and Blake had blown it with one stupid remark.

What O'Brien does on her own time is *her* business, he thought. She's not a date; she's my partner, and all I need to know is whether or not she's solid. What would I say if it were Artie in that seat? And just like that, he knew. "Listen, it's too early to pick up Vayne, and they've all got to be back at the station by now. Want to swing by so they can give us grief for not being heroes last night?"

She smiled for the first time since Blake

had implied she was a 24-karat gold digger. "Yeah, let's start our day with a little abuse from our co-workers. It'll keep us from feeling too cocky about collaring that semi-badass Randall Vayne."

Blake was relieved she was smiling and he wanted to keep the truce alive, so he said, "He may be unarmed but that doesn't mean he can't bitch slap one of us."

Maureen responded in a deep, growling Southern accent. "Dude tries that on me, they gonna find him hung by his own large intestine."

Blake laughed, then realized he'd heard that exact line before. Only he couldn't recall where.

As soon as he saw Det. Johnson's face, Blake knew something was wrong, and the first words that flashed in his mind were the two no cop ever wants to hear, *officer down.*

"Libby, what the hell?"

Det. Johnson grimly nodded toward the break room, and Blake followed her. Maureen hesitated until the tall, whip-thin black woman signaled for her to come, too.

Libby Johnson closed the door and leaned against it, obviously angry and tired. "A total fuck-up."

"Anybody hurt?"

"No, but you can consider that the *only* silver lining."

"What happened?"

"We held back until the undercover inside texted that all the patrons had gone. This was around 2:45. So, we're getting ready to drop our cocks and grab our socks when the front door swings open and Nasilikov steps outside and yells, 'Free drinks for law enforcement,' then he waves us over."

Blake shook his head in disgust. "I'll take dirtballs for fifty, Alex. What is zero cocaine?"

"Not even the hint of a shadow of the ghost of a snort. It was like the Mafia Merry Maids went through there with one of those Dyson tornado suckers."

"You think the u.c. got made?"

"He was sitting with the rest of Dimitri's goons while we tossed the place, so either he's still good or when they made him, they decided it would be more fun to make us look like idiots than to ice him."

Maureen watched the interaction between her new partner and Det. Johnson, deciding there was a strong mutual respect between them. Her observation was correct. Blake and Libby had gravitated toward each other six years earlier when he had joined the squad, maybe because they had both gone to college on athletic scholarships, Blake's for swimming, Libby's for basketball. Fourteen years ago Liberty J, as she called herself back then, had lit up the court at LSU, as well as the eyes of thousands of aspiring young female athletes. There wasn't a team in the WNBA that didn't want to see her signature shaved head in their lineup.

And she would have signed with one of them had some alcohol-fueled cracker moron not gone on what he later told a judge was a "coon hunt" and shot her older brother as he walked home from church with his wife and baby girl.

Blake didn't know Libby's backstory, but he and Artie had asked her for help many times after getting nowhere with one of those smarmy little white boys who thinks he's a gangsta. Sometimes all it took was for Libby to make an ominous entrance into the interview room, bend until her still-closely-cropped skull was almost touching the punk's, then whisper something in his ear. Blake and Artie had never asked her exactly what she said to make them start talking instantly, and Libby had never volunteered the information. Slumped against the door as she was right now, she looked more weary than threatening.

"I'm going in to talk to the lieutenant," Blake said.

"I wouldn't," she replied, crossing to the coffee pot.

The door opened and Det. Willis came in. "Is this a private party or can anyone join?" Blake brushed past him without comment, and Libby didn't look up from the last few dregs she poured into a Styrofoam cup. Willis grinned when he saw Maureen sitting by herself.

"So, Sgt. O. Did you give any thought to my offer?"

"The one about dinner, a movie and, how exactly did you put it? Oh, yes, a moonlight hot-tub skinny dip. I'm still mulling it over." With that, she stood to leave.

"Don't mull too long, babe. I'm a man in demand."

Libby grimaced, maybe from the taste of the java sludge, maybe from Willis' comment. Maureen crossed to the door, Willis' eyes on her the whole way. He couldn't resist taking one more run at the hot redhead before she got away. "O'Brien, you make me want to break my rule about not limiting myself to only one woman."

She stopped at the door, turned back toward him, flashed that dazzling smile, and sweetly responded, "Det. Willis, you make *me* want to break the Sixth Commandment."

Libby almost choked on her sludge as Maureen all-but-sashayed through the door for Willis' benefit. The pudgy detective, totally misreading the situation, looked eagerly at Libby. "The Sixth. Isn't that the one about shalt not doing adultery? Holy crap, is she saying she wants to screw me?"

Libby unfolded her lanky frame from the chair, tossed her empty in the trash can and gave him a grin. "Willis, if you mess with *that* girl, I guaran-goddamn-*tee* you're going to get screwed."

In two long-legged strides she was out of the room, leaving Willis to bask in a fantasy involving red-gold hair, a thong and the hot tub at his apartment building.

Ten minutes later Blake and Maureen were back in the car, and Blake pulled out onto Little Santa Monica heading west. "I never got in to talk to the lieutenant."

"And I never got a cup of coffee."

"You don't want to drink that swill." He checked his watch. "We can swing by that new Starbucks on Camden. It's only a block away from where we're going and we've still got a few minutes to kill."

As he sailed past Rodeo Drive, Maureen pointed. "Camden's one way north. Shouldn't we have turned there and gone around?"

"Normally I would, but Mr. Vayne has an unusually keen cop radar and I don't want to accidentally cruise by him before he's trapped in Carrera's." Blake passed Camden, then put on his blinker to turn south onto Bedford. Halfway down the block toward Wilshire, with the car on the left side of the street, Blake hit the signal again to loop around onto Camden. Two quick, loud, unmistakable pops off to the right caught Blake's attention at the same time Maureen yelled, "Jesus! She shot that guy! Pull over!"

The car slammed to a stop against the curb, and Maureen launched herself out the door, pulling her gun as she ran across the four lanes. "Police! Drop the gun now!"

Blake got out as fast as he could, but he had to go around the back of the car before crossing, so he was a few steps behind his partner as they got to the nightmarish scene on the Beverly Hills sidewalk.

A young woman with a compact Beretta dangling loosely from her lowered right hand stood trembling, eyes wide with horror, and seemingly unaware that Sgt. O'Brien aimed a gun at her from only a few feet away. The woman also appeared not to hear the repeated instructions to drop her weapon.

Blake kneeled to see if the victim was still alive. He tried to find the man's carotid artery, not an easy task with blood still pumping out of where a face used to be. Through the slick wet, Blake felt the tough ridges of the vic's trachea, then slid his fingers an inch to one side and pressed in. He felt a beat, a beat, a beat, then nothing. He reached for his phone, smearing blood on his shirt and tie as he pulled the cell from his inside jacket pocket.

Realizing the shooter was incapacitated

from fear or shock, Maureen cautiously took the .32 from her, touching it only by the barrel.

Blake could feel blood soaking through the knees of his trousers as he stood, calling for backup. Meanwhile his partner cuffed both wrists of shooter-girl, who remained wide-eyed and unresponsive, even as she began to shake more violently.

Only seconds had gone by since the incident, but the street was already coming alive. A dozen women in workout clothes poured through the door of the building next to the crime scene, one woman shrieking "Ali!" as she ran toward the shooter. Maureen kept her right hand on the suspect's biceps, but threw her left out to straight-arm the woman running toward her. Calmly but forcefully, Maureen ordered her to step back.

Blake saw people—lots of them—jumping out of two unmarked white vans that were parked at the curb near the crime scene, and then chaos erupted. As the area was swarmed he tried to maintain a perimeter, barking at the instant mob to stand clear, but with Maureen holding the shooter, Blake had trouble preventing that many people from contaminating the scene. The *wah-wahs* of the sirens grew deafening, and Blake knew he only had to hold off the crowd for another minute or so, but the workout-clothes women were hugging each other and crying, the mob was pressing in for a look, and one man broke free and managed to get by him. Before Blake could turn and grab him, the man darted to the dead man, shouting, "Christ, she killed Dev Roberts!"

When the shooter heard the name, her

eyes rolled up and her knees gave way. Maureen barely got both arms around the woman before they both sank to the ground.

Blake realized a man in the crowd had a video camera on his shoulder, aimed at the victim, so he launched himself in that direction. The last sound the camera picked up was Blake's voice yelling, "Turn it off, asshole!" And the last image it recorded was Blake's bloody palm coming straight at the lens.

The first two questions normally asked following a homicide are who and how. But with fourteen witnesses, including Sgt. O'Brien, who had been looking out the front right window as Ali Garland raised the gun and shot Dev Roberts, they moved on to the third question. Why?

To that end, and with so many people to talk to, the men and women of the Beverly Hills PD utilized every interview room, office and large closet to take statements. For most of them it had already been a long, tough night, and the day was shaping up to be even worse. The crowd of reporters and photographers had been growing steadily in the two hours since the shooting, and as every witness was interviewed and released, a second round of questions fired at them as they ran the media gauntlet in front of the station.

A few reporters stayed at the crime scene with the CSI team, gleaning what details and color they could, but the real action was at the station, where everyone knew by now actress Ali Garland was being held for killing Dev Roberts. Although Dev was a much higher temperature on Hollywood's hot meter, *he* had already been bagged and tagged, so Ali became de facto chum for the sharks.

Ali sat slumped at a table in the main interview room, holding a blanket around her shoulders and staring vacantly at the can of diet soda in front of her. The doctor who had examined her dropped his stethoscope into his case, then patted her shoulder and left the room.

Blake, Maureen and Lt. Rhee waited as the doctor closed the door behind himself. "She's fine. You can have at her."

"Is she going to have another seizure or whatever that was at the scene?" asked Blake.

"No, I spoke with the EMTs. Since she was awake and alert when they arrived, and she claims not to have any history of epilepsy or other seizures, I'm betting she—and forgive the medical jargon—freaked the hell out."

"Dr. Boyce, thanks for your help," Rhee said. "And you'll send me the clearance?"

"Oh, I realize how high-profe this one is. I'll cover your ass by e-mail later on today."

The doctor nodded to Maureen and Blake, then turned and walked down the corridor. The lieutenant looked at his two investigators. "You Mirandize her?"

"Twice," offered Maureen. "But I don't think she heard me either time."

"Okay, go do it again for the benefit of audio and video. I want every T crossed and every I dotted. Ervansky, hang back a minute."

Maureen glanced at Blake, then opened the door to the interview room. When it had whooshed shut, Rhee spoke. "How'd she do?"

"No mistakes, no hesitation. She handled Miss Thing in there, got the murder weapon, controlled the rubberneckers and didn't even pop a curl out of place."

Rhee arched his eyebrow at that last comment but decided to let it go. "Sounds like Wonder Woman did it all."

"You know me, I was leaning against the car eating my doughnut. Only jumped in when it looked safe."

"That must have been when you got all that blood on you."

Blake glanced down at himself. "Shit."

"Speaking of which, I'm going to need a big-ass scraper to keep the fan blades clean on this one. Since you and O'Brien were on scene when it all went down I'm going to let you take point for now."

"For now? Hey, thanks for the big vote of confidence."

"Don't get cute, Ervansky. If she hasn't asked for a lawyer yet, go in there and push her to call one."

"You're joking, right?" Rhee's expression convinced Blake he was serious. "Why?"

"In twenty-three years I don't think I've ever been handed a homicide gift-wrapped as nicely as this." He ticked off his fingers as he continued. "Suspect, murder weapon, live video coverage times four, clear motive and enough eyewitnesses to field a couple hockey teams. We don't *need* whatever she can tell us to nail her, and by hooking her up with counsel ASAP we avoid any hint of strong-arming a fragile young woman and having the public turn on us. And I don't care how good her lawyer is, when he-she-or-it sees what we have he'll advise his client to take whatever the DA offers."

Blake nodded thoughtfully. Everything

the lieutenant said made some kind of sideways sense, but there was a piece of it he was confused about. "You said we have motive."

"The vic and the perp used to be lovers. Apparently he dumped her for another woman."

"How do you know this already?" Blake asked, impressed.

"The TV's been on in my office for the last hour, so I now know more about Ali Garland and Dev Roberts than I ever wanted to. Look, this is a no-brainer and, after last night's costly little outing, I need a quick win."

"Got it. Anything else?"

"Yeah. Woo's Wash and Clean on Third." He stared pointedly at Blake's clothes. "I've seen him get brain matter out of a tweed jacket."

As the lieutenant walked away, Blake called after him, "Who wears tweed in LA?"

When Joe Roberts ran for Governor of California fifteen years ago, he showed the voters a candidate with a transformational platform, a charismatic personality and a willingness to do the heavy lifting to bring about positive changes.

His wife Ellen and his thirteen-year-old son Devlin were among the few who knew the other side of Joe Roberts, the harsh, demanding, take-no-prisoners husband and father, but the two were very different in their responses to him. Ellen understood and accepted the trade-off she made. In return for her pampered lifestyle and elevated position in society, she endured his frequent belittling and the constant judgment, maybe not with a smile, but certainly with a ladylike grace. The sad fact that the grace was bolstered by a slow vodka drip all day—in her breakfast juice, her iced tea at lunch and in her two preprandial martinis—was known only to an elite inner circle. As long as his wife never once appeared drunk, Joe accepted the fuzzy Grey Goose overlay that kept Ellen compliant and serene, and, for her own part, as long as Joe never verbally abused her or the children in front of anyone else, and as long as he never hit one of them, she was willing to be the perfect political wife. Bully that he was, Joe was careful never to violate either of her conditions; he had a lot more to lose than she did if their trompe l'oeil family fell apart.

Susannah Roberts, only nine, adored her daddy, enjoying the endless flow of gifts and privileges he provided. It would be another five years before she saw behind his mask and understood her servitude. Her future choice of anesthesia would be prescription "smoothers," but the results would be the same as her mom's.

Dev was not as accepting and pliable as his mother and sister. He knew he was too young to seriously challenge the alpha male of the house—at least not overtly—but he nurtured his resistance and dislike while playing the part of the good-as-gold son, unconsciously mirroring his father's two-faced persona.

Dev managed to have a cold, a sore throat or a stomach ache every time the family was to appear together publicly for the gubernatorial campaign. His father suspected the boy of faking it, but he would be damned if he'd force the little snot to appear with the family. Roberts would rather have no son at all than show the voters he had sired a sniveling little weakling. With her bouncy curls, cheeky charm and adoring smile at

Daddy, Susannah was all the progeny he needed to show off to the public.

Undeclared war between father and son continued, and when the balloons and streamers fell on election night, they showered down on a smiling and perfect-looking family of only three.

By age fifteen Dev had reached his adult height of six feet and, although he couldn't match Joe's solid bulk, he secretly enjoyed looking down on his father. At five-feet-nine inches tall, Joe was certainly at or above average height for a mortal man, but his image of himself was taller, more commanding. On his annual Europe trip, Joe left his family ensconced in Parisian luxury while he made a quiet side trip to a small shop near Santa Croce in Florence, Italy. There, a talented cobbler received an order for sometimes as many as two dozen pairs of shoes. Several months later, a large parcel from Bondotti di Firenze would arrive at the Governor's mansion, filled with gleaming leather footwear—magical shoes that added nearly one and three-quarters of an inch to Joe's height without any exterior giveaways. He also had his tailor hem all slacks, jeans and trousers almost a half inch longer than necessary, causing them to break more deeply over his shoes and giving an observer less to see, just in case.

Joe Roberts was passionate about many things and angry about even more. There was only one thing about which he was ashamed, and somehow Dev sensed it without even knowing about Senore Bondotti's magical shoes.

The cold war of animosity between father and son turned hot the morning Dev walked into the kitchen and saw his pajama-clad, slippered father reaching up to get a box of instant oatmeal off the top shelf of a cabinet. Joe would have gotten it easily by raising up on his toes, but Dev slipped by him smoothly and grabbed the box, momentarily startling his father, who had believed he was alone. "Here, let me get that for you, Dad."

As the box was handed off from son to father, Dev's condescending smile and Joe's glare marked the opening volley of a battle that would last less than a year. Dev, with financial help from his maternal grandmother, who had always seen right through her shiny-bright son-in-law, declared himself emancipated at sixteen. He never spoke with his father again.

Joe discreetly kept tabs on Dev, disgusted by his son's decision to go into acting, and taking pleasure in Dev's failure to land anything more than a six-line part in an aging actress's vanity production at a "theatre" located at the corner of Melrose and desperation.

The kid deserved to fail. He had been a pain in the ass since he announced, right before first grade began, he would no longer answer to Joe Junior and would enter school using his middle name, Devlin. That was Joe's father-in-law's name, a concession he had had to make to Ellen during her difficult pregnancy, and it explained why the original Dev's widow was financially aiding her grandson in his bid for freedom from Joe's control. This galled Joe, as he knew the sooner the boy crashed and burned, the sooner he'd come crawling back.

Dev Roberts didn't accept the prediction of failure any more than he had bought the rest of the old man's bullshit. Joe might be Governor of

California, but he was never going to govern anything in his son's life again. Grandma Carmichael's generous checks meant he wouldn't have to starve or wait tables while perfecting his craft, but her money couldn't buy him a shot at good roles. His father's name might have opened some doors, but Dev wouldn't give the old man the satisfaction of knowing his son couldn't make it without him.

It took five years for Dev to get his first big break. Five years of studying with the best acting coaches, taking small parts in Equity-waiver productions in the hope that one of the ninety-nine people in the audience was a *somebody*. He endured humiliating little parts in commercials for everything from jock itch powder to antidiarrhea pills. When Dev's break came, he was more than prepared; he was damn good.

The movie was *Don't Kill Me on Tuesday*, the sequel to the prior year's teen-scream smash *Don't Kill Me on Monday*, featuring promising young starlet Ali Garland. The producers had unwisely killed off her character in *Monday*, not realizing she would be the breakout star of a low-budget movie that would surpass expectations, first at the box office and then with DVD rentals and sales. They changed her hair from brunette to blonde and brought her back in *Tuesday* as the cousin of the girl killed off in *Monday*.

Dev was a featured player, but Ali was the star, at least until the film came out. Even the night of the premiere, when Dev and Ali, a manufactured "beautiful couple," walked down the red carpet together, it was obvious the crowd was laser-focused on Dev. Ali still had her rabid, mostly female, teen fan base, but the general public and the critics knew Dev Roberts had the makings of a *real* movie star.

At twenty-two he showed off his acting chops playing a young conscientious objector at odds with his war-loving military father in *Lamb to the Slaughter*. Everyone had predicted the frequently nominated older actor would walk away with an Oscar for his scenery-chewing, Great Santini-like performance, but few had anticipated that Dev Roberts would steal the movie, playing first the principled young pacifist and then, after his hawk father dies in combat, enlisting and transforming into the kind of brutal soldier he had always loathed. Dev didn't win the best supporting Oscar, but everyone who saw the closing scene of *Lamb to the Slaughter* knew he was a bona fide star. His face, as he surveyed the sprawled bodies—some of them children—littering the ground around the Vietnamese village he had helped to destroy, registered horror and shame in equal amounts. He bent to vomit, retching for half a minute before straightening up and taking in the picture of members of his platoon passing among the bodies, delivering a kick or a bayonet stab to anyone who didn't appear dead enough by strict Army standards. Dev's character, Private Jesse Marino, turned away, dropping his rifle into the grass, then walking slowly toward the jungle cover, a place where he was certain to die at the hands of a Viet Cong sniper. As his sergeant screamed at him to come back, Jesse kept walking, the close-up showing tears carving rivers through the mud and filth that darkened all but his eyes. He vanished into the tropical vegetation, threats of a court martial ringing out behind him. The camera stayed on the tree line where Jesse had disappeared, and then a solitary gunshot echoed and credits rolled.

Hollywood insiders were calling Dev the next Heath Ledger and he had dozens of choices for his third movie. He wisely selected a small independent film by an underrated director, a lead role for which he won an Academy Award. At the time of his death at twenty-eight, he had been in seven movies, received another Oscar nod and was getting twelve million a picture.

Dev's success had been annoying but irrelevant to Joe Roberts at first, but he had recently decided to make a bid for a seat in the U.S. Senate and, although he was a prominent figure in California politics, he was relatively unfamiliar to the rest of the American public. His advisors said he needed an edge, the kind of recognizability bump that would pop if he were seen with his famous son.

For once Joe needed something from Dev and was going to have to ask for it himself. Not daring to send an intermediary to blow the deal, Joe tamped down his pride and dialed Dev's number, information he had to get from Ellen, who stayed in constant touch with her son. Even a former Governor of California couldn't get the home phone number of an Oscar-winner without inside help.

The first time he called, Joe reached that stoner Dev had hung out with in high school and was apparently letting live with him. Buddy had promised, in a slow, stumbling voice, to pass the message on to Dev, but after two days of waiting, Joe assumed Buddy's weed-clouded brain had forgotten its simple task.

The second time, Joe got through to Dev's assistant, an efficient-sounding woman who, when she realized who was on the line, politely but firmly referred him to Dev's lawyer, Sam Klein. Joe slammed down the phone, refusing to let that prick of a son and his fucking entourage play hardball with him for one more second.

As Blake Ervansky entered the interview room to question Ali Garland in the shooting death of Dev Roberts, Joe Roberts was in Geneva meeting with three very wealthy former business associates he was soliciting for campaign contributions. In less than an hour he would check his cell, return his chief aide's call and learn his only son was dead.

Blake sat at the table next to his partner and across from Ali Garland, who looked into his eyes with a pained expression on her face. "Ms. Garland, I'm Det. Ervansky. Sgt. O'Brien and I would like to ask you some questions about what happened this morning."

"Oh, God!" she sobbed, her hand snapping up to cover her mouth. "I killed him, didn't I? I killed Dev."

"We'll get to all that in a minute. Has Sgt. O'Brien advised you of your right to have an attorney present?"

"Why did he pull a gun on me? I thought he was the stalker again." She brushed her hand through her hair, blinking frantically, causing Blake and Maureen to exchange a glance. Was she going to collapse? And what was she talking about? Gun? Stalker?

Blake tried again. "Ms. Garland—Ali. We'll get to all that and you'll be able to tell your side of the story. But first, are you *positive* you do not want to call a lawyer? I can provide you with a list of names if you do."

Maureen looked at her new partner with astonishment. Was he actually encouraging this murdering sociopath to get legal protection?

Ali gently rocked back and forth, hands fidgeting with the soft drink can before her on the table. Her voice was lifeless. "I don't want a lawyer. I killed him and it wouldn't be right for someone to try to convince you I didn't."

"Is there anything Sgt. O'Brien or I can get you before we start? Some coffee? Tea?"

She slowly shook her head.

"All right then, if you're *sure* you don't want a lawyer..." He hesitated to give her time to change her mind, and endured a hostile glare from Maureen. "Okay, what were you doing in Beverly Hills so early this morning?"

"I was going to my yoga class. It's, uh, five mornings a week and it starts at seven. We were going to paint one of the walls of the yoga studio today. Blue-green. Almost a teal. Very relaxing color." Her voice had dwindled to a distracted whisper by the time she finished, and her cadence had slowed. She sounded like a person under hypnosis.

"Were you meeting Dev Roberts there?"

"No, no," she said, looking into Blake's eyes. "I had no idea he was going to be there. I haven't seen him in a couple weeks." Now her words came quickly, agitation in her voice. "Why did Dev try to shoot me? We love each other."

"You thought he was going to shoot you?" he asked.

She suddenly seemed to realize her hands

were still fidgeting with the soft drink can, so she pulled them away from it and balled them into fists. "I don't know why he would do that. And why would he have a gun?"

"Ms. Garland," Maureen said, her voice steely, "the man you shot did *not* have a gun."

"But I saw it." Then, to Blake, "I swear I saw a gun."

"What you saw was a cell phone," continued Maureen. "*That's* what he was holding when you shot him."

Ali glanced at Blake, looking as though she needed confirmation what Maureen said was true. With his eyebrows raised sympathetically, Blake nodded. "She's right."

"My, God! What did I do?" She dropped her chin, then slid her hands to the sides of her neck and began sobbing as she stared down at the battered table. Blake showed concern, but Maureen's expression was impassive when she pushed the box of tissues from the end of the table to a spot closer to the weeping woman. Ali took several tissues and dabbed at her eyes, whispering a thank-you.

"Roberts wasn't carrying a gun, but you were," Blake said. "Can you tell me why you had a .32-caliber Beretta Tomcat in your possession when you were only going to a yoga class?"

"I—I have a carry permit. There was a stalker. He, uh, got into my house and I had to mace him in my bedroom to keep him from attacking me." The tissues were shredding in her fidgety hands. "I filed a police report myself. You can check it out. Anyway, I got the carry permit and bought the gun for protection."

"That's understandable," Maureen said,

sounding reasonable. "A lot of people carry guns for protection." Then her voice got hard. "Most of them, though, don't whip them out and shoot anyone holding a cell phone."

Ali looked stung, so Blake tried to calm the waters by speaking to her as if he were addressing a confused child. "She makes a good point. Why were you so quick to fire?"

"To be perfectly honest, I thought I was shooting the man who tried to snatch my purse a few minutes before that."

"Where?"

"In front of Starbucks."

"Wait, wait a minute. You were mugged *today?* This morning?" As Blake tried to wrap his mind around this new development, Maureen leaned back in her chair, crossing her arms over her chest and telegraphing that she didn't buy a word of it. By now the tissues had been reduced to a pile of fluffy bits, and Ali locked her fingers together, presumably to stop their fidgeting.

"Yes. A real tall man in jeans and a black hoodie grabbed my handbag. And I know you're supposed to let go so you don't get stabbed or something, but today I had a whole bunch of cash in my wallet. I was going to pay for my next two months of yoga classes." She looked into Blake's eyes, an embarrassed smile on her face. "I know most people think celebrities are rich, but not all of us are. My, uh, career kind of went on hold when I moved in with Dev two years ago, and I haven't had time to get it back up to speed since he and I broke up in February."

"And the purse?" Maureen asked, to bring her back from her rambling tangent.

"The strap broke, but both of us were still

holding onto it when a couple guys came out of Starbucks and chased him off."

"So, why didn't anyone call the police?" Maureen challenged.

"Well, I was okay. I mean except for my broken purse. And my skinny latte, which got knocked out of my hand when we struggled. Oh, yeah, and the can of paint spilled when it hit the sidewalk."

"What can of paint?" Blake asked.

"The one for the yoga studio, remember? The blue-green paint? The other women were supplying brushes and drop cloths. Bringing the paint was my job."

"Okay," Blake continued. "The mugger runs off and you walk around the block."

"Yes. I walked up to Little Santa Monica, then a block west to Bedford. I crossed the street and turned left, then walked past the big parking building where I always leave my car. I was almost to the yoga sudio... studio, and then a tall man in jeans and a black hoodie lunges out of the alley and points a gun at me. At least I *thought* it was a gun. I already had my hand on my own gun inside my purse because I was, uh, scared the mugger would follow me. I kept looking behind me the whole way." She licked her lips nervously and blinked back tears. "I thought he was going to kill me, so I didn't even think. I pulled out the gun, closed my eyes, and hoped I'd hit him when I pulled the trigger." She shrugged helplessly, then looked at Blake. "What should I have done? What would *you* do?" Ali's hand covered her mouth as she broke down in sobs.

"Let's take a little breather," Blake said. "I'm going to send in Officer Ortiz and she'll escort you to the ladies room if you'd like to freshen up. And if you're getting hungry, we have a menu from the sandwich shop down the street. Officer Ortiz can send someone to pick up whatever you want."

"Thank you," she said, blinking furiously as she tried to regain her composure.

Blake and Maureen left the room and, as they entered the corridor, Blake nodded to a young Hispanic woman in uniform who was waiting outside. She nodded back and went into the interview room. Blake and Maureen could finally speak privately.

"What the hell was going on with you in there?" he demanded.

"With *me?"*

"You went into that room with a hard-on, and you made damn sure she knew it!"

"Oh, you want to talk about a hard-on? She turned those teary big browns on you and you were falling all over yourself. 'Can I get you some tea, Ali? Can I get you a sandwich, Ali?' I was expecting you to offer her a pillow and a blankie next. And why did you keep encouraging her to get a lawyer?"

"Because the lieutenant told me to. He's making a preemptive strike against anyone looking for us to make even the tiniest mistake on this. He says we can afford to be magnanimous because the case is so cut and dried. Although, hearing there was a mugger dressed exactly like the vic makes the whole thing a lot less cut and not nearly as dried."

"You don't really *believe* any of that, do you?" Maureen asked, astonished by his naiveté.

"I don't know yet. But all that stuff about

home invasions and muggers is easily disproven if she's not telling the truth, so if she knows she can be caught in a lie, why would she bother?"

"I don't know *why* she's lying, but I know for sure she is."

"Are we talking psychic powers here," Blake said with a sharp edge, "or are you going by your *women's intuition?"*

"You're a real dick, you know that?"

"Hey, it's a legitimate question. You're positive she's lying, and I'm asking how you can be so sure."

"Okay, her voice. The tangents with TMI. The fidgeting. Her hand over her mouth. The blinking. My God, she demonstrated virtually every tic, twitch and verbal cue a liar can give. Didn't you learn this stuff in college? Freud? Fast? Lieberman? Nirerenberg?"

Blake deflated, doubly screwed. He had automatically assumed his partner's negative reaction to Garland had been some unconscious attractive-woman-disliking-another-attractive-woman dynamic. Then he had challenged the basis of her response and been squashed like an intellectually deficient bug. At least Blake had *heard* of Freud. "Uh, I basically faked my way through college on a swimming ticket, so I might have missed the course on body language," he said sheepishly.

"Yeah, well," Maureen said, as close as she was going to get to apologizing for coming on so strong. "Anyway, let's check out the whole mugging story. But I'm telling you, that woman is not being truthful about *anything*."

He tried to regain some ground with a charming smile. "How about her name?"

She could tell this was his version of an olive branch, so she smiled back but slipped in a last zinger. "I wouldn't bet money on it."

Sam Klein slapped his parking chit down onto the gleaming black surface of the post-postmodern reception desk, causing the woman sitting there to flinch. She put her hand flat on the romance novel she had been lost in, then smiled. "I'm sorry, sir, but we don't validate."

"Of course not," Sam spat out, snatching back the ticket and storming toward the chrome and glass double doors. "Why should *anything* go my way today?" When he got to the elevator bank he jabbed the down button and, when the car didn't arrive within a few seconds, he gave it an additional three or four irritated pokes. He knew his crappy mood wasn't only because of the unproductive four-hour deposition he had gone through; his blood sugar was also low and his stomach growled. As soon as he got out of this mid-Wilshire architectural in-joke, he'd call his half-wit assistant and order something to eat.

Attorney Sam Klein didn't usually handle divorces, and as he rode the twenty-two stories down from the penthouse to the parking garage mulling over his lost morning, he remembered why. The man he had deposed was one of those masterwonks of the internet. His software, in more than a billion computers around the world, had put him in the top ten on America's income roster. Unfortunately, it was that same software that hid his true financial worth from Sam, a canny cyber obfuscation of how much and where.

Klein represented the man's future ex-wife, a woman who had married him when he was still playing *Dungeons and Dragons* and tinkering with code in his father's basement. Two children and fourteen years of nerd-sitting entitled her to half of that massive financial pie, and even the much thinner slice Sam intended to carve off for himself would be a substantial part of his income this year. That is, *if* he could find the money.

From 8:00 that morning till noon he had charged the bastard from every direction, and had still walked out with the same phony forty-nine-million-dollar figure the little jerk and his patronizing attorney had presented to Sam's client at the start of this divorce. Sam wasn't stupid; he knew half of forty-nine million was getting dangerously close to *real* money, but he also knew his client should be getting ten times that amount. She was still willing to gut it out, scraping by on the seventy-thousand-a-month maintenance and child support he had won for her, but Sam was tired of being yanked around by that jackwad and his lawyer.

God, I need a cigarette, Sam muttered, handing his ticket to the valet, then patting his pockets till he found the Nicorette. By the time his silver Mercedes rolled to a stop in front of him, the gum was already taking a bit of the edge off. For the hundredth time he wondered why he lived in a city where smoking ranked somewhere between child molestation and elder abuse, and for the hundredth time the one-word answer was money. Only New York City could boast a bigger cauldron of bubbling cash, and he didn't like the weather there.

As soon as he had cleared the gate of the parking garage, Sam checked his cell phone and found five urgent messages from Dennis. Why did I ever agree to hire the nephew of my third-most-profitable client, he asked himself. The fussy little drama queen thought running out of Splenda packets at the office constituted an emergency, and Sam was fed up with his over-the-top responses to those little glitches of everyday life. "Call Dennis," he told his phone, and it did.

"Oh, Mr. Klein, I'm so glad you finally got back to me," Dennis blurted out breathlessly. "We have a bit of an emer—"

"Dennis!" snarled Sam, cutting off his assistant's yammering. "Whatever it is can wait till I get there."

"But Mr. Klein, you don't know—"

"White meat turkey!" he barked. "Kaiser roll, light mayo, no lettuce. Make sure it's there in fifteen minutes, and tell Karen to put up a fresh pot of coffee in exactly ten minutes. Did you get all that?"

There were two beats of silence before Dennis responded, having used the time to switch from panic to snippy mode. "Of course, Mr. Klein," he smarmed into the phone. "I'll get right on it, *sir*."

The connection broke and Sam wondered if there were any way to fire Dennis without losing his uncle as a client.

Once back in Century City, Sam opened the polished mahogany door of his own suite of offices and was immediately comforted by the warmth and hominess of the lobby. None of that stark, minimalist, contemporary crap for Sam Klein. He had selected the Jaipur carpets himself, as well as the Victorian camel-back couches and the softly glowing Venetian glass sconces on the walls. He gave himself a few seconds to absorb the calming vibe, then walked past the way-too-perky receptionist—Judy, Jody, something like that—and headed toward his private office.

Sam had barely rounded the corner of his outer office when Dennis popped up from his desk like a Whack-a-Mole rodent.

"Turkey sandwich and coffee. My office, now!" Sam ordered, a preemptory strike to cover him as he crossed to the safety of his office.

He was able to open the door right before Dennis' nattering started—"Mr. Klein, there's something you should know"—and shut it before he could finish.

Sam enjoyed nearly a full nano-second of relief before the skeletal form of "supermodel" Brianna launched itself from one of his leather wingbacks and started screaming at him from a foot away. Not for the first time, he thought: *Jesus, she looks like a coat hanger with a head.* The description, as always, pleased him, and he fought the urge to smile until he finally processed what she was saying.

"Dev's dead! Didn't you *hear* me? That stupid bitch killed him!"

"What?! Dev's dead?"

"Shot to death! Where the hell have *you* been this morning? It's all over the news! The police arrested Ali for killing him."

Sam set his attaché case down and sank heavily onto the nearest chair as his sucky day got suckier. He calculated his losses, above and beyond the monthly twenty-grand retainer. He'd been helping a broker churn stocks on Dev

Roberts the past couple years in return for a tidy fee which he billed as legal services, although a stickler for the truth might call them kickbacks.

The coat hanger was in his face again, and Sam snapped back to the disaster at hand.

"I *said*, what about the money? Am I getting it? 'Cause I'm not keeping this kid if I don't get the money."

Sam scanned her scrawny midsection, wondering first what other men found attractive in these stick women who dominated the media, and second how the fetus was surviving on two raisins and a Wheat Thin every other day. The kid might be born anorexic and have a whore for a mother, but little Dev or Deb would be filthy rich before the first diaper change. "Of course the money goes to you and Dev's unborn child."

"All of it? I'm not losing my figure and my modeling career for a measly few million bucks."

Her "modeling career." It was all Sam could do to keep from laughing. The coat hanger was too dimwitted to have noticed the only cover she had ever gotten was a second-tier women's magazine that had miraculously scooped the bigger and better mags with an exclusive Dev Roberts interview two months later. At Dev's request, Sam had brokered the deal. Prior to that Brianna, who insisted the press always refer to her as *Supermodel* Brianna, had done some lingerie ads and, for all Sam knew, pole-dancing at bachelor parties. "Yes, with the exception of a half-million-dollar bequest to a children's hunger initiative, you get it all."

"What about the house?"

"Dev's life insurance will pay the mortgage off and then it's yours, free and clear."

"How much are we talking about here? Bottom line."

"I'll need to check the investment portfolio and factor in the chalet in Vail, but I'd say in the neighborhood of sixty or sixty-five million."

The coat hanger visibly relaxed and got a dreamy look on her face. "Yeah, that's what I figured."

As if this twit had the ability to calculate anything more than a ten-percent tip for her acrylic nail technician, Sam silently observed.

Supermodel Brianna, real name Brenda Schultz, left happy, with thoughts of lynx coats and Lamborghinis filling the nearly empty space between her two-carat diamond earrings. A moment after she left, Dennis entered with a turkey sandwich and coffee, and Sam told him to pull the Roberts will from the safe.

As Sam hungrily tore into his overdue lunch, he did an assessment of the situation. If he could convince the coat hanger to keep him on to handle legal matters and manage the money, he'd be in the same cushy position as before. Plus, he had that little nugget of his own buried in Dev's will. He hadn't expected it to pay off for another twenty or thirty years when a much older Dev Roberts overdosed or had an M.I. in the saddle, but what the hell, Sam deserved this. Who cared about one more dead actor anyway?

As Sam chewed a bite of his sandwich, a single thought pressed to the front of his mind: *the turkey's a little dry today.*

Blake and Maureen pulled into the parking structure at the corner of Bedford and Little Santa Monica. They cruised each level slowly, as Ali had been too shaken to say for sure where she had left her car. They checked each black BMW until they found the one with the *CUL8R* license plate, then parked as close to it as possible.

They could see the parking receipt laying on the dash, so Maureen unlocked the driver's side door and, careful to disturb nothing else, pulled out the receipt while Blake phoned in the car's location to the impound officer. Maureen closed the door and examined the ticket, then turned to Blake as he hung up. "6:32."

"Okay, a minute or so to get down to the street. Two minutes to Starbucks, however long it takes the barista to skinny up a latte, quick struggle on the sidewalk, then three or four minutes to get to the crime scene. Timeline seems about right."

Maureen held up Ali's car keys, a sterling silver ring from Tiffany with five keys and a two-inch-tall naked troll doll with another inch and a half of neon yellow hair sticking straight up from its rubber head. "Where should I leave these?"

"Front left tire. Impound should be here within fifteen minutes."

"If memory serves, I was promised coffee hours ago."

The first thing they noticed when they approached the Starbucks was a drying puddle on the sidewalk, maybe three feet wide. There were orange traffic cones surrounding the still-tacky paint, presumably to keep customers from stepping in it. "Looks like she wasn't lying about the blue-green paint," he observed.

Maureen flashed him a grin. "*Is* it blue-green? I see more of a teal."

"Very relaxing, though," Blake replied, playing along. Then he looked more closely and saw a clear footprint at the far edge of the spill. Moving around to that side, he squatted for a better look. "See this?"

"A shoe print."

"And a little extra. Come here."

Maureen got on one knee, mindful of the sticky paint. She noticed Blake hadn't been quite as careful and had now added to the knees of his trousers a blue-green counterpoint to the drying blood from earlier. Blake indicated the center of the print. "That letter C in the middle?"

"Yeah."

"It started out as a G. The shoe is made by a local company called Glendale Feet, and they specialize in making cheap kicks that look like the hundred-and-fifty-a-pair shoes all the little would-be gang-bangers want. There's a branch of the Crips called the Rolling Forties, and after a new member is initiated he has to buy a pair of these and carve away the rubber from the cross-piece of the G."

"So, unless they cut with a template, each shoe should have enough irregularities to make it unique."

"Yep," Blake said, standing.

"Roughly how many Rolling Forties are we talking about?"

"Only three or four dozen actual gang members. The problem is that half the fourteen-year-old boys in Hollywood and BH carve their own Glendales so they can feel like gangsters."

"Should we get CSI on it?"

"Yeah. The print may not be relevant to our homicide, but maybe it'll link up with some other crime."

As Maureen phoned the ID bureau, Blake went inside to talk to the barista who had served Ali Garland that morning. He was already questioning a bland-faced boy of around twenty when Maureen approached.

"Yes, I make Ms. Garland a venti skinny latte every morning. She's an excellent tipper, not at all the kind of person you'd expect to shoot somebody."

"Did you see anything that happened out front after Ms. Garland left this morning?" Blake asked.

"No, by the time I got outside it was all over. I saw her latte on the sidewalk and I offered to make her another at no charge, but she said no thanks and left."

"She told us a couple gentlemen came to her assistance and chased off the mugger."

"Three of my other regulars, yes."

"Can you give me their names?" Blake asked, pulling a small spiral notebook from his pocket and patting around for a pen.

"I only know them as Kona, macchiato, and half-caff house blend. Sorry." He looked disappointed for a second, then brightened. "But they're here almost every weekday. You could come back Monday morning, say, sevenish, and talk to them."

"I'll tell you what, take three of my cards and give them to Kona, Mac and Half-caff on Monday and ask them to give me a call."

"Sure," the boy said, eagerly taking the proffered cards. "Do you think the mugging had anything to do with the shooting?"

"They're probably unrelated, but we have

to check out every possibility."

By the time the kid had made coffees for Blake and Maureen and retrieved the files from the store's interior and exterior CCTV cameras, CSI was on-scene photographing the shoe print and taking a sample of the still-tacky paint.

Joe Roberts sat heavily on the bed in his eleven-hundred-dollar-a-night hotel suite, no lights on even though the sky over Geneva had darkened a while ago.

So, Dev was dead. As a father, Joe knew he should be feeling more, but what? Weren't good parents supposed to love their children unconditionally? And maybe Joe *had* loved his son once, in some hazy past where Ellen was happy and sober as she held his firstborn for him to see. Maybe that initial, tiny-fingered grasp of Joe's own little finger had been a moment of joy and love. Perhaps there had been a time when a wobbly toddler needed the balancing hand of his father to help him stay upright. And maybe that long-lost child had even smiled up at Joe with adoration.

Where had he gone, that boy Joe might have loved? When had he become the sullen brat who liked nothing about his father except the luxury goods and services his money provided?

Had it all gone wrong when Joe Junior was six? When he decided to use his grandpa Carmichael's name instead of his own father's? Could a first-grader possibly sense the magnitude of the disrespect? Joe would have preferred that Dev had spat in his face, because then he could have delivered one ringing slap and sent the boy crying to his room. The lesson would have been over in an instant, and Dev would have learned the consequence of showing disrespect to his father.

Ellen had claimed the name business was only the boy expressing his independence, that Joe should be proud their son was capable of making decisions beyond whether to wear the Spider-Man or Batman pajamas. Ellen. What the hell did *she* know about parenting? Thanks to her inspiring example, Susannah had been consuming prescription pills as though they were Tic-Tacs since she was fourteen.

Quite the family, thought Joe. A wife who only endures her marriage by feeding an eighty-proof buzz, a medicated daughter and a dead son. Dark emotions simmered in Joe Roberts, but he refused to let them boil over into pain and grief. Instead, he tightly channeled their power into an estuary of anger, the emotion which had driven him his entire life, the emotion with which he felt most comfortable. Grief is weakness, but anger is strength.

Alive, Dev was too full of himself to help me out when I needed him. Now that he's dead, I can make him over into the son I deserve.

Joe reached for the phone on the night stand. He'd get the next flight out of Switzerland and, once back in LA, he'd make sure Dev helped him get elected.

Any hope Blake and Maureen had of finding ten minutes to eat the burgers they had picked up on their way back to the station evaporated when they were accosted by Det. Willis as soon as they came through the door. "I found that file on the break-in," he said, holding up a thin folder.

"Give us the highlights," Blake said.

Willis skimmed the first page as he spoke. "Okay, 911 call received 2:15 A.M. April eighth this year, squad car responds to a home on Roxbury where they find Ali Garland in her nightgown," he glanced at O'Brien, bouncing his eyebrows up and down, a buffoonish attempt at lasciviousness before he continued. "She claims to have scared off an intruder, and officers find a broken window where the alleged intruder gained entry. Vic's description of the perp is thin because her bedroom was dark when he entered, and he ran out as soon as she maced him." He looked up from the file, then handed it to Blake. "She couldn't help the sketch artist, but said the guy was muscular and tall. Of course, when you're five foot zip, I guess *everyone* looks tall."

"CSI find anything?" Blake asked.

"No DNA, but there was mace residue consistent with Garland's description of the confrontation and a pretty fair set of footprints in the mud outside the broken window."

Blake quickly flipped through the file to find the photos of the crime scene. He pulled one out and handed it to Maureen. Willis noticed which photo they were looking at. "Yeah, it rained a couple hours earlier that night, so the ground was wet enough to take an impression. And dry enough to hold it," Willis added.

Maureen looked up from the photo, and she and Blake exchanged a knowing glance, before he turned to Willis. "Thanks for pulling this. Can I ask you to do one more thing for me?"

"Anything for you and the lovely Sgt. O," Willis said. Maureen smiled noncommittally, but

Blake was stone-faced.

"Ask Sherry to compare these shoe prints with the ones from the Starbucks mugging as soon as she can."

"Will do. Oh, by the way, Roberts' doctor came in and positively identified the stiff. Lucky he had a birthmark on his ass, 'cause facial ID was not gonna happen."

Blake looked at Willis with disgust, then he and Maureen walked away, Willis' eyes glued on her retreating form.

"What do you think?" Blake asked.

"It's definitely the same *kind* of shoe, and if it turns out to be the same one we saw in that paint spill, I guess things are starting to get complicated."

They checked in with Officer Ortiz, who told them Ali was resting in one of the pay-to-stay rooms, then went looking for Libby Johnson. While Blake and Maureen were at Starbucks, Libby and her partner Jim had already begun to interview the producer of the TV show that had gotten Dev Roberts killed.

Libby opened the interview room door to let Blake and Maureen in. "Mr. Kentner, this is Det. Ervansky and Sgt. O'Brien. They're the lead investigators on this. Blake, Sergeant, meet Kenny Kentner, creator and executive producer of *Yanked*."

A weighty title for a guy who didn't look to be over thirty, thought Blake, as he reached out to shake hands. "Mr. Kentner."

"Oh, please call me Kenny," the man said, pumping Blake's hand vigorously. He treated Maureen's hand more gently.

After they sat, Blake turned to Libby.

"Where's Jimbo?"

"His wife went into labor so he left for the hospital. Kenny here has been telling me all about his TV show. Take it away, Kenny."

"Well, as Det. Johnson told you, I'm the creator *and* executive producer of *Yanked* on ZGN. Have you seen it?"

"I've never heard of the show *or* ZGN," Blake replied.

"You don't know about the Zeitgeist Network?" Kenny asked, incredulous. "It's the next FX, according to *Variety*. I mean, ZGN is grabbing the eighteen to forty-nines like crazy."

"Kenny," Libby interrupted, "can we stick to anything relevant to this morning's shooting?"

"Absolutely. Okay, *Yanked* uses big-name celebrities to play jokes on *other* famous people. It's *Yanked*, liked yanking your chain. Get it?" Three impassive faces told him that although they "got it," they didn't find it as amusing as he obviously did. Kenny took a deep breath and soldiered on. "*Any*hoo, Dev Roberts was nagging me literally *forever* to be on the program and, with my second-season pickup on the line, I thought he'd be a great incentive to wave in front of Zeitgeist."

"And what exactly was this morning's joke supposed to be?"

"Well, everybody knows Dev and Ali Garland were an item for a long time. And even though they broke up and are both seeing other people, they've stayed pretty close. So, the yank was that Dev would step out from the alleyway next to her yoga studio, hold out a cell phone and say 'It's for you'."

"That's it?" Blake asked skeptically.

"When you have a movie star big as Dev Roberts, that's all it has to be."

Maureen leaned forward with her elbows on the table and spoke for the first time since the intros. "All bullshit aside, Kenny, how did your copycat program on a no-name network get an Oscar-winning actor, who, by the way, hasn't appeared on television for the last five years, to embarrass himself with a joke as uncreative and unfunny, as"—and here Maureen pushed her cell toward Kenny and did a pretty good impression of Homer Simpson—"D'oh, it's for you."

Kenny Kentner's body went stiff during Maureen's attack, and it was obvious her words had pissed him off. Libby and Blake, however, looked at Maureen with impressed surprise.

"It's true," Kenny began, his voice tight with the effort of telling the truth, "that *Yanked* follows in the wake of some better-known shows of the genre, but even Ashton-effing-Kutcher would have to admit he stole from—oh, excuse me, I should have said was *inspired by*—Allen Funt and *Candid Camera.* And I don't care how big the star is, he or she wants the exposure my show gives them."

"Really?" asked Maureen. "What other big stars have you had on the show?"

Kenny squirmed uncomfortably in his chair. "Well, there was Heidi Montag."

"Right. How about a person known for something other than plastic surgery and temper tantrums?"

Kenny glared at Maureen, but didn't try to fool her with another lame name. "What? No one? So kill the spin and tell us why Dev Roberts *really* did your show."

Kenny's pleading eyes darted to Libby, then to Blake, hoping one of them would put a stop to the redhead's demeaning interrogation. When they didn't offer to save him, he slumped and a sigh of defeat whooshed through his lips. "I have no idea. You're right, the show's a piece of dreck and no self-respecting celebrity would ever consent to appear on it. All I ever get are the dregs and the desperate. On probation after smacking your wife around? Career in the toilet? Coming out of rehab? Call Kenny and get your face on TV again."

"But Dev didn't fit any of those criteria," said Maureen, patient and conciliatory now that she had gotten him to start telling the truth. "So why did he do it?"

"Because I begged him. Literally begged. Zeitgeist was about to pull the plug and I needed a miracle." He looked at Maureen, then spoke defensively. "It isn't only me, you know. A few dozen people feed their families off this show."

"And you wanted to protect everyone's livelihood. That's a real stand-up thing to do, Kenny." If there was sarcasm in Maureen's mind, it didn't leak into her words, and Kenny appeared to be at least partially placated.

"Well, I try to be a stand-up guy. Dev and I went to high school together. I was three years ahead of him, and I was kind of a mover and a shaker. Directed the plays, put on the talent show, all that kind of stuff. Anyway, Dev looked up to me so I gave him small parts in a couple school productions. After graduation I worked as a production assistant at Stephen Cannell's company before I went out on my own. I thought *Yanked* would put me on the map, but ZGN was the only place low-rent enough to buy it, and even *they* were losing faith. I figured Dev owed me, so I ambushed him at The Ivy one day. He remembered me, but didn't invite me to sit down and join him for lunch, so I had to stand there and make my pitch while he kept eating and everyone at the other tables smirked. He didn't bother to palm me off on his agent for the big 'no thanks,' just asked me to leave. Next day, he calls, apologizes, says he had been in a lousy mood, then asks me if he could pick the celebrity to be *Yanked.* I couldn't say yes fast enough. Went over to his house that same day and made a handshake deal to yank Ali Garland."

"Kenny," asked Libby, "is there any possibility she knew about this beforehand?"

"No way. All my people understand their jobs depend on keeping everything secret."

"What about Dev?" Blake asked. "Could he have tipped her off in advance?"

"Why would he do that? The whole point is to capture a shocked look on someone's face and then the relief when they learn it's only a joke. Dev was totally down with catching Ali off guard."

Libby and Blake exchanged a look, then she turned back to Kenny. "That's all we need for now, but we may want to talk to you again."

"Det. Johnson, could I ask him one more thing?" Maureen said.

"Of course."

"We confiscated the digital files from four cameras this morning. Isn't four kind of overkill for a reality show on a small cable outlet?"

"Well, normally we'd have two, but when I dangled Dev's name in front of Zeitgeist, they ponied up the extra bucks for me to hire some freelancers. They wanted me to put as much Dev Roberts face time as possible on ZGN."

As Libby stood, she reached out to shake Kenny's hand. "You've been very helpful, Kenny. And we'll be in touch if we need anything else."

"Uh, when exactly will I be able to get those video files back from you?"

"You're not *really* thinking you could air them, are you?" Blake asked.

"I'm not saying what I'd do with them. I'm only saying what any good lawyer would tell you, that those files are my property. Well, technically, Zeitgeist's property, but you know what I mean."

"And you know what I'd tell that lawyer? Those digital files and all the images they contain are now material evidence in a homicide investigation."

Kenny shrugged sheepishly, then crossed to the door. "Can't blame a guy for trying."

Once the door had closed behind him, Libby Johnson turned to Maureen. "Impressive. And how do you know so much about TV?"

"Det. Johnson," she said, flashing that dazzling smile and speaking with the mock sincerity of a television pitch man. "It's not TV... it's *Zeitgeist*!"

Libby shook her head, then aimed her thumb at Maureen as she spoke to Blake. "It's always the quiet ones, huh, Blake?"

"Thanks, Lib."

"De nada."

She left and Blake turned to his partner. "Okay, I didn't want to embarrass myself in front of Kenny, but what did that long number mean?"

"What long number?"

"Eighteen-two-forty-nine. He said ZGN was getting a lot of them."

For a second, Maureen looked puzzled, then she smiled. "Not eighteen, *two*, forty-nine," she held up two fingers. "It means the age group eighteen to forty-nine. That's the prime target market for pretty much everything but Ensure and Polident."

When Sam Klein woke, he noticed his lunch plate and coffee cup had been taken away and the manila envelope labeled "Last Will and Testament of Dev Roberts" had been placed on his desk. That meant Dennis had caught him napping, probably took a couple open-mouthed drool shots with his cell phone. Sam shook his head to clear it, pissed at himself for dozing off at work. Jesus, he thought, I'm only forty-two, I shouldn't be falling asleep in the middle of the day. He blamed the tryptophan in the turkey for making him drowsy and resolved to go back to corned beef and pastrami as of tomorrow. Screw that buzzkill cardiologist. And no more of that lame decaf, either.

Klein unwound the string on the old-fashioned double-loop closure and opened the envelope containing Dev's will. As soon as he glanced at the top page, he realized Dennis had brought him the wrong one.

"Dennis!" he shouted, never one to bother with the intercom when bellowing could do the trick. A moment later Dennis opened the door.

"Yes, Mr. Klein?"

"Wrong will," he said, holding up the document. "This is the one from last year. I need the new one."

"Yes, sir. I'll go find it. And, uh, you *do* know Brianna is holding a press conference right now, don't you?"

"Damn it!" Sam lunged for the TV by his wet bar and grabbed the remote.

"Oh, it's almost over. But I DVR'd it in the conference room if you'd like to watch it from the beginning."

Sam followed him to the conference room, then impatiently waited while Dennis pushed buttons on the remote and brought up a still image on the TV screen—the front gates of Dev's Bel-Air home. Dennis handed Sam the remote. "I'll go pull that new will."

Before the door had closed behind his assistant, Sam punched the remote and saw the large crowd of paparazzi and legitimate reporters milling around in front of the locked wrought-iron gates. One of the reporters apparently saw something in the driveway and pulled his cameraman into place, as an awakening spread through the ranks. When Brianna approached the other side of the entrance, dozens of cameras and microphones were aimed at her.

"I would like to make a brief statement, then I ask that you please give me privacy to grieve." She smiled wanly, turning slowly from left to right, giving each camera a full-face and a profile. So far so good, thought Sam. Then Brianna read from the paper in her hand. "As I'm sure you all know, Dev Roberts was murdered this morning. He was gunned down by Ali Garland, a has-been actress that Dev dumped in February."

The coat hanger's voice grew more shrill

and agitated as she disregarded her script and began winging it. "She hated Dev for throwing her out on her giant butt, and she hated him for turning her down when she came here begging us for money. I know some lawyer will come up with a phony defense for that bitch, but don't you believe it. She hated him and she wanted him dead and she murdered him in cold blood!"

The coat hanger got herself back under control, approximated a brave smile, then did the head turn again, this time right to left. She ignored all the shouted questions, turned away from the gates, and walked back up the drive toward the house. Sam hit the off button and left the conference room, running into Dennis on the way back to his office. "Uh, Mr. Klein? I can't find any record of another will for Mr. Roberts."

In the larger of the two guest houses on Dev's property, a disconsolate young woman sat at a small desk, eyes puffy and red, but finally dry after almost eight hours of crying. In all the world, only Dev's mother and this woman, Lily Sims, would truly grieve for the man. Millions of fans would mourn the loss of their superstar until Channing Tatum had a sex change or Justin Bieber punched a cat. The stockbrokers, agents, lawyers and all other beneficiaries of the trickle-down economics of Dev Roberts' career would speak respectfully at the funeral, then hurry off to plug the money hole with another actor or heiress or lottery winner. But Ellen Roberts and Lily Sims would never be able to leave the day's horror completely behind.

Lily had been Dev's personal assistant for seven years, hired while he was shooting *Lamb to the Slaughter* and needed someone reliable to pay the bills and coordinate with his people. While he was on location in Myanmar for three months, Lily had never seen him. Their business was conducted by phone, fax, e-mail and courier, but she fondly recalled the day he hired her.

As soon as she landed the interview, Lily rented *Don't Kill Me on Tuesday.* It was her first glimpse of the man with whom she would later fall in and out of love, and she made up her mind to take the job no matter how low the salary.

He had been charming and flirtatious at that initial meeting in his small apartment on Formosa Drive. He apologized for not having an office, and offered ten thousand a year more than Lily was requesting to offset the incon-venience of her having to work out of her home, a studio apartment in the not-so-great part of North Hollywood.

A year later, with the successful *Lamb* behind him and gross-profit participation in the indie film he was working on, Dev bought the exclusive property on Bay Court in Bel-Air and invited Lily to move into one of the guest houses. With free rent and another five-thousand-dollar salary bump, Lily knew she had one of the best jobs in Los Angeles, but it wasn't only the money that made her love it.

Lily knew she wasn't a raving beauty, but when she looked in the mirror she saw a serious, reliable woman, the kind a man could marry and spend his life with. She wore her hair in the style most flattering to her round face, dressed nicely, and knew how to apply makeup in a way to highlight her best features (full lips, great skin), and shape and shade the flaws (squarish jawline, apple cheeks), but she would never be competition for any of the gorgeous actresses and models with whom Dev was seen around town.

Still, he always comes home to me, she thought those first few years. And it was true that Dev haunted the club scene and dated the way any suddenly rich and instantly famous guy was expected to do, but he never got serious about any one woman.

From the window of her bedroom in the guest house, Lily would watch the headlights of Dev's Ferrari wipe the front of the main house, then go dark. She observed the upstairs window of Dev's bedroom until the light came on and then, presumably after he had undressed and slipped into bed, was turned off again.

Sometimes she stood there a long time, thinking about him naked, tucked into his 800-thread-count Frette sheets. She had no idea if he actually slept naked, but she was sure about the sheets, as she had paid the bill for them.

It took years for her to understand Dev's flirtiness was equally applied to any female from three to ninety, and to accept the idea that he wasn't going to one day ask her to remove her glasses and then, in a *"Why Miss Sims, you're beautiful"* old-time movie moment, take her in his arms and kiss her. And with each passing year, his girlfriends got prettier and thinner, and Lily got older and five pounds heavier.

The final proof for Lily that the pumpkin was never going to morph into a gilded, horse-drawn coach and take her to the ball came the afternoon two-and-a-half years ago when she slipped into the big house with that day's mail for Dev. She had always come and gone freely, mostly entering from the side door because it was closest to her cottage. Her habit was to put the preculled mail on Dev's desk, check his out box for any memos requesting her to take care of something, then chat up the housekeeper before going back to work. That day, however, after she dropped off the mail, Lily decided to go to the kitchen to make sure plans were progressing for that Friday's party. While most other celebrities lay low the week before the Academy Awards show, Dev always threw a lavish soirée a few nights before. With less pressure to look perfect, and no photographers, the stars were able to eat, drink—often to excess—and be merry without fear of showing up in the tabloids looking sloppy drunk or smiling with a front tooth blacked out by half-chewed Osetra.

To get to the kitchen, Lily walked through the hallway that crossed behind the living room, and as she did she heard voices. Slowing down to listen, Lily heard Dev and his friend Buddy, the occupant of the smaller guest house, laughing. It took her only a moment to realize *she* was the butt of the joke the two men shared, and she stiffened with humiliation at the cruel nickname Buddy used when he referred to her. She waited, hoping Dev would defend her, chide Buddy for the insult, but the conversation shifted to the oral talents of the Kim Kardashian look-alike Buddy had banged the night before. With her cheeks burning and her heart breaking, Lily quietly retreated to her cottage.

Before the end of the day, she had written her letter of resignation, intending to leave it on Dev's desk the next morning. But that night, while she lay in bed unable to sleep, she thought it all through again. With her annual automatic increases, Lily was by then making nearly one hundred thousand a year, most of it staying in her savings account. She might be able to find another job as a celebrity's assistant, but would they offer housing, utilities and a car? Even if she could get someone to match her current salary—and that was iffy—she'd have to burn much of it on the things Dev provided her. Lily was approaching thirty. She needed to quit fantasizing and begin getting serious about her future. Three more years of banking most of her salary and she'd have a half-million-dollar nest egg. If she pulled her focus off an unattainable movie god and started considering mortal men, she might even find love.

Lily got out of bed and went to her desk. Quitting was foolish and self-indulgent, and she had never been either. She hit the power button on the shredder, then fed the single page of her resignation letter into the chattering teeth.

As she climbed back in bed, certain she had made the correct decision, Lily began the rationalization process that would enable her to continue working for Dev without resentment. After all, *he* hadn't used the hurtful name for her. Maybe he hadn't wanted to embarrass his old friend by correcting him, she thought, then drifted off to sleep.

A few months later, Ali Garland reentered Dev's life, and any leading-lady fantasies Lily might have still harbored were sublimated into a supporting-actress reality. Unlike so many of the prior girlfriends, Ali was *respectful* to Lily, spoke to her as an equal, even sought her advice on a birthday gift for Dev in the early stages of their relationship. When Ali told Lily she had been invited to move into the big Tudor house, Lily realized she was happy for the first time in a long while.

Lily began taking care of Ali's personal business in addition to Dev's. Rather than expecting it as one of the perks of living there, Ali paid her a thousand dollars a month, cash and off the books.

Lily soon felt like an older sister and a confidante rather than an employee, and she became protective of the actress, whose gamine looks and tiny stature made her seem more like a girl than a woman. When Ali confided she was pregnant with Dev's child, Lily was genuinely pleased. Ali was the tie; she made Lily feel like part of a family, and Lily would have done anything for her.

Lily knew long before Ali did that Dev was sleeping with Brianna, because Lily was the one who wrote the checks for the credit card bills. She paid for the tickets to Vail, for a ski trip Ali couldn't go on because of morning sickness. She knew about the diamond necklace that had not been given to Ali for Christmas. She knew what New York hotel Dev was in with Brianna the night Ali miscarried the four-month fetus.

Ali was kicked to the curb, Brianna was placed on the throne with King Dev and, for the second time, a fantasy life collapsed around Lily.

So now, Dev was gone and Lily, to whom deception did not come easily, had a decision to make. What she had done was done in a moment of anger at her boss for his cavalier treatment of someone kind and good. She could cop to it right now and accept the consequences or she could keep the secret and move on with her life.

A pounding on the door snapped her back to reality, but before she could cross the room to answer it, Brianna had used the housekeeper's key to let herself in. The two women, unlike in every way, came face to face in the middle of the small living room.

"Free ride's over, fat ass. I want you out of here in a week."

When Lily froze, too shocked to respond, Brianna moved in closer, stabbing a bony finger in her face. "And don't think you're gonna get anything from Dev's will, either, because I finally convinced him you've been taking advantage long enough. I get *everything,* so leave the car keys when you clear out your shit."

Brianna glanced around the cozy room—was she judging Lily's decorating or taking inventory?—then spun around like a runway model on fast forward and walked out, slamming the door behind her.

Angry determination was a new feeling for Lily, but she let it wash over her, dispelling her doubts. She crossed to her desk, opened the top drawer, and took out the envelope marked "Last Will and Testament of Dev Roberts."

Unwinding the string and loop closure, Lily pulled Dev's will from the envelope. She hit the power button, then watched resolutely as the shredder's gnashing teeth greedily devoured Brianna's future.

By 3:30 Friday afternoon, **Blake and** Maureen had viewed every image from the four *Yanked* cameras plus the CCTV footage from Starbucks—both interior and exterior—and all the coverage from the outside cameras of the chic little shops between the location of the shooting and the high church of caffeine. The story those images told was irrefutable.

Ali Garland, smiling a thank-you at the man who pushed open the door from the inside to let her exit the coffee shop, had a can of paint hanging from one hand and her to-go cup in the other. Once the door holder had ducked back into the shop, she was alone on the sidewalk. Ali carefully shifted the strap of her large leather bag higher onto her shoulder and turned to walk north. Before she could step out of the frame of the Starbucks exterior CCTV camera, a tall man in a black hoodie and jeans rushed her from out of camera range. Although his skinny jeans clung to a trim lower half, even the baggy hooded sweatshirt couldn't disguise his broad shoulders and muscular upper body.

He grabbed the strap of the purse, jerking the young woman sideways. The to-go cup and the paint can hit the sidewalk simultaneously, both splashing their contents everywhere, as Ali held onto the body of the handbag. When the strap snapped in two, the thug was temporarily knocked off balance and Ali fell to the sidewalk. By the time the mugger made a second lunge for the purse, three men were hurrying out of the shop.

The assailant ran out of frame in the direction from which he had appeared, with two of the men chasing after him. The third man pulled Ali to her feet as several other people came out to help. Ali seemingly assured the Good Samaritan that she was all right, while the two who had taken off after the mugger walked back into frame. Their labored breathing told the viewer they had been no match for the speed of the fit young mugger.

Ali surveyed the mess on the sidewalk as the barista Blake and Maureen had talked to earlier said something to her. She placed a hand on his arm and smiled warmly, but shook her head and started walking north again.

The crowd drifted back inside to their croissants and laptops as the story continued in the eye of the next CCTV camera.

The two cameras between Starbucks and Little Santa Monica showed Ali hurrying north, but stopping twice to look behind her and all around. She apparently thought she heard something, because the second time she paused she slipped her right hand into the purse held against her chest, obviously locating the gun in case she needed it.

No images from the short block along Little Santa Monica, but Ali was picked up again by the camera at the entrance to the car park as she turned south onto Bedford. A push-in by the tech showed Blake and Maureen Ali's frightened face as she stopped again to check that no one was lurking in the parking structure. Shifting the purse, probably to make sure she had the gun securely in her hand, she moved out of that frame.

She immediately walked into an establishing shot—Maureen had to explain the term to Blake—from one of Kenny Kentner's cameramen, and within seconds four cameras were digitally recording the shooting.

Blake and Maureen watched themselves playing small parts in the reality show fiasco,

Maureen running with her gun drawn, Blake's bloody hand moving toward a camera lens and, of course, unlike the CCTV cameras, Kenny's had sound, so Maureen's shouted commands for Ali to drop the gun were clearly heard, as well as Blake's "Turn it off, asshole!"

Three times Blake and Maureen went through the grisly scene of Dev Roberts being shot in the face, once for each of three slightly different camera angles, but it was the fourth camera, the one behind Dev, the one that had captured the "over the shoulder"—another term Maureen had explained to him—that finally sickened Blake.

Any monster movie buff will tell you it is the *implied* horror, not the in-your-face tearing out of throats or the flailing of a bloody knife, that shakes you to your core. The screaming girl, snatched hither and yon through the dark water by the unseen nightmare below the surface, is much more deeply disturbing than later close-ups of the massive shark biting the back of a boat, a truth successfully exploited by films like *Don't Kill Me on Monday*.

The fourth cameraman had been up on a thirty-two-inch-high riser placed about six feet behind Dev, close enough to see Ali's face when she got yanked but far enough back not to be noticed by her before it all went down. At first, all that showed in the frame was a high-angle view of the sidewalk, then right before Dev shouted "It's for you!" the very top of his right shoulder came into the bottom of the shot. At the same time, Ali's terrified face turned into the frame, a reaction triggered by the sudden sound and movement. It would have been a bust shot, but Dev's shoulder blocked out everything below Ali's chin, so the gun was heard but not seen as it was fired blindly. Literally blindly, for Ali had closed her eyes tightly and grimaced the split second before the two shots rang out.

The most hardened homicide cop would have felt the quick punch of shock, and tasted vomit in the back of his throat at the sight of what splattered onto the camera lens—a ghastly mix of blood, hair and brain—and Blake was far from hardened. The tech had to play it three times before Blake could watch it through, and he never glanced to the left to see how his new partner was handling the appalling footage.

The camera angled down quickly, the operator—probably fearing for his own life—having jumped down off the back of the riser. From the lower angle, Dev's body completely blocked Ali for a second, but then, before the cameraman turned and ran down the alley and away from the shooter, Dev dropped out of the frame, revealing Ali. She was trembling, as if waiting for return fire, her eyes still tightly shut and the now-visible gun aimed upward. A crazy swipe of brick, then pavement, then black.

"Again?" asked the tech.

Blake glanced over at Maureen. Her eyes were closed, and her lips made a tight line, so he assumed she was responding to the video with the same sense of horror he had. Blake was half right. Maureen's eyes *were* closed in horror, but hers was born of memory and guilt. She shook her head. "I've seen enough."

"Okay, you can put those back in evidence with the originals," Blake said to the tech. "The lieutenant will probably want to see it all, but it's getting late and he was at that bust all night, so I'm guessing not until tomorrow."

"Uh, tomorrow's Saturday."

"Crap. Okay, don't leave until I find out if he wants you to come back in the morning or stay. But go ahead and put them away. I don't want a frame of this winding up on YouTube or the 6:00 o'clock news."

The tech gathered up the labeled bags, each containing one copy of an SD card from a digital video camera. Blake waited until he left to swivel his chair toward Maureen. "So?"

"So, I don't think there's a grand jury in the country that would indict her on more than involuntary manslaughter, and only a strong prosecutor could make *that* stick."

"Oh, Lt. Rhee's going to love this," he said ruefully, as the door pushed open and Officer Ortiz looked in.

"Det. Ervansky?"

"Yeah."

"She wants to know if she can have her purse back."

Blake looked at Maureen. "Did you bring it in?"

"No, I assumed the CSIs would take it."

Blake turned back to Ortiz. "Ask Sherry in ID if she has everything she needs from it. If so, you can give it back to Ms. Garland. Oh, and Ortiz?"

"Sir?"

"See if she's done a comp yet on the two sets of footprints."

When the door shut behind Officer Ortiz, Maureen stood and said, "I guess we can't put off breaking the news to the lieutenant any longer."

"Okay, but you stand in front of me in case he decides to shoot the messenger."

Once Sam Klein turned out of the demolition derby that was Sunset Boulevard traffic on a late Friday afternoon and passed through the stone gate of Bel-Air, he could finally drive by rote and focus on the problem at hand.

He and Dennis had torn the office apart looking for Dev's will, even enlisting the aid of Jody or Judy to go through the messenger service receipts to find out when it had come back signed and witnessed. Jodyjudy had produced a receipt showing the service picked up the will from Sam's office September twenty-sixth, delivering it to Dev's assistant that same day, but there was no record of its return. That made Sam feel a little better, but he wished he had been able to get through to Lily on the phone.

Sam knew Lily Sims was dependable and thorough, and she wouldn't have mislaid the will. She probably spent weeks getting that ditz Dev to stop and sign it, and it was most likely laying on her desk, already addressed to Sam's office. The events of the day would have distracted her so much that she forgot to call the messenger service for the pickup, Sam reassured himself.

Lily was always on top of things, and was the only decent woman in Dev's life. No looker, but dependable as the tides. He wondered if he could hire her as his own assistant now that she was out of a job. He couldn't picture prim Lily staying on to work for the coat hanger. If Sam could only fob off Dennis onto someone else, maybe even offer that phantom employer a check for part of Dennis' first year's salary.

These musings had distracted Sam from the potential disaster of a missing will, but as he slowly edged through the crowd at Dev's gates and punched in the security code, careful to shield his action from prying eyes and camera lenses, the anxiety came back. If that will found its way into the wrong hands—wrong hands being defined as those belonging to any lawyer with even half a brain—things could get sticky for Sam. He had been very careful to stay within the letter of the law, if only by a zillionth of a millimeter, but he was well aware that if his actions were measured by his embracing of the *spirit* of the law, his career would be over.

When the gates swung open, Sam Klein eased his silver Mercedes through, turning left to the drive that accessed the two guest houses in back.

"Let's see, it's 4:00 P.M. now, so that's what, sixteen hours since midnight? And in that time, the drug bust that might have gotten me promoted goes all to hell, costing the city a load of cash, the served-on-a-platter murder turns out to be only a tick above self-defense, and Randall Vayne slips through my fingers. *Again.*"

"Oh God, Vayne! I forgot," said Blake. "Didn't you send—"

"Of course," Rhee interrupted, "as soon as you phoned in the shooting. But before Willis and Lang could get there, Vayne must have heard all the bells and whistles from two blocks over and said sayonara. Apparently, he took the time to change out of his Men's Wearhouse suit and into a four-thousand-dollar Valentino before slithering out the back door." He sighed. "Are you *sure* Ali isn't an evil genius murderer?"

"Do you want to look at the video?"

"No. From what you two say, it's pretty conclusive. Send the tech home and I'll look at it all on Monday."

"If there's anything positive here, sir," said Maureen, "it's that Garland hasn't asked for a lawyer. Det. Ervansky and I can take another run at her, find out if there's any chance she knew about the show ahead of time."

Before Lt. Rhee could respond, his office door burst open, banging against the wall as a short, heavyset black woman rushed through, barreling toward Rhee's desk. "Keesha, what's going on?"

She had already pushed herself between the lieutenant and his computer and tapped the keys rapidly. "You are *not* going to believe this," she said, then stepped aside and indicated the screen. Maureen and Blake watched along with the lieutenant, immediately recognizing the clip from the over-the-shoulder of Dev's shooting.

"I am going to kick the snot out of Kenny Kentner!" Blake exploded. Then he turned to Keesha. "Is Det. Johnson still here?"

"She went home."

"Would you mind looking on her desk for a contact number for Kentner?"

"I'm on it." Almost as quickly as she had burst into the room, Keesha was gone.

Rhee glared at Blake. "You *said* you got everything from those cameras."

"I did." Blake turned to Maureen. "Could you go find that tech and see if the breach was ours?" She nodded and left, then Blake turned back to Rhee. "There were four cameras and four operators. I had them dump the cards at the scene and they were bagged and labeled within ten minutes of the shooting. We only made one copy of each and those are with the originals."

The lieutenant looked more defeated than angry. "Why didn't I listen to my mother and become an accountant?"

"I'll sort everything out before I leave," Blake said.

Exiting Rhee's office, Blake crashed into Mrs. Gail Hatcher, arguably the toughest, most high-profile defense attorney in Los Angeles. Contrary to the urban legend, she did *not* have the dried scalps of vanquished prosecutors hanging from her belt, but her lupine features and aggressive manner intimidated people as much as if she did.

Recovering her balance, Gail grinned at Blake as if he were about to be the next tasty vole to slide down her gullet. "*Just* the man I'm looking for."

"Mrs. Hatcher. To what do I owe—"

"I'll be representing Ali Garland," she interrupted. "As of right now, your"—and here she pointedly checked her watch—"eight-and-a-half hours of browbeating my client are officially done."

"Be sure to photograph the bruises where I worked her over with a nightstick."

"You're always so entertaining, Detective. I don't know how I live without you between cases."

"And I wasn't aware Ms. Garland had asked for counsel."

"Oh, she hasn't," trilled Hatcher. "But I'm about to go change that. So, the next time you want to talk to *her* you go through *me*." Even the clicking of her high heels as she strode away down the hall was ominous, the staccato rat-a-tat of distant rifle shots.

Blake realized Keesha had materialized by his side sometime during the brief exchange. For an overweight forty year old, she moved with the speed and stealth of a ninja. "I took the liberty of calling Kenny myself and telling him to haul his no-talent ass back down here now."

"I take it you've seen his show?"

Keesha snorted derisively. "It makes *Here Comes Honey Boo Boo* look like *Masterpiece Theater*."

"You're a jewel, Keesh."

"And yet you have still not proposed to me." She walked away, muttering something about commitment-phobic white boys, but Blake knew it was only part of her act. Keesha had been in a relationship for more than ten years, and it wasn't with a white boy. In fact, it wasn't even with a *boy*, but only Blake and Lt. Rhee knew that.

As Blake headed back to his desk, he saw Maureen coming toward him and shaking her head. "It wasn't us."

"You sure?"

"No, I made that up so you'd feel better."

"Sorry. I'm having a crappy day."

"I know; I've shared every minute of it with you, remember? Anyway, those SD cards were logged in at 8:40 A.M. Came direct from the scene. Copies logged out for us by the tech at 2:51 and back in at 3:38, each one accounted for."

Officer Ortiz approached, carrying a large manila envelope she handed to Blake. "From

Sherry in ID"

"Thanks."

"And about Ali Garland's purse," Ortiz continued, "it's not with the evidence and nobody remembers seeing it at the scene."

"Would you mind checking again? I really don't need Gail Hatcher accusing us of losing her client's personal property."

"Sure."

After Ortiz left, Maureen got a thoughtful look on her face. "I don't think we lost it. I think someone in the crowd grabbed it off the ground before the cavalry showed up."

"Ali said she was carrying a lot of cash. We'll have to find out exactly how much in the morning," Blake said.

"The handbag alone is worth forty-five hundred dollars."

"You're joking, right?"

"Seriously. It's an Etienne Volanté, and if you add in the tax it'll cost you five grand to buy it, with maybe enough change back for lunch at Mickey D's."

"How do you *know* that?"

"I've been on the waiting list for one since June. Soon as Fergie and Beyoncé get theirs, I'm next in line."

"Then you recognized it in the Starbucks footage?"

"Yes."

"And you didn't think to mention that?"

"Why? It wasn't relevant. Do you want me to tell you the make of the shoes she was wearing and how much she paid for her earrings? 'Cause I can do that, but doesn't it fall under the category of who gives a hairy rat's ass?"

Sam could tell Lily had been crying as soon as the door of the guest house opened, and it reminded him to fake-up a bit of human concern before diving into the more important business. "Lily, I'm so sorry."

"Mr. Klein. Please come in."

He did, and upon entering the room saw a half-dozen cardboard boxes, some already filled with books, framed photos and knickknacks. "What are you doing? You don't have to leave."

"The new owner begs to differ," she replied, trying but not quite succeeding to keep the bitterness out of her words.

Brianna, Sam thought. Doesn't even have her bony hands on Dev's money yet and she's already channeling Scrooge McDuck. "You let me handle Brianna. And don't even *think* about moving."

Sam could tell she was about to start crying again, so he gently guided her to the couch, his hand light against the small of her back. As soon as they sat, she pulled a tissue from her pocket and blotted her eyes. "I'm so sorry," she said. "It's just that Dev was... he was such a..."

"I know, it's a tragic loss and we're all going to miss him so much." He patted her hand, calculating how much more milk of human kindness he was going to have to pour before getting to the nitty-gritty. "And I don't know if this will be of any comfort to you, but Dev always spoke about you with genuine respect and affection."

"He did?"

The look of hope on her face told him her feelings for Dev had been more than strictly professional. It was precisely the leverage he needed. "My God, every time he came to the office, it was 'Lily took care of this' and 'Lily handled that.' If I had a dollar for every time he said he didn't know how he'd get along without you..." Sam trailed off, as if he were recalling something that had never even happened. In fact, he couldn't recall Dev ever referring to Lily as anything other than "my assistant."

Lily's shoulders lifted and she took one bracing breath to regain her composure. "Thank you so much for telling me that. It means the world to me."

"Well, I thought you should know how much he cared about you."

"Can I get you some coffee? Or a drink?"

"No, no, sit. I'm fine. I'm actually here in my capacity as Dev's attorney. I mean, we're all heartsick that he's gone, but you know the legal system. It keeps chugging along."

"What can I do to help?"

"I'm hoping you have Dev's will here. The signed copy doesn't seem to have made its way back to my office and I need it to get the ball rolling." He saw the fleeting nervous look on her face and interpreted it as embarrassment. I was right, he thought. The reliable assistant had not performed with her usual efficiency and had not yet returned the will.

"Mr. Klein, I don't have it." At least *that* was true, Lily rationalized, as she had burned the contents of the shredder an hour earlier.

"But, surely you know where it is; you signed for it last month."

"Oh, I remember it being delivered, but it took me almost two weeks to get Dev to sign it. I witnessed it, but then Dev took the will and said he'd handle getting the second signature. After about a week, I asked him if he'd gotten the other witness to sign, but he was kind of busy and I didn't get much of an answer. I had it on my calendar to ask him about it again on Monday."

"Any idea who he was going to ask to be a witness?"

"He didn't say. I assumed either Brianna or Buddy."

Buddy, of course, realized Sam. That jerk-off had probably been rolling doobies on the envelope, too stoned to remember what it had inside. Sam stood to leave. "You're right. It has to be one of them. I'll walk over to Buddy's and pick it up."

She accompanied him to the door, where he paused and smiled at her. "Unpack those boxes. I'll be in touch."

As she closed the door behind him, Lily hoped he had not seen through her lies. Let Buddy take the fall. Buddy, who considered her subject material for a cruel joke.

By the time Blake and Maureen were finished grilling Mr. Kenny Kentner about the appearance of the macabre video on the internet, it was 6:30 and they were exhausted. They'd have to come in on the weekend to deal with a whole list of things, starting with the freelancer Kenny had blamed for the leak. Then they'd have to sit through all the footage again, hoping to get a look at the person who had snatched Ali Garland's purse. And the tech had not been thrilled to hear he'd be working on Saturday. They had learned the footprint from the mugging scene was an exact match for the one from the break-in at Ali's house back in the spring, so they would have to decide whether or not to pursue that avenue. The intruder-mugger might have indirectly caused the shooting, but he wasn't really a part of it.

Then there was Gail Hatcher to contend with. She had already sent an e-mail demanding they either charge or release her client, but Blake knew that decision could be legally stalled for another twelve hours. Gail had attached an addendum telling them she would be billing the police department for the careless loss of her client's valuable handbag and its contents, a figure totaling nearly nine thousand dollars, according to her. So, a day that had started with a bang was ending with a groan.

Maureen hung up the phone. "Voicemail again."

"We'll find him tomorrow. What the hell was he thinking, posting that video online?"

"Oh, I'm sure he made some quick-and-dirty cash deal with someone."

"You know, the lieutenant kept us out of the raid last night so you could have a quiet first day to get acclimated."

"We sure screwed him on that, didn't we?"

"That we did," Blake said, getting up. "I vote we call it quits and hope tomorrow is less dramatic."

If Buddy's bloodshot eyeballs weren't enough of a giveaway, the marijuana cloud that wafted out of the guest house doorway would have cinched it. "Mr. K," he rasped on the intake. Then he coughed out, "Dude."

"Buddy. May I come in?"

"Knock yourself out," he said, stepping aside and waving ineffectively at the ganja reek. "Sorry about the weed. Grief and all, you know."

"Yes," Sam replied dryly. "I think Queen Victoria did the same thing when Prince Albert died."

"Those fuckin' paparazzi shouldn't of been chasing that car."

"Buddy, I need a little focus here. Do you remember Dev asking you to sign as a witness to his will?"

Buddy thought hard. Sam could tell he was thinking hard because his face scrunched up and he slowly bobbed his head, as if to shake free a memory that had lodged in one of his few remaining brain cells. "Would it have been with like pens and stuff?"

"Yes, Buddy, he would have asked you to sign your name with a *pen*, as opposed to, oh, let's say a dildo."

"Dildo. Good one, dude." A vapid chuckle came out of his mouth, followed by a burp that sent pot breath and the smell of half-digested junk food Sam's way.

"We're going to focus, remember? Did you sign something for Dev?"

"I think I did. It was a couple years back, though. Or maybe yesterday. You want some Cheetos?" He reached for the open bag, pulled out one of the day-glow squiggles and popped it into his mouth.

Sam realized strangling Buddy would be a selfish pleasure, but it wouldn't get him closer to the goal line. With a clenched jaw he ignored the open-mouth crunching, speaking patiently and slowly. "Good. You signed it. Now I need you to tell me where it is."

"I'm kind of sure I don't have it."

"*Kind of* sure?" Sam looked around at the clutter in the room, knowing the will could have been covered with two inches of detritus by now.

"Yeah. I think maybe Dev took it to give to the Pooch."

"Who?"

"That chick in the other guest house."

"Lily Sims? Dev's assistant?"

"Right. The Pooch." Through his bubble of mellow, Buddy saw Sam's look of disapproval. "Oh, come on, man, you must've seen her. Woof. Yeah, yeah, I *know*, it's not politically collect to say stuff like that anymore."

Jesus, Sam wondered, how stoned *is* this ying-yang? "Are you *sure* Dev took the will back from you to give to her?"

"Dude, I'm not even sure what color my pants are."

Sam told his phone to call Dennis, then realized he must have already left the office. I'll call him in the morning, he thought, and have him search this place until he finds the will. "Buddy, as much as I'd love for you to keep living here, I'm legally required to tell you that you've got to move now that Dev's dead."

"Dev's dead? That's harsh."

Sam left without another word. Buddy waited a moment, then tilted his head up and closed his eyes. "Green," he said out of nowhere, then looked down at his blue pants. "Shit."

As Blake eased his car into the Friday going-home traffic, the normal maddening slow-crawl felt almost soothing after twelve hours of nonstop tension. He steered them through the flow of Sunset Boulevard heading east. "I hope you don't expect me to provide today's level of excitement all the time." He grinned at Maureen and she flashed back that dazzling smile. It was the first time all day he'd really looked at her, and he realized he'd been wrong about her eyes yesterday. They weren't electric blue at all, more of a smoky gray-blue. Or maybe it was the mid-October post-sunset darkening that made them look that way.

"Hey, I'm sorry I went all Robocop this morning with Ali Garland," Maureen said. "I swear I thought she was lying about everything."

"But you were right about Kenny. Libby and I were buying all his b.s. until you yanked his chain. Yanked. Get it?" Blake added dryly.

"Fifty percent doesn't feel like a very good average for my body-language skills. I may have to hunt down and kill a couple psych professors at UCLA."

"You went to UC?" he asked.

"Yeah, you?"

"Champeen of the intermural swim team. When did you graduate?"

"Two and a half years ago. I took a couple years off halfway through," Maureen replied.

"You go backpacking through Europe?"

"Something like that. So, when did you graduate?"

Blake slowed to wave in a driver on a side street who might otherwise have grown old and died waiting for the next opening. "Seven years ago. I came here from St. Paul, Minnesota, frostbite capital of America."

"No wonder you stayed. The lure of the

endless summer."

"Yeah, the weather was a big factor, but it was more that I wanted to escape my parents' expectations for me."

"They wanted you to grow up to be a circus clown?" she asked.

"A dentist. Like my dad; like my mom; like my older brother. What made *you* become a cop?"

"Nothing as satisfying as killing parental aspirations. I was influenced as a child by a TV show called *The Brothers Gunn*."

"I *loved* that show. I was maybe in second grade when it went on the air, and I wanted to be like Max Gunn."

"I wanted to grow up and marry Danny Gunn."

Then it came to Blake. "Wait a second, that's where I heard that line before. That hang-him-by-his-own-intestines thing you said this morning. I should have recognized you were doing Max's gravelly voice."

"That was from the third-season opening episode called 'Kill Or Be Kilt'."

"Was that the one with the Scottish serial killer?" he asked.

"Very good!"

"God, I haven't thought about that show in years, but who knows? Maybe it *was* a subliminal influence on my young mind."

"I know it was on mine. I never missed an episode and I actually believed real cops did all that jumping-onto-moving-cars stuff, and talking in jokes. Anyway, I decided on law enforcement when I was six."

"And saved your folks a fortune in tutus."

It was nearly dark by the time Blake pulled onto the circular drive of the big Spanish, and the lights of the porte cochere were already on. A fit-looking man watered rose bushes on one side of the entrance. He turned, squinting, as the headlights swept his face, then waved as the car slowed and he saw Maureen.

"Come on," she said, her hand on the door release, "I'll introduce you to Charlie."

"That's okay. It's been a long day and I think I'll head home."

Maureen reached across to the ignition and turned off the key as the man locked the hose nozzle and walked toward the car. "What I meant to say was get out of the damn car and meet Charlie."

As Maureen jumped out and closed the passenger side door, Blake saw the man put his arm around her shoulders and give her a quick peck on the cheek. Great, he thought, now I have to pretend I'm thrilled to meet my partner's sugar daddy. Blake stiffly rounded the front of the car and walked over to where the two stood. He was relieved to see the guy at least had the decency to take his arm from around Maureen for the intros.

"Charlie, this is my new partner, Blake Ervansky."

"Hey, Blake." The handshake was firm, and Blake could see he was a good-looking guy, but he had to be at least twenty years older than Maureen.

"And Blake, I would like you to meet my father."

Her *father*. Of course. Blake rearranged his face from a rictus of tolerance to a friendly smile as quickly as possible. "Nice to meet you, Charlie." He snarked his eyes at Maureen, who smiled back innocently.

"I'm about ready to throw some steaks on the grill, so if you'd like to stay for dinner, there's plenty of food."

"Thanks, but maybe some other time. I have to get going, and I believe your daughter doesn't need to spend any more time with me today."

As he pulled out of the circular drive, a bone-deep weariness settled over Blake and he realized he wanted to be home. For the first time all day, he thought about Jane and hoped she'd be there at his house.

It used to be that twenty-five laps after work had been enough to transition him from detective mode to relaxed human being, but as the homicides, drug overdoses and child-abuse cases stacked up over the years, Blake needed fifty laps in the pool, then seventy-five. It was certainly better than the escalating alcohol intake many long-time cops used to anesthetize themselves, but Blake was finding that wearing himself out in the water at the end of the day wasn't calming him down anymore.

The nights Jane was there were the best. Her patience and calm could drain away the poison of even the worst days, and feeling her head tuck under his chin, breathing in the rosemary scent of her hair, those were enough to soothe him. Her sweetness reminded him there was a safe place for him, a place where women aren't beaten by their own husbands, and meth moms don't raise their children in squalor.

He had met Jane almost two years after

buying his house. The kitchen had been his first big project and, once it was done, Blake bought a beginner's cookbook and started living on more than his previous two staples: drive-through and take-out. Once a week he took Laurel Canyon to Ventura Boulevard in the valley and loaded up on groceries at the big Ralph's a block north of there.

He was in the produce section, debating whether to spend the extra money for the organic carrots, when he noticed a girl, maybe seventeen or eighteen, standing in front of the bin of avocados. She had a suspicious look on her face as she picked one up and brought it to her nose for a furtive sniff. Having gathered no useful information from that, she turned it in her hand for a bit of hard scrutiny. Blake had come up next to her, pretending to be selecting a mango from the adjacent bin. She was way too young for him, but she was adorable in her produce befuddlement, and his only intention was to help her. "Guacamole," he said quietly, startling her out of her exam.

She looked at him with an unsure smile. "English, por favor?" she said hesitantly.

"Guacamole *is* English. Well, American. And it's an avocado's highest and best purpose on Earth."

"I have never seen one of these things before in my life."

She didn't know what an avocado was, her voice had a slight country lilt, and her hair was that very light blonde many starlets preferred. "Let me guess. You just got to LA and you're an actress."

That opener had usually gotten Blake a

positive response, the flattered smile, the fluttery lashes, sometimes even a light touch on his arm to accompany the giggle, so he was caught off guard when avocado girl looked insulted.

"Now let *me* guess. You've been here a long time and you're a Chippendale's dancer."

"What? No! I'm a police officer," he said, taken by surprise.

"Well, lookee there, neither one of us is a very good judge of character, because *I* am a kindergarten teacher."

With that, she pushed her basket away and Blake understood three things in rapid succession, he *had* insulted her, she was at least four years older than he had guessed, and he didn't want her to get away. He quickly threw four avocados in a plastic bag, grabbed a couple limes, then headed for dairy, where he picked up a container of sour cream. Garlic and onions he had at home.

Blake walked by the aisle ends until he spotted her between two walls of canned goods, then waited to see which way she turned at the other end. Swinging his cart around sharply, he rounded a chips display and started down the flour, sugar and spices aisle, moving slowly, as if he were deciding which brand of baking soda to buy, but always keeping her in his peripheral vision as their carts approached each other.

She considered all her choices carefully, checking prices, then putting the smallest bag of flour in her cart. While she read the label on a jar of something Blake couldn't see, he crossed the aisle and nosed his basket almost up against hers. "I'm sorry," he said, loud and clear, no hesitation. There wasn't any hostility when she looked at him, only respectful wariness.

"I really am a cop, my mother will vouch that I am the second-most reliable of her three children, and my lifelong dream has been to make guacamole for a kindergarten teacher." The wary look had softened to one of skepticism, so Blake pushed his advantage, taking out his business card and thrusting it toward her. "These avocados will take at least four days to ripen, so you have plenty of time to think about it, but when Friday rolls around and you're ready to try what many have called nature's most perfect food, dial that number. You can bring a bodyguard, a chaperone or a Rottweiler."

She didn't say a word, but she struggled to keep the amused smile off her face as she dropped his card in her purse, then pushed her cart around Blake's and continued walking down the aisle.

"Don't shatter my dream," he called after her, but she didn't look back. Then, before she rounded the corner and disappeared, he yelled, "Do you really think Chippendale's would hire me?" He turned back to his cart to find a woman of at least eighty giving him the old once-over.

"They'd be crazy not to," the woman said, leaning heavily on her cart for support.

Jane's phone call finally came through on Thursday and, though she wouldn't go to Blake's house, she agreed to meet him at a park in Van Nuys on Saturday afternoon. Blake introduced her to guacamole and tasted the sweet, slushy Kool-Aid-based beverage she had brought in a Thermos, a family recipe, she said, for something called Baptist Sangria.

As those first few weeks went by, Jane

exploded a number of myths and misconceptions Blake had about women, without even realizing she was doing it. She talked matter-of-factly about her hardscrabble upbringing in a West Virginia mining town, but had neither the bitterness nor the need to conquer the world so often seen in people who grow up knowing what a terrible hand of cards they were dealt at birth.

Since she shared an apartment with two flight attendants, she always came to Blake's house rather than the reverse and, even though they began spending every Saturday together, winding up for the night at his place, she never left anything behind. No hairbrush or perfume or change of clothes, all the things Blake was used to finding when he had dated a woman for more than a month. Jane showed none of the usual signs of trying to settle in to his space, which Blake appreciated. At first.

There was a genuine joy in Jane. Not the "OMG, I have a second callback" elation of the actresses Blake had dated in the past, but the deep satisfaction she had from having worked her way through college and finally becoming a teacher, a position as distant and unattainable as astronaut to her family back in West Virginia.

Half of her salary every month was sent home to her mother. One of Jane's brothers had already joined her father in the mines, but she was determined her younger siblings would have an easier time than she had had if they wanted to escape a dead-end existence digging coal or marrying a man who did. First-year kindergarten teachers don't make a fortune anyway, and with half of it going back east, Jane lived on the tightest budget possible.

Blake was used to inviting broke young women out to dinner and having them order a massive steak or a huge pasta dish, only to fill up after four bites, then take the doggy bag home "for lunch tomorrow." And it wasn't something he had ever minded. But as he and Jane settled into a regular weekend routine, she insisted on bringing Friday night's dinner. She would let him take her to a restaurant on Saturday night, but Blake noticed she always ordered the least expensive entrée on the menu.

She never took advantage, never crowded him, and never once asked where their relationship was headed. That was everything Blake had always wanted in a woman, but now he wanted more. Lately, he had found himself wondering why she wasn't pressing him for a commitment and, surprisingly, wishing she would. He had been toying with the idea of asking her to move in with him, but she had never given him any indication she wanted to.

As Blake rounded those last few turns before his house, he knew how disappointed he'd be if her little Honda wasn't in his carport. Even though it was Friday there was no guarantee, as she sometimes had school functions to attend and occasionally she spent an evening with other teachers. Blake had unsuccessfully tried to winnow out information from her about those nights. And although he thought his questions about her "girls' nights out," were subtle, she had seen through his ruse, cocked an eyebrow at him and never clarified whether any of the teachers on the nights out were male.

For the first time in his dating life, Blake realized *he* was the one who needed clarification, reassurance and forward momentum, and as he put the last curve behind him and saw her car, relief lifted his spirits. It was short-lived.

Jammed next to her Honda was an older-model Chevrolet, missing a rear bumper and with a patch of rust alongside the license plate. With nowhere to park, Blake cruised by slowly, then turned left into the driveway of his nearest neighbor. She was the elderly widow of an early rock legend and didn't own a car. Her caregiver would have left at seven after making her dinner, so Blake hoped it would be okay to leave his car in her driveway for a couple minutes while he checked out Jane's company.

He felt annoyed as he walked the hundred yards down to his house. Of all the rotten days for her to invite someone over. He badly wanted her attention, her dinner, her soothing and her body, and he was pissed-off that he would now have to play jovial host to one of her friends.

As he approached his house, he noticed movement in the living room, but it wasn't Jane. He stopped and looked, trying to make sense of what he *thought* he saw: a man holding the biggest knife in the world. Where was Jane? He couldn't see her and his heart began pounding with fear-triggered adrenalin. Ducking below the top of the shrubs so as not to be seen, he ran the last fifty feet to his front door. He heard no screams or scuffling when he put his ear to the door, so he quietly tried the doorknob. The door was unlocked, and he stepped softly into the entryway. He could hear low voices from the living room and one of them, thank God, was Jane's. Moving carefully along the wall of the foyer, Blake slid out his Glock and raised it alongside his right ear pointed upward. At the entrance to the living room, he flattened himself more closely to the wall, ventured a peek into the room, then pulled his head back as soon as he'd taken in the scene. Jane was sitting on the couch, but Blake had only been able to see her legs from the knees down, so he didn't know if she was tied up or hurt. The guy with the knife was apparently the only other person in the room, but Blake braced himself to go after anyone else who might be ransacking the rest of the house. He sensed movement as the punk, who stood on the other side of the coffee table from Jane, leaned toward her, knife extended.

One quick breath to steady himself, then Blake pivoted on the ball of his left foot, swinging his right around to plant it solidly, crouching slightly and bringing the Glock down. "FREEZE! DROP THE KNIFE! DROP IT!"

Blake was familiar with the slow, surreal unfolding of critical moments like this. The punk, who appeared to be in his late teens, turned toward Blake, the knife still in his hand, but at the sight of a six-foot-four-inch man with bloodstains on his suit pointing a monster gun at him, the kid froze in terror, everything paralyzed except his bladder. While the front of his jeans darkened with involuntarily released urine, Jane stood, ignoring the knife and putting her arm protectively around the kid's shoulders. Unable to process what was happening, Blake maintained his defensive crouch until Jane's voice overrode the pounding in his ears.

"Blake," she said, as if introducing him to someone they had just run into at the mall, "this is Johnny Buffington. He's the son of one of my fellow teachers and he's been demonstrating these fantastic knives for me. This one, for instance," and here she gently took the knife from the still-motionless boy, "can cut a penny in half."

Blake straightened, slowly lowering his gun while Jane turned the boy around and pointed down the hallway. "Go right in that first door and I'll bring you some dry clothes." She watched Johnny disappear down the hall, then turned back to Blake. "Cap'n Crunch on a cross, Blake, what were you thinking?" Even with the enormous knife in her hands, she seemed more like a kindergarten teacher admonishing a child for eating a crayon than a woman confronting her lover for almost gunning down a salesman.

"I *thought* I was saving the life of the woman I love."

If Blake assumed tossing in the woman-I-love bit would get him off the hook, he was mistaken. She shook her head, then placed the knife in his hand. "I'm going to find some dry pants for that poor boy while you get out your checkbook, 'cause you're buying that knife."

As she turned and walked down the hall, Blake stood with a gun in one hand and a knife in the other. With all that weaponry, he should not have felt as helpless as he did.

Swiss Air flight 928 landed at 6:14 Saturday morning, only ten minutes late. There were no reporters or paparazzi around to note former Governor Joe Roberts disembarking, and the distracted, sleepy passengers wouldn't have cared even if they had known.

No liveried limousine driver held up a

square of cardboard with Joe's name scrawled on it to give away the game; the man who fell in step with Joe as he strode through Terminal Three at LAX wore a dark blue pinstriped suit and a blue and silver, diagonally striped tie. Only if you had observed the man's deferential nod upon greeting Joe, and his swift movements in relieving the former Governor of his suit bag and briefcase, would you have deduced he was an employee rather than a business associate.

In defiance of all the posted signs, the stretch limo was parked in the red zone, its government license plate a warning to any zealous airport cop with ideas about enforcing the rules. The pinstriped man opened the back door and held it as Joe Roberts got in.

As the heavy door closed solidly behind him, the aroma of fresh-brewed coffee filled Joe's nostrils and he was thankful he had declined the oily black liquid that passed for coffee in first class. Two other men were already seated in the well-appointed interior, one about Joe's age and another much younger. The younger man began speaking immediately. "All right, we have a lot more information since we called yesterday. The woman is being held in..." He trailed off as the older man laid a hand on his wrist and shook his head. The younger man realized Joe was glaring at him as though he had made some kind of mistake.

"Coffee only, for now," the older man said, a movement of his head indicating the driver, who had put Joe's valise in the trunk and was walking to the driver's side door.

"Of course," said the younger man as he reached for the carafe and poured a cup of Joe's favorite blend. Joe took the coffee, but shook his head at the proffered plate of croissants and Danish. As soon as the driver had slid in, closed his door and started the engine, the older man pressed a button on the grid by his elbow and the privacy panel rose smoothly to separate the forward cab of the car from the compartment where the three men sat. Simultaneously, soft music began playing in the background, additional insurance that what was said in the limo *stayed* in the limo.

Joe drank his coffee and listened as his two aides updated him on what they had been able to find out concerning Dev's murder since yesterday. He nodded occasionally, emotionally disconnected from the fact that they were discussing the death of his son. When the last of their information had been passed on, Joe set down his cup and spoke, not like a bereaved father but like a canny politician.

"Here's the way I see it. They have that actress dead to rights, but Hatcher is a good enough attorney to put up a fight. She knows she'll lose but she wants the publicity. Let's make sure the DA pushes this. I want to be in that courtroom ASAP, looking for justice and grieving like hell. And I want the press to ambush me as I leave the courthouse every day." He turned to the younger man. "Get Seigler on it now. Figure out what they're most likely to ask, then have him start writing up my answers. Tell him to make certain they're sincere-sounding, heartfelt. I also want a statement for a press conference Monday morning. There's no way to ignore the elephant in the room, so I'll have to acknowledge the estrangement, but have Seigler frame up something that sounds as if my son and I were finding our way back to each other. Makes his death more poignant if a reconciliation was imminent." Now he spoke to the older man. "I want them to sympathize with the grieving father, but they shouldn't see me as weak."

"Maybe you can announce some changes to your platform," the older aide suggested. "Get tough on crime, appoint stronger judges, close legal loopholes, that kind of thing."

"Good thought. And come up with some legislation we can propose and name after Dev, like they did with Megan's Law or Amber Alert."

The younger aide got all that down, then sat back and looked at Joe. "I see one problem with this plan."

"And that is?" Joe asked.

"Well, the public's going to love you while you're sitting in court doing your impression of Ron Goldman's father, but what happens to the campaign if the trial drags on for months?"

The older aide shook his head, sad that it was getting harder and harder to train the new puppies to speak to their masters properly. He would talk privately with the younger man later, tell him that although men like Joe Roberts know they are venal, soulless bastards, they do not appreciate having it pointed out to them. "It won't last for months," the senior aide said wearily. "The police have the murder weapon, motive, witnesses and more surveillance footage than the NSA. Two weeks, tops."

Joe had a second cup of coffee, and the three of them rode in silence to the Roberts compound in the Pacific Palisades.

They had not gone to bed still mad at each other, but they hadn't been all lovey-dovey either, so Blake was not surprised to wake up with raging morning wood. He looked over at Jane, who was still asleep, deciding that waking her for sex would not endear him to her any more than his ill-chosen words last night.

After he had written out a check for a hundred and thirty dollars for a knife he didn't need, and the kid had left wearing an almost new pair of Blake's jeans—Jane had told the boy he could keep them—the long day finally caught up with him and he was primed to spar.

As usual, Jane did not ruffle. Blake had a theory kindergarten teachers take some secret training that enables them to remain calm and reasonable in the face of most childish behavior, but he had sorely tested her equanimity with his irritated complaints about a stranger in his home, his parking spot being commandeered, getting blackmailed into buying an overpriced knife and losing what he falsely claimed were his favorite jeans.

Normally Jane would have reacted to the message beneath the complaints: *I had a crappy day and I need you to hold me,* but Blake crossed an unspoken line after she had explained she was doing a favor for a colleague whose oldest child was trying to hone his selling skills. The colleague had assured Jane she didn't have to buy anything, just let the kid rehearse his spiel. She had told the boy to come to the house at 6:00, thinking she and Blake would listen politely to a fifteen-minute pitch and that Blake might then generously offer to buy one of the little paring knives for twenty bucks before they enjoyed a romantic dinner and a moonlight swim. Of course, this was before she learned the cheapest knife he had was seventy-five dollars.

Then Blake had been over two hours late getting home, Jane had been reluctant to send the boy away without at least a small sale and, knowing she had less than ten dollars in her wallet after picking up food from their favorite Thai restaurant, Jane decided to stall until Blake finally arrived to help her out. She listened to the boy's sales pitch several times, giving what she hoped were helpful suggestions and wishing Blake would hurry up and get there.

Once they had each said their piece, the evening might have been salvaged, except Blake wasn't quite ready to back down. "If you weren't the only person in LA without a cell phone, I could have called and told you I'd be late."

Blake knew he had blown it as soon as he saw the look on her face. She walked quickly to the kitchen and started plating their dinners for a microwave warm-up, trying to act as though she were not on the verge of tears. As the old saying goes, you can't suck the bullet back into the gun once it's fired, though Blake would have given anything to do so.

Jane could not afford a cell phone. Even the offers of "free" phones were beyond her reach because of contractual monthly fees, so earlier in the year Blake had decided to surprise her with a cell phone and a check for the first year's service, expecting if not a delighted squeal, then at least a thank-you kiss.

Instead, she had handed the phone and the check back to him and said, "Do I look like a ho to you?" He assured her she looked nothing like a ho, and that's when she surprised him by saying, "Then why are you treating me like one?"

Blake suggested she was being overly sensitive; they had been dating for six months and he could easily afford the gift.

Jane sat with him and explained what it was like to grow up dirt poor, or as they called it back in West Virginia, *coal* poor. Blake, having been blessed with parents whose thriving dental practice ensured their three children didn't go without, had never given much thought to those little urchins he had seen in school, the ones whose lunch—if they even *had* a lunch—often consisted of nothing more than a mayonnaise sandwich.

For the first time he heard the urchins' perspective, as Jane assured him she had been one of them. She described what it was like to wait with her mother for the government surplus distribution every few months. It was usually either cheese or peanut butter, so meals for the following ten days or so would be built around that federal largess. She told of looking forward to Christmas and Easter, not for any religious reasons, but because the Christian charities saw to it each poor family had at least a frozen turkey and whatever trimmings could be packed into a can or a box.

The wealthier people of the town tried to be sensitive to the plight of the needy children, and one of them came up with a program called Backpacks Full Of Love. Every Friday morning people would drop off nonperishable food at the school office. In the afternoon, while the children had their last playground period, the teachers discreetly put food in the backpacks of the kids most likely to have little to eat over the weekend.

Sometimes Jane and her brothers would find true treasures when they got home: instant macaroni and cheese, ramen noodles, fruit roll-ups, individual bags of fish-shaped crackers. Some weeks it was only neon orange squares filled with a crumbly distant cousin of cheese, but every morsel was eaten.

By slipping the food in when the other children couldn't see, the kindly teachers hoped to mitigate the stigma of taking charity, but Jane told Blake she avoided the eyes of any adult other than her parents, always embarrassed that one of them might have been the provider of the items which had stood between her and hunger the weekend before.

Starting at fifteen, Jane had waitressed after school and full time in the summer. She had put herself through her state college with a bit of help from a stipend that was funded by one of the mining companies and earmarked for the college-bound offspring of coal miners, not that there were many of those.

As a direct result of those small childhood humiliations, Jane had decided she would never again be a taker. No matter how little she had, she knew she was better off than many other people, including her family in West Virginia. She could afford to be a giver, even if on a modest scale.

Blake's offer, though well-meaning, had shamed her, conjuring up not only memories of having to accept help in order to survive, but adding the uncomfortable idea of accepting money from a man with whom she was sleeping. Blake tore up the check, returned the phone, and had never mentioned it again. Until last night.

He looked over at the face of this tough little cookie who made him so happy and was so exasperatingly proud and independent. A thick tress of hair covered one of her eyes, the hair he had assumed was bleached until he saw her college graduation photo, with her in a cap and gown, and her beaming parents and four siblings all crowded together for the photographer. The youngest three were tow-headed, Jane and her oldest brother were light blonde, and even the now-darkening hair of her mother and father told him her color was a gift from Mother Nature, not Lady Clairol.

He had not known until she told him, that numerous Swedes had migrated to West Virginia during the Great Depression, backbreaking work in the mines and minuscule wages preferable to starvation.

Blake thought about gently brushing the hair back off her face, maybe waking her, but not seeming like he was trying to. As he considered the ploy, his cell phone rang. Snatching it from the night stand, he turned away from Jane, and spoke as softly as his morning croak would allow. "Hello?"

"Where the hell were you last night?"

Artie Lassiter's voice boomed out of the phone, straining the capacity of its speaker, and Blake realized he had forgotten the retirement dinner at Roy's. "Oh crap, Artie, I'm sorry."

"I'm screwing with you, guy. After you caught that shitstorm yesterday, and with everyone else in the squad dead from the all-nighter, we scrubbed the mission. Do it again another time. How's my replacement working out?"

"She looks better than you, she doesn't fart in the car, and she offered me a blowie."

"Yeah, in your dreams. Give Janie a hug for me and I'll call you as soon as the cool cats reschedule."

"Cool cats? Artie, you're an eighty-year-old beatnik trapped in a fifty-year-old body."

"Suck my—"

Artie hung up, cutting himself off before the final word like he always did, and Blake glanced at the clock. He was supposed to pick up Maureen at eight, so he knew he had to get into the shower. He put his cell phone back on the night stand, then turned to see if his phone conversation had awakened Jane. It had, and the look in her eyes told him he was out of the doghouse.

"Hey, Detective," she murmured, "want to help a girl cut a penny in half?"

"God, I hope that's a euphemism," Blake replied, sliding over and reaching for her.

By 8:00 A.M. Buddy's bungalow had been tossed, and Sam Klein had not found Dev's will. Enough seeds under the couch cushions to replant a Mexican pot forest, but no will. Sam sat down to think while Dennis paged through a vintage porn magazine, one of many they had found next to Buddy's water bed.

"I thought for sure it was here," Sam said, more to himself than to Dennis.

"Should we go through Lily's place next?"

"No. If she says she doesn't have it, she doesn't have it."

"So where is it?"

"Well, I don't think it walked away on its

own. We know Dev had Lily sign it. We *think* he had the stoner sign it, so what if Dev took it into the main house? He might have intended to give it back to Lily and then forgot."

"Is *La Supermodel* going to be happy if we search the house?"

"She's never going to know. Call the limo service and get someone over here as soon as possible."

"Town Car or stretch?" Dennis asked, pulling out his phone.

"Town Car. Let her see how poor people get around."

Blake was running late, but it had been worth it. The girl who had told him on their third date she was a "virgin once removed" was no schoolmarm in bed, and it always surprised him that someone so innocent-looking had such a healthy, uncomplicated approach to making love. She had none of the rules he had run up against with other women, rules about what and where and how.

If Jane was up for sex, there was nothing taboo, and if she wasn't in the mood she told him so. At first Blake had thought that meant she wanted to be begged, seduced or forced, but he quickly learned a no from Jane did *not* mean "convince me." Luckily, the yes-to-no ratio was quite favorable to Blake's desires. Last night's no was disappointing at the time, but he knew that tired and aggravated as he had been, he wouldn't have made an impressive showing. And this morning's yes had more than made up for it.

He stopped in front of the O'Brien house and his partner climbed in the car. "You're a half hour late," she said.

"Yesterday I was thirty minutes early, so I'm averaging right on time."

"Well, ain't you slicker'n snot on a door-knob." She used the words and voice of Max Gunn, bringing a smile to Blake's face.

"You know, you could have let me know you live with your dad so I didn't feel like a jerk all yesterday."

"I was going to tell you when we stopped for coffee, but then that whole shooting-in-the-face thing popped and it slipped my mind. Besides, you deserved to feel like a jerk."

"Mea culpa. As I was recently reminded, I have a tendency to say the wrong thing when it comes to women."

"How 'bout trannies?"

Blake ignored her. "So is your father retired?"

"He was, then he started this blog and suddenly it's the second-largest liberal site after *The Huffington Post*."

"He must have something worthwhile to say."

"Nah. Charlie'll tell you he says the same old progressive stuff you get from Matthews, Maddow and everyone else on MSNBC. Only he says it in a funnier way. And now that all his comedy writer friends are posting, there's a pretty high laugh content."

"Why does he know so many comedy writers?"

"Because he used to write sitcoms before he started producing TV dramas."

It took a minute for the tumblers in Blake's brain to click. "Charlie O'Brien. Wasn't the guy who created *The Brothers Gunn* named Charles O'Brien?"

"I'm impressed. Most kids don't bother reading credits."

"And that's why you know all those lines from the show," he said.

"I grew up on the *Gunn* set. Remember that goofy little Puerto Rican kid who used to get into Danny's house through the dog door?"

"That was you?"

"Don't be a dick. Charlie wrote him into the series so the studio would have to hire an on-set teacher and I could go to school right there. Ricardo and I were the only students at Gunn Elementary."

"So, *my* father handed out dental floss for Halloween, and your dad produced the number one show on television."

For the remainder of the ride, he asked questions and got juicy, insider answers.

"What the hell do *you* want?"

"Good morning to you, too, Brianna." Dev always said she was a total bitch until her second cup of coffee. "May I come in? I have a surprise for you."

"You have my money?" she asked eagerly, glancing at his briefcase.

"No, dear, sixty-five million in currency wouldn't fit in a briefcase."

"Oh."

Brianna sounded disappointed, and Sam thought: *beautiful face, stick for a body, nothing above the brain stem.* She stepped aside and let him in. "So when do I get it?" she whined.

"You know, the will doesn't get paid out

automatically. First I'll have to file a Baranski writ," he ad-libbed. "Then a judge will call for a DeNiro hearing. And if the twelve-seventy forms are all in order, the funds will be released."

Brianna wilted in the face of the bogus legalese. Then she remembered. "So what's the surprise?"

"*You* are going to The Golden Door for a few days. My treat. Massages, facials, anything you want. The car is outside and you need to leave right now."

At first her face lit up at the idea of people waiting on her hand and foot, then a spark of feral intelligence hitched a ride on a neuro-transmitter, making the unaccustomed leap across a synapse somewhere under that frothy mane of hair. "Why?" she asked, narrowing her eyes with suspicion.

"You've suffered a tragic loss and I know Dev would have wanted me to send you away for some pampering."

"No-o-o," she said, dragging out the word. "You're trying to get me away from my house."

"It is *not* your house, damn it!" He hadn't meant to lose it like that, but Sam was sick to death of coddling overprivileged idiots.

"You said Dev left it to me!"

"And *if* I can find his will, you'll get it!" Great. Now it was out. Well, maybe this would get her attention and make her a little more cooperative.

"You don't know where the will is?" Her voice had shot up into Alvin-and-the-Chipmunks range.

"I believe it's somewhere in this house and I need to search for it before the police decide to come here to look around."

"Why would the police want Dev's will? He didn't leave them anything, did he?"

Patience, Sam prayed. "They won't come looking for the will. They'll be looking for evidence to use in the trial."

"Oh. What happens if you don't find it?"

"The money and property will be distributed according to the stipulations of Dev's *prior* will."

"Who gets the money then?"

"Ali Garland."

Brianna staggered, then sat hard on the nearest chair, her eyes watering while visions of Lamborghinis, diamonds and Beluga-grade blow faded and winked out. Her breathing sped up and he feared she was about to have a panic attack.

Sam got down on one knee and held her emaciated hands in his. He would make one last attempt with the avuncular approach before grabbing her twig-like ankles and slamming her head into the wall. "Brianna, sweetie, we can make this happen, but I'm going to need you to do a little acting. Dev told me you wanted to be an actress, and he thought you'd be great at it."

Brianna blinked a couple times, obviously flattered by the lie, but she wasn't ready to go off point. "Ali's going to get all of Dev's money," she brayed.

"No. No she's not. According to the law, she can't inherit if she's found guilty of killing him."

"So then *I* get it?" she asked, brightening.

"Not automatically. If Ali is found guilty, all that does is negate the old will. If we don't find the new one, you and I will have to make a case before the court that Dev *intended* for you to get everything."

"Dev said you were a good lawyer. You'll be able to do it, won't you?"

"Not with you looking very *un*pregnant and holding press conferences to say Ali is a murderer. So here's what's going to happen. First, don't say anything bitchy to Lily Sims. We may need her to testify that she witnessed the missing will and knew what was in it."

"Uh, I may have already—"

"I know," he interrupted. "I've smoothed things over with her for now. So don't get in her face again. You want to prove you're a good actress? Then *act* like you're her best friend."

"Okay."

"Now here's the really important part. You go to The Door to grieve privately. And eat some damn food for a change. I need you to come back looking like a glowing mother-to-be, not a survivor of Auschwitz."

Brianna searched her memory. She was sure she had watched every season of *Survivor* but Auschwitz didn't ring a bell.

"While you're there buy some maternity clothes, *real* maternity clothes, none of that is-she-or-isn't-she bull, and start wearing them every single day. Are we clear?"

"Yes."

"I'll send down a selection of engagement rings from Cartier; you pick one, *only* one, and you put it on and don't take it off. No more clubs, coke, booze or partying. When you come back, you're the Madonna."

"Huh?"

He saw his mistake. "Not *that* Madonna. The mother of—never mind. When you come back be ready to play the role of Dev's bereaved and pregnant fiancée."

Once Sam was sure she understood what the stakes were, he hustled her into the Town Car and sent her off. He told the cook to bring coffee, called Dennis at Buddy's, and prepared to search. He hoped Brianna thought he was doing all this to protect *her* interests, but if the second will didn't turn up, Sam would lose a half-million dollars.

Saturday was a long day for everyone. Sam Klein looked high and low for a will that no longer existed. Joe Roberts prepared for a press conference he hoped would make him seem like a loving father. The "supermodel" rehearsed what she assumed were maternal expressions in the mirror of her spa suite and forced herself to eat an entire scrambled egg. Lily Sims paced her living room, fear and guilt gnawing at her. She understood she had done something horrible, irreversible. *And* she had destroyed Dev's will.

Blake and Maureen looked at the videos again, hoping to see the person who had taken Ali's purse. Unfortunately, not one of the shots was wide enough to include the ground where the purse would have fallen. As Maureen explained to him, in television, faces are money, geography is bullshit.

They interviewed the freelance camera guy, who admitted running back to the truck and making a quick copy for himself before turning the camera's file over to Blake. What he had done was reprehensible, but not prosecutable.

The only apparent good news came when they watched Brianna's press statement from the day before. Her suggestion that Dev had turned Ali down when she needed a loan gave them hope for a new motive and a chance to turn this loser case around.

Gail Hatcher denied them access to Ali, telling them Brianna was too ignorant a twat to understand that Dev and Ali were putting a business deal together. She gave them Ali's agent's phone number so they could confirm what she said.

Tracking down an agent on Saturday is not easy. The good ones play as hard as they work, and the lousy ones don't check their messages often enough, so it was 4:00 o'clock before Rudy Claytor returned their call and confirmed what Gail Hatcher had told them. Rudy e-mailed a copy of the agreement between Dev and Ali in which Dev was to put up a million dollars for Ali to produce and star in a Michael Moore-type documentary. The contract had only been drawn up a couple weeks earlier, and it hadn't been signed yet, but it showed intent. Blake and Maureen knew it blew a big hole in their last hope for a motive. Why would Ali Garland shoot the guy putting up the money for her pet project?

As they sat in Lt. Rhee's office at the end of the day, the three agreed the whole case was a steaming pile, but there was no evidence of intent and no murder. They figured Hatcher would stall a grand jury hearing as long as she could, leaking details that would win public support for her client and making the police look like heavies for having gone after a terrified young woman who had feared for her life and defended herself with lethal force. The evidence would add up to nothing more than a tragic series of events, ending in the accidental shooting of Dev Roberts.

While Blake drove Maureen home, Gail Hatcher paid a visit to her client. As everyone had expected, earlier that day she tried to have Ali released on bond. And although no one would have guessed from her commanding performance, Gail had not tried very hard.

When she had explained her strategy to Garland, she expected resistance, but her client understood she had temporarily replaced Ann Coulter as the most polarizing woman in America, a situation that would only change with the release of mitigating information and photos of her looking helpless and frightened. It would take time, so they were both relieved when bail was denied. But Gail had discovered a problem.

She entered the interview room and sat across from her client. Once the door had closed, she leaned toward Ali and, in a venom-laced voice asked, "Why didn't you tell me Dev Roberts' will leaves virtually *everything* to you?"

"It doesn't, I swear! He's leaving it all to Brianna. He even waved the thing in my face and told me so."

Gail Hatcher listened to the shock in Ali's voice, observed her body language, and parsed her words carefully, finally deciding her client was telling the truth, very likely for the first time. "The will you are referring to is missing. And if the old one is made public, the police will have the one thing that could nail you, motive."

"So they don't know about the old one?"

"Honey, I didn't get where I am by staying two steps *behind* the cops. The minute I decided to represent you, I put one of Dev's maids on my payroll. She's afraid she'll lose her job and I can be very generous."

"But Dev's lawyer knows about it and, trust me, he's no friend of mine."

"For some reason, Sam Klein's trying to keep a lid on this whole thing, probably running a greedy little scam of his own. As long as the old will doesn't surface, I can still get you off, but eventually Klein's going to have to produce a will. And if it's the wrong one, you're screwed."

"What can we do?"

"You can stay here looking helpless and forlorn. *I'm* going to move heaven and Earth to get the grand jury convened *before* the old will turns up."

The leather Week-at-a-Glance planner on Joe's desk had only three listings for the third week of October: *Mon–Press Conf, Tues–Funeral, Wed/Thur/Fri/Sat/Sun–Grieve.* "Home" was *actually* written above the arrow that stretched from Wednesday morning to Sunday night—you never know who might come across your planner and read it—but Joe knew what he meant.

There were already checkmarks through Monday and Tuesday, and as Joe watched the TV replay of his eulogy, he thought Dev wasn't the only one in this family who can act. Ellen had not attended the funeral. Joe tried to sound sad and protective as he told the reporter who asked about his wife that she was prostrate with grief. Joe had been completely truthful about the prostrate, but unless it comes in one-liter bottles, less so about the grief.

Standing in for her mother, twenty-three-year-old Susannah embodied the picture of bereavement, leaning heavily on the arms of the two men—Joe's top aides—who flanked her, and keeping her face hidden behind a black veil. Joe had insisted on the veil when he realized she had so much Valium in her that a trickle of drool tracked from her lip to her chin. His aides had been specifically instructed to make it look as if she were leaning on them lightly for support, but they all knew diazepam and gravity would have dropped her like a pregnant pole-vaulter had they taken their arms away.

Joe was used to the combative interaction of press and politician, and so was surprised by how respectful those jackals could be when they saw him only as a father who had lost his son.

The real take-away from the funeral for Joe was the kind of juice only royalty and movie stars can provide. More than a hundred major players from the entertainment industry had shown up to pay their respects, and at least half of them came over to speak privately to him, expressing their condolences and promising him support if he decided to continue his campaign for the Senate. Joe, not realizing an actor will promise you a kidney right up until you need one, assumed he was locking in the kind of star power whose presence at a fundraiser guarantees success.

The only thing left on his calendar was to stay in seclusion at his house for five days. With the knowledge that his wife would be blackout drunk and his daughter wouldn't leave her seat on the bus to Downer Town, Joe wondered what he would do to fill the time.

By the day of the funeral, Sam Klein had given up on trying to find the new will. Whatever Dev had done with it, he'd taken the secret to his grave. Sam had attended the service, mostly to keep a tight grip on Brianna's arm, as her instinct had been to throw herself on the casket in a play for public sympathy. With her black dress and her skeletal body, she had the potential to turn the tearful service into a reenactment of *The Corpse Bride*, so he held on and kept her from going airborne.

Sam's biggest disappointment was that he had only been asked for his business card by three people. Trawling for clients at a funeral turned out to be much harder than working the crowd at a party.

Since the grand jury was convening the following week—the District Attorney was going for manslaughter rather than one of several possible murder charges—Sam had decided to keep the old will on the DL for now. As soon as Ali was indicted, he could begin the process of getting Brianna named as Dev's beneficiary. He had been surprised to learn how quickly the grand jury would hear the case. Apparently, in a rare confluence of desires, the police, the DA *and* the defense attorney had all pushed hard to get it over and done with as early as possible.

"Mr. Klein?" Dennis stood in Sam's open doorway.

"What?"

"Unless you need me for anything else, I'm going home."

"You couldn't reach Mrs. Chastain?"

"Voicemail. Twice."

"All right, you can go. I'll stick around for a while in case she calls back."

Since there was little to do until the grand jury ruling, Sam had decided to jump back into his high-dollar divorce case, churn up a little cash. But the future former Mrs. Chastain had been dodging his calls for two days. Rich bitches, he thought, always too busy with their shopping and their Juvéderm injections to keep their eyes on the prize. Sam wished he hadn't gotten her so much interim support money. Seventy grand a month was taking the edge off her incentive to close the deal.

Mrs. Chastain *did* call back at 7:00 P.M. when she had been certain she would only get voicemail. But the very real Sam Klein picked up the phone, so she was forced to tell him face to face—well, ear to ear—that she and her husband were reconciling. Once again for Sam, the dulcet sound of *ka-ching* had become the wet swish of a toilet flushing.

Twilight. Blake stood on the once-rickety deck and looked down at his back yard. He had watched all the news highlights of Dev Roberts' funeral and was thinking about going for a swim, although he knew the water was already getting cold. High leafy walls of oleander protected his privacy, but they also blocked out all but an hour or two of sun.

One eight-hundred-dollar electric bill the previous winter had discouraged Blake from leaving the pool heater on twenty-four/seven, and he wished he could afford a retractable cover. It would be at least another year before he finished all the repairing and remodeling, so maybe then, barring the demise of the air-conditioning system or an invasion of termites, he could get the pool covered. It would be nice to swim year-round without dumping a big chunk of his take-home into the coffers of the LA Department of Water and Power.

The Roberts case was all but put to bed, and the police had breathed a collective sigh of relief when the District Attorney decided to go for manslaughter. The mitigating circumstances and compelling videos would most assuredly preclude an indictment on that charge, and the grand jury would have to be pretty hard-assed to push for involuntary manslaughter or reckless endangerment. No, this one would be history in another week and Blake would be glad to move on to some clear-cut crimes and central casting perps. He and Maureen had spent yesterday and today going over all the witness statements the other detectives had taken, speaking to the three Good Sams who had rushed to Ali's aid at the Starbucks, and generally tying up all the clerical loose ends to be boxed and buried as soon as the grand jury ruled.

It was only Tuesday and he was already looking forward to seeing Jane on the weekend to clear away the bad juju from the previous one. The fight was not their first, but it *had* been their worst, and the make-up sex would have been better if he hadn't had to rush off and spend Saturday at work. Dinner out that night had been okay, but spending all Sunday together was what Blake had been looking forward to. So when Jane told him she had to leave by 11:00 A.M., he had been disappointed.

In his head he knew the two weeks before Halloween are for a kindergarten teacher what a looming April fifteenth is to an accountant, and he guessed she had used the afternoon to cut out paper ghosts and witches. In his heart, though, he felt resentment toward those grubby little kids who got to spend every day with *his* girl.

Blake finally decided braving the chilly water would not be worth the annoying scrotal contraction, so he went back inside to put in an hour on the second bathroom's tub installation.

Lily Sims sat in the dark in her living room, still wearing the somber gray suit she had bought for the funeral. At least Brianna hadn't been rude to her at the service. Lily didn't know what Sam Klein had said to her, but the self-styled supermodel had steered clear of Lily since returning from The Golden Door this morning.

The maternity clothes were a surprise, as was the engagement ring Brianna told reporters Dev had given her a few days before his death. Lily knew there had been no diamond ring on Brianna's finger when she told Lily to clear out. And no invoice for jewelry had come across her desk. Lily tried to recall if there had been a ring in evidence during the impromptu press conference, the one in which Brianna had called Ali a murdering bitch.

Ali. What would happen to her? Lily's own actions would be dictated by the grand jury's verdict, as she had decided to keep her secret if Ali got indicted. But if she went free, with poor Dev cold in the ground, Lily would have no choice but to come forth and tell the truth, despite her former closeness to Ali and despite the possible legal consequences for herself.

The tide of public opinion turned during the week before the grand jury met, and although many people still mourned Dev, most of them had seen or heard at least a part of the story behind the story. The prime-time access entertainment shows competed for interviews with the women in Ali's yoga class, women who told of Ali's "stalker." The young barista spent his fifteen minutes confirming the attack on the actress only moments before the shooting. Cable news programs tried to get interviews with Ali, Blake and Maureen, but did not succeed.

By the time the grand jury ruling came down, only two people were surprised by Ali's exoneration: Joe Roberts and Sam Klein. Each of them watched on TV—Sam in his office and Joe at home—as a beaming Gail Hatcher, a protective arm around her client, declared her satisfaction with a legal system wise enough to look past the surface mirage to the truth below. She also announced her client was turning in the weapon used in the fatal shooting to the police reclamation program, an anti-violence gesture she hoped would inspire others to do the same. She then hustled Ali into a limousine, and left the jostling, shouting reporters on the courthouse steps.

Blake turned off the TV in the break room where he, Maureen, and a few other detectives had watched the scene. "Well, thank God *that's* over," he said.

But it wasn't even close to being over, and within twenty-four hours Blake and his partner would no longer be on the police force.

For a few moments Joe Roberts was furious. He would have no high-profile presence throughout a trial. No chance to play the strong, dignified father figure. No continuing national coverage to augment his recognizability with voters and his own party.

As he calmed down and thought things through, a smile spread across his face, then he picked up his phone.

An hour later, the stretch pulled onto the grounds of the Roberts compound and stopped at the front door. Joe slid into the car, turning first to his two aides and saying mysteriously, "New plan." Then he touched a button on the control grid, waiting until the privacy panel had come all the way down, before speaking to the driver. "Sacramento."

Although Sam Klein had lost two of his biggest clients in as many weeks, he had hoped to convince the coat hanger she needed him to manage the sixty-five million from Dev's estate. Fucking moot point now, he brooded, acid reflux kindling a fire behind his sternum, because Ali Garland would get nearly everything. And she would run that cash through a wood chipper before she'd let him anywhere near it.

After Dev got Ali pregnant, he had asked Sam to make up a will to be sure she and the baby would be well taken care of in the event of his death. He wanted everything airtight and in writing to prevent his father from coming after the money. Not that Joe Roberts needed it, but Dev knew his old man was capable of deriving satisfaction from even posthumous power over his son.

Sam had drawn up a tentative document and given it to Dev to look over. Two days later, Ali came to his office and slapped the will down on his desk, flipping it open to page three and pointing to paragraph XIV-b. People thought she was a ditz because she kept that whole naive ingénue thing going, but she was a smart bitch, all right. She had sussed out Sam's lagniappe and, having caught him with his hand in the cookie jar, held the ultimate bargaining chip. If he didn't want to lose Dev as a client and have her go public so that his other clients started looking more closely at their *own* wills, he'd have to rewrite the damn thing per *her* instructions. And Sam had.

After Ali had been dumped and Dev had knocked-up Brianna—and by the way, had the guy never heard of a condom?—he asked Sam to do another will. Luckily, since the coat hanger didn't have the brains of a Toll House cookie, Sam wrote the will the way he wanted without fear the skanky girlfriend would spoil his plans. Dev barely looked at these things anyway, and even if he did, there was little chance he'd spot something hinky in the innocuous two lines that left half a mil to what *appeared* to be a charity.

So, Sam had two phone calls to make in the morning. One to tell Ali she was getting everything, and God, how he would hate making that call. The second one would be to tell the coat hanger she was out on her bony ass without a peso. Now *that* call was going to be fun.

Reporters and photographers were on alert outside Ali's house when the limousine pulled up. The two guards Hatcher had hired kept the hounds at bay while the women got out of the car and walked to the front door, ignoring the shouted questions. Hatcher strode with her usual don't-mess-with-me verve, but Ali kept her head down and stayed close to her lawyer, a baby chick seeking safety with its mother hen. The two exchanged a few words at the door, then Hatcher walked back toward the car while Ali let herself in.

As soon as she had closed and locked the door, shutting out the noise from the rabble, Ali leaned back against the solid wood and took what felt like her first deep breath in weeks. Her head tilted back, her eyes closed, and she finally allowed herself the satisfied smile she had been holding in since the minute she had shot that smug son of a bitch. She brought her fist up over her head and pumped it as she triumphantly crowed. "*Yes*!"

Det. Libby Johnson entered the hushed squad room, heard what everyone was listening to, then crossed to Maureen's desk. "What the hell's going on?"

"No clue. We rolled in five minutes ago and Keesha told Blake the lieutenant wanted to see him."

Even with the muffling effect of Lt. Rhee's closed door, Blake's voice could be heard. "Bullshit! This is total bullshit!"

Inside the office Rhee sat behind his desk while Blake angrily paced. The lieutenant had expected a reaction like this, and was waiting for the first blast to dissipate so he could explain the situation. "I could not agree more. It *is* bullshit. But when it's the Governor handing it to you, you call it foie gras and you eat it with a smile."

Blake's initial anger flamed out, exactly as Rhee had known it would. Now he was simply pissed-off and the lieutenant had dealt with *that* mood enough to know the steps ahead by heart. Blake folded his arms across his chest in a confrontational attitude. "What if I say no?"

"It wasn't a request and you don't have that option."

"So what you're saying is that if somebody offers enough cash, the Beverly Hills Police Department will sell him a detective as a pet."

"Sell, no. Lend, yes."

"But I *will* be Joe Roberts' pet, right? Or would bitch be a more accurate description?"

The lieutenant had a twelve-year-old son and two teenage daughters, so he was inured to sarcasm. "The job you'll be doing for Roberts is the same as what you do here, but with only one case to deal with."

"LA must have dozens of working private investigators. Why can't he hire one of *them?*"

Lt. Rhee put both arms on his desk and leaned forward. Now was the point in the dance to put some steel in his voice—part tough boss, part reasonable older brother. "Because none of them had a hand on his son's pulse when the last blip went flat."

Blake didn't respond and Rhee, having successfully made the stop, now went for the deflection. "And *they* didn't take the gun away from his killer."

It took Blake a moment to make the connection. "Ah, jeez, not O'Brien, too?"

"Both of you."

"Please, give him the gift of me, but don't

send her down the tubes. I've got six years in, four as a deet. I'm solid. But she's been with the county less than a year and only made sergeant six weeks ago."

"The Governor assured me your careers and pensions will not be affected."

"And we know how politicians keep their promises, don't we?"

The lieutenant flipped open a file folder, pulled out a sheet of paper, and slid it across the desk. "There's your guarantee, signed by the Governor *and* the Commissioner, both close personal friends of Joe Roberts." Blake glanced over the document, knowing the battle was lost. "Spend November and December looking into the shooting again. Go over the details, look for any inconsistencies, play follow-up and reinterview. Then, sometime in January, you give him a final report and you and O'Brien are back on the job."

"We can look, but there's nothing to find."

"You know that and so do I, but Roberts is still in the denial stage of his grief. Maybe by the time you show him proof of what we already know, he'll have moved on to acceptance."

"And what was the sticker price?" Blake asked with a sigh, flopping into the chair in front of Rhee's desk.

"The Joe Roberts Foundation donated two hundred and fifty thousand dollars to the Fallen Officer Fund last night."

Blake's eyebrows lifted in surprise. "I may be a prostitute, but at least I'm commanding top dollar."

"Ervansky, you more than *anyone* should understand what that money means. Oh, don't look so surprised. Do you really think I didn't know about all those on-duty visits to her house? About Artie still buying those kids presents at Christmas and on their birthdays?"

Blake remembered his first days riding with a detective whose partner had died, Artie's feelings of guilt, his tortured belief that it should have been *him* shot in that jewelry store, not Bob Nolan, not a man with a beautiful wife and three kids under ten. He had understood why Artie checked on the family at least once a week, always bringing something—candy, DVDs, a stuffed animal—but Blake had thought those swing-bys were their little secret.

"I know Barbara appreciated everything Artie did to help her before she remarried last year. When a cop dies, though, the widow—or widower—needs more than that. You've worked the phones here on a Sunday, you know how hard it is to get donations anymore."

"Ten say no for every one who says yes."

"Exactly. And that yes might only be a five-dollar check. In case you haven't noticed, the State of California is in the shitter, and it no longer funds programs it calls *nonessential*."

"Thanks to the jackasses we keep sending to the State House," Blake grumbled.

"And we both know Joe Roberts was one of the worst."

The two men looked at each other. They were still on opposite sides of the desk, but were now on the same side philosophically. "I guess this is happening, then," Blake said dispiritedly.

"It's happening. You and O'Brien take the day to wrap up anything you can on your cases, then hand off what you can't. I'll need your guns and badges before you leave tonight."

"As a newly minted civilian toady, will I be allowed to keep my testicles?"

"Nobody else wants 'em," Rhee snorted, as he reached into a drawer. "Here. Brand new laminated IDs. They prove you and O'Brien are state-licensed private investigators." He slapped the cards down on the desk.

Blake took one and passed it under his nose. "M-mm. It still has that new whore smell."

"Your checks will come from Joe Roberts until you're back here, and because I'm *such* a great guy, I gave him figures twenty percent higher than the salaries you and O'Brien are getting from the city."

"If I'd known about the extra money, I would have applied for a lackey position years ago."

"That's right, Ervansky, piss out all the funny in here. Because Joe Roberts is not a joke-around guy."

Blake picked up the second ID, stood, and clicked his heels. "I will serve my new overlord with all the seriousness and respect I can fake."

"By the way, as of today your car is in the shop."

"Why? Nothing's wrong with it."

"Yeah, you know that and so do I. But department paperwork is going to show the vehicle being worked on until the day you're back on official duty."

Blake realized he was being given the okay to keep driving the city-owned car while he played P.I.

"One more thing; there's a bit of a poison pill built into this exercise."

"Why am I not surprised?"

"*If* you somehow prove this was a murder and not, as Lemony Snicket might call it, an unfortunate series of events, the Fallen Officer Fund gets another quarter million, and you and O'Brien each get fifty grand."

"That sounds great. Where's the poison pill?"

"If the BHPD botched a homicide and let the murderer get away, we look incompetent and Joe Roberts makes a political stink."

"Well, as much as I could use the money, you and I both know it ain't happening."

"I know," Rhee said wistfully. "I know."

Ali pulled aside the curtain to see if the reporters were still camped out at the edge of her lawn. They were, but the guards kept them from getting any closer. Flies, she thought. Or maybe vultures. Something that fed off the dead anyway. They had briefly fluttered to life when her car was brought back the night before, but after the officer who had driven it got into the escort patrol car and pulled away, the vultures settled down to wait.

She went back to the kitchen and poured another cup of coffee, then sat to call Sam Klein. She had spent the previous evening hoping the second will had turned up. Gail Hatcher was right, the first will might provide enough motive for the police to start looking more closely into the shooting. Not that they would find anything, but still. Then, right before falling asleep, Ali had come up with a plan, and her first thought on waking an hour ago was that she hoped the incriminating will *did* go public. She now had a way to turn that big lemon into the sweetest lemonade ever. To bypass the annoying Dennis, she dialed Sam's private line.

"Sam Klein."

"Hello, Sam. Long time no speak."

"Ali." Sam crammed as much loathing as he could into the two syllables.

"You sound judgmental. Didn't you hear? I'm an innocent woman."

"Is there a point to this call?"

"Yes, which version of Dev's will are you going to be unveiling?"

"The one that gives you every last dime," he snarled.

"You're sure on that? Not going to fake me out and produce the new one, are you?"

"Go to hell."

"Ah, same old charming Sam."

"Are we done here?"

"Almost. I have two requests. I'd like to be the one to break the news to Brianna, and I want to make the public announcement about my inheritance."

"Well, you can tell the world, but I already called Brianna ten minutes ago. She's probably slashing her wrists as we speak."

"Oh, I wouldn't worry about that. She's too stupid to cut lengthwise, so all she'll wind up with is a few horizontal nobody-loves-me scars."

Brianna was not hacking at her wrists with a razor, although that had been her first idea after she hung up. All that time and work invested in Dev. All those disgusting blow jobs, for Christ's sake, and she was going to wind up with nothing?

Not to mention that she was ballooning

fast with her ace in the hole, the baby she had counted on to secure a proposal from Dev. Shit, she thought, nothing ever goes my way. Brianna picked up the pen to continue making the list of things she needed to get done quickly, before Ali showed up and kicked her out. So far the list had only two items: *get aborshun* and *sell jewlry.*

The first one was easy. The doctor in Canoga Park who had helped out Brenda Schultz several times before, and since he was willing to barter, it wouldn't cost her a cent. Hell, a couple more BJs won't kill me, she thought.

Forty minutes later, doctor's appointment secured and jewelry gathered together—e-Bay would take too long, so she planned to cruise a couple pawnshops before her D&C—Brianna was about to leave when she heard a knock on the front door. Assuming one of those annoying reporters had figured out the gate code, she was in full harpy mode when she yanked open the door.

"Morning, Brianna," Ali chirped. "May I come in?"

"Well, since it's your house, I guess I can't say no."

The "supermodel" stepped to one side, the actress entered, and the big door shut solidly.

Knowing there were spies on the staff, Ali made sure she and Brianna were completely alone and unable to be overheard when she laid out her proposition.

Even in his best suit Blake felt like a poser sharing space with Joe Roberts and his expensively dressed aides. Maureen, standing next to Blake, blended right in with the moneyed crowd as they all waited for the press conference to begin. Her black jacket with matching knee-length skirt projected professionalism and confidence, while the lavender silk blouse with ruffled jabot sketched enough femininity to keep her from looking too severe. When Blake had spoken with her earlier, he noticed her eyes had an almost violet glow, making him wonder if it was not only different lighting that made her eyes seem slightly changed each day, but the color of her clothes. Were her eyes reflecting the lavender of her blouse?

Blake tried to pay attention as the press conference began, Joe Roberts was introduced, and the man himself stepped up to the podium. But it was only a lot of blah-blah-blah to Blake, so he let his thoughts wander.

Maureen had taken the news much better than Blake had, even saying she was happy to take a crack at emulating her childhood hero, P.I. Max Gunn. The two of them had sat with Libby Johnson, who would be their point person on the force, and worked out all the details. Their computer codes had been cancelled so no future investigation could claim noncops had had access to police-only information. They were promptly issued a new code, which gave them exactly the same access as before, but could only be traced back to an innocuous arm of the office of the Police Commissioner.

They could use labs, files and personnel, but they would have to be discreet about it. In other words, Blake and Maureen *were* and were *not* still affiliated with the Beverly Hills Police Department.

Last night they had met with Joe Roberts,

whose only two directives were to look closely at all aspects of his son's shooting and to hand in a report every Monday on the prior week's findings and activities. A young aide had told them who to call for petty cash—which he defined as anything less than ten thousand dollars—and handed them each an envelope. Joe Roberts paid a week in advance.

The blah-blah-blah was ending, so Blake tuned in as Joe gave his final statement about not resting until he had uncovered the truth about his son's death.

Inside the Bel-Air mansion of the deceased Dev Roberts, a deal was struck with the devil, although given the two women involved in the bargain, one would be hard-pressed to say who was the devil and who was the dealmaker.

Certain she could now sidestep even a whiff of motive and still get the funding for her project, Ali Garland exited the back of the house and took the path toward Lily Sims' bungalow.

Lily was surprised to see Ali when she opened the door, unsure how to greet the woman who had once been like a little sister to her. Ali had no such doubts; she stepped forward and put her arms around Lily, embracing her warmly. "Oh, Lily, this must have been awful for you."

When Lily stiffly endured the hug, Ali noticed, but still hoped she could bring down the barrier between them, win Lily to her side like she always had before. She would try sympathy and friendship first and, if those didn't work, she'd bring out the big guns. When Ali let go, Lily wiped at her eyes and asked, "Why did you have to kill him?"

Ali closed the door, not wanting anyone to accidentally overhear what needed to be a *very* private conversation. "You know what he was planning to do to me."

"Yes! And I told you what you needed to protect yourself."

Taking Lily's hand and leading her to the couch, Ali said, "And if the worst thing Dev had ever done to me was to set me up to be caught on TV with unwashed hair, no makeup and baggy workout clothes, I would have tricked myself out that morning to look adorably surprised when the cameras appeared."

"That's what I thought you were going to do," mumbled Lily.

"And I *was*. That was my only intention, I swear."

"Then why? Why kill him?"

"Three weeks before the taping, Dev asked to meet me at my house, so I had the contract waiting, the one for him to put up the funding for my documentary. I thought he was coming over to sign it. You know what he did?"

"No."

"He tore it up in front of me and laughed, then said he had never intended to give me the money. Don't you see? He strung me along just to get my hopes up, even had my agent convinced he was serious, all so he could destroy me."

Ali's eyes now brimmed with tears. Lily saw her shoulders slump, saw her struggle to maintain her composure and that old desire to protect Ali bloomed anew. Still, Lily thought, she killed Dev. Sensing Lily's ambivalence, Ali pushed on. "After he tore up the contract and threw it in my face, he called me a bad actress and a lousy lay. And then he said... he said—"

She broke down in sobs and Lily couldn't help herself; she slid closer and put her arms around Ali. "You don't have to tell me. It's all right," she said soothingly. But Ali pulled away and wiped at her eyes.

"No. You have to hear this. You need to know what he was really like. He said I wasn't even a decent mother, that I couldn't keep his baby alive inside me."

Lily's arms went around Ali again, and this time both of them sobbed. She remembered so clearly the night Ali had miscarried, how she'd held onto Lily's hand in pain and fear, how she kept saying, "Where's Dev? You've got to find him for me, Lily." Lily had known where Dev was and she knew who was with him, but she lied to Ali, told her she couldn't reach him on location.

Lily cried with the remembered agony of losing what had felt like a family to her. She recalled Dev's coldness when he had thrown Ali out of his house. She cried at the knowledge that he could pretend to do a fake business deal to inflict more pain on this sweet and fragile girl.

Ali wept only for effect.

When they had cried themselves out, they sat back on the couch, Lily conflicted, Ali wondering if her performance had been persuasive enough. Throwing in the miscarriage had been an inspired bit of ad-libbing. Dev had never mentioned the baby the night he tore up the contract, but Ali thought her rewrite of the scene had been solid.

"You have to tell all that to the police,"

Lily said.

"What?!" Ali was stunned by the calm and unexpected pronouncement.

"They'll understand why you did it. I'll testify about how badly he treated you. You can tell them about the contract, and I'll tell them how he deliberately set out to get you on TV looking terrible."

Ali could not believe this idiot actually thought the two of them were going to skip hand in hand to the cops and spill their guts. It was time to bring down the hammer. "We're not going to say anything to the police."

"Ali, we have to."

"Why is that? Because your conscience is bothering you? You tell the cops I knew in advance about the *Yanked* taping and you'll be charged as a co-conspirator in a premeditated murder."

"But I didn't do anything except tell you to dress nice and put on makeup."

Ali stood and started pacing, all pretense of warmth and friendship gone. "Didn't you, Lily? Didn't you have good reason to want Dev dead and to coerce me into carrying out your wishes?"

Horrified by Ali's transformation and the implications of her words, Lily tried to defend herself. "No! I never wanted him dead."

"You know Dev's nickname for you, don't you?"

Lily's flaming cheeks confirmed what Ali had only guessed. "The Pooch. He and Buddy called you that when you weren't around. A name that made you feel so worthless and degraded you plotted his murder."

"STOP!" Now Lily jumped up, suddenly terrified. How much trouble was she in?

"And then, of course, there's the money," Ali said with a nasty edge.

"What money?"

"The two hundred thousand dollars you're going to get from Dev's will."

"That's a lie! I saw the will; Brianna gets everything."

Ali pounced, a delighted smile on her face. "So, I'm right. *You* have the second will."

Again, Lily's autonomic nervous system betrayed her, and guilt blazed on her face. "No, I...I shredded it. And then I burned the pieces."

Ali laughed. "Oh, my God, I couldn't have planned this any better myself. See, I'm the one who told Sam what to put in the old will. *I* protected you; *I* made sure you got a bequest. Me, not your precious Dev. And now, when that will is revealed, everyone will know what you stood to gain from his death."

"But I didn't even know about it."

"Who's going to believe that? Especially since you destroyed the new will, depriving Dev's fiancée and unborn child of their rightful inheritance. Bitch, you are going to look downright vengeful."

A bewildered Lily backed away, trying to put distance between herself and this monster. Ali didn't bother to follow. She knew her taunts would be effective even from across the room; she had done live theater. "Oh, the stories I'll tell. About how you tricked me into believing Dev was going to renege on our contract. Dev, who was thrilled to partner with me in a movie project, as my agent will confirm in court."

Lily backed against the wall, unable to retreat any further, unable to escape the hateful lies. “No,” she whispered. “Brianna hates you, and she'll testify Dev did, too. That he never would have given you a penny.”

“Oh, Lily, you poor, deluded girl. Brianna *adores* me. Watch us this afternoon when we talk to those reporters at the gate. You can slip into the bushes and see it live, or you can catch the highlights on *Entertainment Tonight.* Either way, you'll realize you can't say a word without making yourself look like the mastermind behind a murder.”

Lily's knees went wobbly, and she slowly slid down the wall. Ali walked to the door with only a dismissive glance at the trembling woman crumpled on the floor. As she put her hand on the doorknob, she stopped and smiled at Lily. “Look on the bright side. If you keep your mouth shut, you don't go to prison, you *do* get a lot of money and, as a parting gift, Brianna and I are going to let you keep the car.”

“So, Monday morning, your place or mine?”

“Why, Ms. O'Brien, this is so sudden. And I've vowed to stay chaste until marriage.”

“Put your Y chromosome back in your pants, Bunky,” Maureen said, reaching for a garlic roll. “We no longer have an office out of which to work, remember?”

They had stopped at an expensive Italian restaurant in Westwood on their way back from the Palisades, figuring they were both dressed up anyway, might as well do lunch in style. “Well, the perks of my place are a swimming pool and a

Foosball table."

"Tempting as that is, my father's house has the video equipment, monitors and computer we'll need to do this."

"The O'Brien manse it is then."

Their waiter arrived with steak pizzaiola for Blake, veal parmigiana for Maureen and two large sides of spaghetti.

"A sit-down lunch, Friday afternoon free. I could get used to being a private dick."

Maureen raised an eyebrow, but didn't touch the line. "I don't know about you, but I'm going to spend my afternoon spreading that advance all over Rodeo Drive."

"I'm going to attempt to plumb a toilet," Blake said around a mouthful of steak.

"Not sure I know what that means; really glad I'm not the one doing it."

"It means I'm going to install one."

"You don't currently *have* a toilet?"

"Only in the master bath, which I recently redid in masculine, black-granite splendor."

"So, you're a do-it-yourselfer."

"Out of necessity. After I put up half the down and signed on for a mortgage, I didn't have enough to hire contractors to do all the work the house needed. Still needs."

"Your parents pay the other half of the down payment?" she asked.

"My grandfather."

"Another dentist?"

"Not *just* another dentist. He once did an emergency veneer for Weird Al Yankovic."

The crowd of reporters at the gates of Dev Roberts' estate had thinned in the weeks since his death, but the few who remained were about to see their persistence pay off.

In the unfinished second bathroom of his house, Blake realized the two pipe ends he was attempting to join did not match, leaving him two choices. He could pull up the flooring and muscle off all the connections he had spent ninety minutes fitting and sealing, then move the lower pipe three-quarters of an inch, *or* he could say goodbye to his temporary raise and rehire the guy who had installed the Midnight Sky power-flush in the master bath.

He leaned back against the cool porcelain curve of the Snowflake White, considering both options. His eyes drifted to the small TV he had brought in so he could listen to CNN while he worked, and saw the front gates of Dev Roberts' place over the words: "Breaking News." Blake pawed through tools, rags, Teflon tape and instructions until he found the remote, then kicked the sound louder as Ali Garland and the so-called supermodel walked up to the gates.

"Good afternoon," Ali said. "My name is Ali Garland, and I believe you all know Dev's fiancée, Brianna." The stick-girl smiled, placing a protective hand over a bump in her midsection that was smaller than the one Blake still had two hours after his Italian lunch.

"Today I received a phone call from Dev Roberts' attorney, telling me I have inherited the bulk of Dev's sixty-five million-dollar estate."

Blake heard the gasp and buzz from the crowd as he scrabbled in the junk on the floor, this time looking for his cell phone. When he found it, he hit speed dial. "Come on, come on. Pick up."

"O'Brien Prosthetics, can we give you a hand?"

"Are you near a TV?"

"No, I'm driving on Sunset. Why?"

"Ali's inheriting sixty-five million bucks from Dev."

"Mother of God, if that isn't a motive I don't know—"

"Shh, let me listen."

The crowd had hushed after Ali's shocking opener. "I know what you're thinking. What a travesty, what a miscarriage of justice. That the very woman who...who..."

Her hand went to her mouth to stifle a sob, and Brianna's arm curled around her protectively. A tearful Ali looked to Brianna for encouragement, getting it in the form of a nod and a squeeze. Ali mouthed the words "thank you" to Brianna, then turned to the reporters and took a bracing breath. "The woman who by accident killed her good friend and business partner, and took away this wonderful woman's future husband and this baby's father." Here she paused to place her own hand over Brianna's, which still rested on the world's flattest baby bump. "That such a woman should profit from Dev's death is unthinkable."

"Blake, what's happening?"

"I don't know. But Ali and that girl who called her a murdering bitch are suddenly BFFs. Wait, she's talking again."

"...agree with you more. That's why I am relinquishing my rights to the inheritance and signing it over to Brianna. Every dollar that was bequeathed to me will now go to her."

The crowd gasped, erupting into shocked

chatter.

"...ake? ...oing on? ...hear you..."

"Maureen, you're breaking up. Call me when you get home." Blake put down his phone, eyes never leaving the TV.

"All other details in Dev's will are to be honored as written. The generous bequest to his long-time assistant Lily Sims, the amounts to members of his household staff, those won't change. That's all I have to say, but we will be happy to answer all your—"

"If you could hold those questions for one moment," Brianna said, interrupting. "Ali, this is an unexpected blessing for me and my precious child. I know Dev cherished your friendship, as do I. And I also know that his accidental death occurred *before* he had the chance to sign the contract for the documentary film you two were going to produce together."

Ali looked into Brianna's eyes, preparing to feign surprise and gratitude. So many words, she thought, and so few IQ points. Please let her get it right.

"Ali, I would like to write you a check for one million dollars—"

The reporters had by now almost run out of gasps.

"—so that the project near to Dev's heart and your own can go ahead as planned."

The women fell into each other's arms, weeping. Reporters began calling out questions, and the two pulled apart, continuing to hold hands in a show of solidarity and affection.

"Brianna, not long ago you called Ali a murderer. What changed?"

Brianna lowered her head and put her

free hand over her eyes, a gesture demanded by Ali when she realized the twit wouldn't be able to pull off the embarrassment necessary to make her response believable. "I am *so* sorry for saying those hateful things. With my hormones raging," she dropped her hand to her baby bump in case anyone had forgotten she was pregnant, "and having lost the only man I ever loved, I lashed out at someone who has been like a sister to me."

Blake's cell phone rang and he snatched it up. "Maureen?"

"It's Jane."

"Oh, sweetie, I'm right in the middle of something."

"What should I pick up for dinner?"

"Surprise me."

"Bye."

Blake hung up and turned back to the strangest press conference he had ever seen.

As Ali had expected, the reporters left as soon as the press conference ended. She slipped away unnoticed and drove to the Brentwood post office, arriving a few minutes before closing time.

The bills, threats, fan mail and catalogs filled a plastic postal bin, but it was the box she picked up at the counter that most interested Ali, a small package she had mailed to herself the day before she shot Dev Roberts.

Hatcher's guards were still on the scene when Ali arrived home, but the vultures had dwindled to only a few. Setting the heavy bin aside, Ali cut the tape on the box and opened it. Inside was a disposable prepaid cell phone she had not wanted the police to find when they searched her house after the shooting.

"Hello," a deep male voice answered.

"Tommy?"

"Ali! Oh my God, are you all right?"

"I'm fine. It's over. There's no way they can prove anything now *and* I have the money for the film."

"But how? I thought he—"

"I'll tell you everything when I see you. And Tommy? You were perfect. I never could have pulled this off without you."

"Ali, I'd do *anything* for you; I love you."

"And I love you."

"When can I see you?" he asked.

"Day after tomorrow, 3:00 o'clock."

"Same place?"

"Yes. If I'm not there by 3:15, it means I'm being followed and I can't risk stopping."

"Can I call you?"

"Not on my cell. Let me give you a new number that can't be traced."

Standing at the wall mirror, Blake could see Jane sitting up in the bed behind him. She was paging through *Ladybug*, jotting notes on a pad when she found anything she could use for her kindergarteners.

When Jane showed up with lasagne for dinner, Blake had tried to look hungry, even telling her he had eaten a salad for lunch. Now, after two heavy meals, he felt uncomfortably full and not as romance-ready as he liked to be on a Friday night, especially when a sweet young thing was in his bed warming herself up for him with dot-to-dot panda bears and help-the-bunny-find-his-mommy mazes.

He stroked his chin as he angled his face in the mirror. "I was thinking," he said.

"Mm-hmm?"

"Now that I'm going to be a private eye, probably with a tortured past full of dark secrets and three ex-wives, maybe I'll grow some face fuzz. Nice 'stashe, a little soul patch. What do you think?"

She looked up from her reading and met Blake's eyes in the mirror, holding the look for several seconds. "We-e-ell, that's kind of a coincidence, because *I've* been thinking of letting my underarm hair grow out three or four inches."

Jane looked innocent enough when he turned from the mirror to meet her gaze, but he wasn't so clueless as to miss the point she was making. "Am I to assume, then, that you would *not* quiver with desire if I sported facial hair?"

"No more than you would pop a chubby if *I* sported Wookiee pits."

She smiled and went back to her magazine. Blake slipped into the bed and looked over her shoulder. After a moment he pointed to the open page. "That one and that one."

"No, this one's wearing a bell and this one only has one horn," she said.

Blake scrutinized the page for another moment, then leaned back against the headboard with a sigh. "School is hard."

"I know. You're lucky you got out before they came up with these cow-matching tests."

"Get that out of my bed," Blake growled as menacingly as he could without wiping the grin off his face. Jane tossed the magazine away in a careless arc, turning off her lamp and snuggling down against him. Still propped back on the headboard, he put his left arm around her and held her close, her head resting lightly on his bare chest. "I was thinking..."

"Oh, poosh, that's what you said right before you suggested the porno star look."

"We haven't gone to the beach in a while. Maybe we could pack a lunch, pop some corn for the seagulls, roll a few winos. Spend the whole day beach bumming."

"That sounds like fun. If you'll make the popcorn in the morning, I'll fix sandwiches."

Blake hesitated before replying, "I was thinking more about *Sunday* afternoon."

"Oh."

"Sunday not good for you?"

"Gosh, I have so much to do for Monday. I was hoping to get out of here by 11:00."

"That's fine. We'll do it tomorrow."

But it wasn't fine at all. This would be the third Sunday she hadn't stayed all day. Like most men his age, Blake considered himself an expert in the art of easing out of a relationship while still *seeming* to be fully engaged. He was afraid Jane might be doing exactly that to him.

Sunday afternoon at 2:45, Ali lingered over her second glass of chardonnay as the late lunch crowd slowly disappeared. She had noted every car that pulled in after her and seen all of them leave except for the one belonging to the family on the outdoor deck. She doubted the parents of three children wearing Universal Studios caps were following her, so she relaxed and looked out at the foaming surf, but kept part of her attention focused on the T-intersection a few hundred yards down the road.

When the familiar motorcycle roared by on Pacific Coast Highway, then turned left onto Sunset, Ali signaled for the check.

A few minutes later she pulled into the nearly empty parking lot of the Lake Shrine, a ten-acre, multidenominational meditation garden that most Angelenos don't know exists. The last religious service let out at noon, and the Shrine closed at 4:30, so this was the best time to meet Tommy without being seen.

As she entered, Ali passed the small Court of Religions where the Buddhist Wheel, the Christian cross, the Jewish Star, the crescent moon and star of Islam, and the Sanskrit symbol for Hinduism shared space harmoniously, maybe the only place on Earth they did.

A couple people were still in the gift shop by the exit, but when Ali stepped onto the path that bordered the lake, she was alone. Looking like an ordinary seeker of serenity, she moved along slowly, enjoying the beautiful gardens and watching the swans glide over the glassy surface of the water.

The view was dominated by the huge archway that fronted the thousand-year-old sarcophagus holding some of Mahatma Gandhi's ashes, but Ali only glanced cursorily at its gleaming blue tiles and the three massive gold lotus blossoms that topped it. Her goal was the area west of the sixteenth-century Dutch windmill replica.

The only sounds were the plashing of the waterfall and the even more subtle whirring of hummingbird wings near the feeder. Statues of Jesus and Buddha watched benignly from the colorful shrubbery, along with numerous other deities she didn't recognize. She paused between the lily pond and the rose garden, making a last visual sweep of the grounds before taking the brick steps down to the sunken grotto. Lush ferns flanked the path.

A young man in motorcycle leathers stood as Ali entered. In a heartbeat, the two closed the gap between them and embraced, his athletic six-foot frame contrasting with her fairy-like delicacy. They held tightly to each other, her face buried in the black leather that hugged his chest, his in her hair.

When they broke the embrace and sat on the stone bench, they held hands, each looking at the other's face as if etching the images in memory to tide them over until next time. "I was so worried about you. Why didn't your lawyer get you out sooner?"

"It was too dangerous. Half the people in America hated my guts and we were afraid some vigilante fan of Dev's would come gunning for me. Then when we knew the grand jury was less than a week away, we thought sitting in jail would make me more sympathetic."

"Was it horrible?"

"Mostly boring. But it's over; we did it."

"I saw the press conference. How did you get the superslut to give *you* money?"

"That's a long story for another time."

"And when is that time? When can we start being seen together in public?"

"Soon. In January I'll begin prepping the movie, and if we can start shooting by April, I'll bring you in to work on it. Let people gradually get used to seeing us together."

His face showed disappointment.

"I know it seems like a long wait, but you have to get through these last two semesters, so how much time are you going to have anyway?"

"I'll always make time for you," he said.

"I'm working on a way for us to spend Christmas together. Dev has a house in Vail and I still have the keys."

"Skiing, that would be awesome."

"I'll call you if I think it's safe to meet here again."

"Are the police still looking at you?"

"No, they're done, don't want to appear any more thuggish than they already have. It's Dev's father. He's got some political campaign going and he's trying to make himself look all law and order for the voters. Before we leave, did you get rid of that purse?"

"Multiple dumpsters. And each piece was sprayed with sulfuric acid."

"And you didn't think that chemistry class would pay off. How about the shoes?"

There was the briefest hesitation before he said, "Of course."

"Good. Okay, I'll leave first. Give me five minutes." She reached into her pocket and grabbed a few bills. "Here, something for the donation box on the way out."

They hugged again, and Ali looked up at him. "I love you so much, Tommy."

"You'd better," he said with a roguish grin. She thwacked his leather-clad arm, then blew him a kiss as she disappeared onto the ferny path.

When Maureen got to the door Monday morning, Blake was slouched against the jamb, an electric-green bucket hat angled rakishly over his forehead. "Blake Ervansky, private eye."

"How sweet. You mugged a pimp." She stepped aside to let him in.

"The surf shops in Malibu have a surprisingly small selection of tasteful headgear."

"There's coffee in the kitchen. Come on." As Maureen padded away in bare feet, Blake dropped his day-glo chapeau onto the foyer table and followed her.

"We ran out of half and half, but Charlie went to pick some up," she called out.

Blake entered the kitchen, looked around at the gleaming appliances and endless granite countertops and whistled appreciatively. "Right up until this minute I liked my little kitchen."

"Coffee now, or do you want to wait for the cow juice?"

"I'll wait." He sat at the island and looked across at Maureen. She wore sweats and her hair was down—the first time Blake had seen it that way—but, as always, he was drawn to her eyes. Today, possibly reflecting the black of the granite and the gray of her sweatshirt, her eyes looked almost steely. "Can I ask you a question about your eyes?"

"Uh, okay."

"Do they change color in different light?"

"No, they change color when I put in different lenses. I think today's are Rain Cloud."

"Jeez, all this time I thought you were some kind of mutant alien eyeball morpher."

"So sorry I can't live up to your Comic-Con expectations."

"Here I come to save the da-ay," Charlie's voice sang the opening line of the Mighty Mouse

theme song as he came into the kitchen with a small paper bag. "Hey, Blake. Good to see you again."

"Hi, Charlie."

Charlie leaned against the island while Maureen opened the half and half and poured three cups of coffee. "Maureen tells me you two are going to catch a murderer."

"It's more likely we'll shuffle paper and tap dance until they let us back on the force."

"Well, you never know."

Charlie took his coffee and walked out of the kitchen, and Blake and Maureen looked at each other. "So," she said, "where do you think we should begin?"

"I guess we call Libby and get copies of everything. Then we slog through it all again."

That's how the long, boring week opened for them. Copies of all the CCTV videos, witness interviews and CSI reports on the footprints and gun arrived Monday afternoon. Tuesday they catalogued all of it, making a schedule of what to do and when. Not relishing the idea of viewing the gory videos again, they put those off until the next week and concentrated on looking for any red flags or inconsistencies in their witness statements.

They fell into a daily routine. Charlie joined them for coffee each morning, then worked on his blog until lunch, when the three of them met back in the kitchen to eat. Afternoons, Charlie left to play tennis or hang out with his buddies while Blake and Maureen continued reviewing the material without any results.

By Friday morning they were going stir crazy from all the reading and no action, so they made a few appointments for the following week, beginning with Kenny Kentner on Tuesday, so they could feel as though they were *doing* something. A messenger arrived midday with their paychecks and new business cards. Apparently, they were now E&O Investigations, LLC. The delivery brought Joe Roberts to mind and they realized they had to write their first weekly progress report to turn in on Monday.

When Charlie came into the kitchen for lunch, Blake and Maureen were staring at a nearly blank laptop screen and looking discouraged. "What's up?" he asked Maureen.

"We're trying to write a progress report, only we haven't made any progress."

"You looked pretty busy to me all week. What do you have so far?" He stepped behind Maureen and looked over her shoulder to see the screen. "Made appointment with K. Kentner. Re-read all witness statements."

"Maybe if we put it in a larger font, it'll look like more," Blake suggested.

"All you need is a rewrite and punch-up."

"I love you, Dad, but this isn't a script."

"Kiddo, *life* is a script," Charlie replied mysteriously, then he reached into his pocket and pulled out a couple fifties. "Why don't you two go down to Musso and Frank and bring me a chopped salad. Get whatever you want, and by the time you're back I'll have the report."

Forty-five minutes later, when Blake and Maureen returned with the food, they found two single-spaced typed pages on the kitchen island. They read their report while Charlie unpacked the lunches and put out napkins and utensils.

"Crikey, this makes it sound like we *did*

something," Maureen said.

"Straw into gold, sweetheart. Nothing Rumpelstiltskin couldn't do."

Blake laid the pages down and turned to his partner. "I didn't realize how good we are. Let's ask Roberts for a raise." He then looked at Charlie. "Seriously, how did you do this?"

"When you produce over three hundred episodes of prime-time comedy and drama, you learn how to turn nothing into something. And if you're lucky enough to be handed *something*, you learn to make it *wow*."

With their report done, and having made a decision to dive into all the videos on Monday, Blake and Maureen decided to call it a day. Blake was glad to leave early. He had been thinking about Jane all week, trying to figure out what might be going wrong and how he could fix it. Yesterday he came to the conclusion that what he saw as a comfortable pattern might have begun looking to her like a rut.

Every Friday night she brought take-out; every Saturday he took her to a restaurant for dinner; and Sunday nights—at least until she started ducking out before noon—they scrounged in his fridge for a makeshift meal. Blake realized he needed to step up his game before Jane got bored enough to leave him.

I'm not even thirty, he thought, driving north toward the valley. I shouldn't be this dull. He considered his parents' marriage, which had always seemed calm, solid, safe, the kind of relationship that was fine—even preferable—for older people with children, but looked like slow death on toast to Blake when he was a teenager. He wondered if his dad had ever dazzled his mom. Had he pursued her with flowers and love notes when they were young? Had she been flirtatious and exciting? Or had their proximity in dental college and shared professional goals inexorably vectored them toward the same point on some big life graph, a point where getting married was merely the next box to tick with a checkmark?

Blake loved his parents, but he didn't ever want to be like them. And he knew age was no insurance against that. His brother Ethan, only three years older, was already working in the family dental practice and playing the male lead in what looked, to Blake, like a play about a stultifyingly boring marriage.

Maybe it runs in the family, he thought. Maybe I'm doomed to be a dull guy and Jane has already figured that out.

At his first stop, a liquor store, he picked up miniatures of cognac for Steak Diane, and dark rum for an island interpretation of Bananas Foster. And a split of Moët & Chandon Imperial to oil the wheels of seduction. When the clerk saw the two teensy bottles of booze and the one-serving champagne, he muttered something that sounded like "big spender."

At the grocery store, Blake selected two long-stemmed red roses from the flower cooler after he had gathered everything else on his list. The romaine was prewashed and bagged, the Caesar dressing was bottled, and the brown rice came ready-cooked in microwavable cups, but Blake was going to turn out a main dish and a dessert by himself.

He e-mailed Jane at 3:00, telling her not to bring take-out, then showered, shaved and changed clothes. By 3:45 he was butterflying two filets and slicing mushrooms.

Sunday evening. Blake sat on his deck in the falling dark, trying to decide if the weekend had been a success or a failure. The November air was a little too cool for him to be sitting there in a long-sleeved cotton shirt, but not cold enough to spark up the fire pit, so he knew he'd have to put on a jacket soon or go inside for the night. There was probably enough time to grout the tub if he got started on it now.

Usually the thought of knocking one more item off his home-improvement to-do list was motivation enough, but not tonight, not when he was in such a brood mood.

The dinner on Friday had been a romantic success, although in hindsight he wished he had bought a candle for the table and that the smoke alarm hadn't gone off when he finally got the rum to flame on the bananas. He had installed a rheostat on the dining room light switch, so he could provide a flattering—if not flickering—glow, and he was tall enough to shut off the shrieking alarm without dragging in a ladder.

He had watched Jane's face when she saw the table laid out with a champagne flute, real plates, and a single rose on her napkin. She smiled and put her arms around him, but before her face nestled into his shirt front, he saw tears. Why haven't I brought her flowers more often, he asked himself. It's such an easy thing to do. The second rose was in a skinny vase next to the sink she used in his bathroom when she stayed over.

Blake had hustled her out of the dining room, saying he had cooking to do, and suggested she take a relaxing shower while he finished up. When she came back in half an hour, wrapped in his old flannel robe, hair still damp and with her faced flushed pink from the hot shower, it was all he could do not to pick her up and carry her to bed right then. Instead, he handed her the glass of champagne. "To the chef," she toasted.

"To us," Blake said, clinking his ginger ale against her bubbly.

Soft lighting, soft conversation and soft music filled the next two hours, but then the soft part of the evening ended when Blake *did* pick her up and carry her to the bedroom. He paused at the light switches along the way, kissing her briefly as she turned off each one, tasting brown sugar and dark rum on her lips.

They had maintained the sweet romance of the evening as they made love the first time, but by the second round, youth and passion had kicked romance out on its ass and were partying like bunnies.

They made love again Saturday morning, setting the tone for what became a lazy, intimate day. When they finally got motivated enough to dress and drive to Griffith Park, they held hands and walked slowly, enjoying the lovely fall day and unburdening themselves to each other.

Blake spoke of his unhappiness about the sudden job shuffle. He didn't care much for Joe Roberts and he disliked feeling like a rich man's stooge. He wanted to be back on the police force doing real investigating, not playing games.

Jane talked about an autistic boy in her class. Her success or failure with Jaden would determine whether he would be mainstreamed into first grade the next year or put into a special school, a responsibility that weighed on her.

Sharing their separate burdens had made each feel closer to the other. When they returned to the house at the end of the afternoon, neither felt like pulling it together for their usual Saturday night dinner out, so Blake ordered a pizza to be delivered. Later, he boxed with his Wii while she used a Bedazzler to make circles of denim into sparkly merit badges for her kids.

In Blake's opinion, the evening had ended perfectly when she told him she would be in LA for Christmas. Last December, Jane had flown back to West Virginia to spend the holidays with her family, but this year, instead of going home, she would send them the money she would have paid for an airline ticket.

A perfect weekend in almost every way, except that Jane had left shortly after 11:00 that morning, citing the now-familiar "things to do." From the day he met her, she had been the most open and honest woman he had ever known, but now he felt in his gut she was hiding something. Blake had brought out his A game and it was not enough.

The first stars were already floating in the pool, their light crinkling as the surface of the water shimmied in the breeze. He needed to swim off his angst, but he knew the water would be like ice. He decided to turn on the heater next weekend—screw the electric bill—so he could lose himself in the punishing rhythm of push-off, stroke, touch, turn, push-off, stroke, touch, turn. Twenty-five times, fifty, a hundred. However long it took to numb his fears.

Was Jane's decision to be with him for Christmas a good sign, he wondered, or was she only setting him up for a gentle letdown? He thought of Brandy, his last serious girlfriend. They'd had a good run a couple years back, nearly eight months before he started feeling tied down and wanted to move on. She was a singer and actress, and when she landed a major role in a revival of *A Little Night Music*, Blake had seen an opportunity to leave without inflicting too much pain. He would wait until after opening night to let her down gently, confident in the knowledge that six-weeks of standing ovations would more than outweigh the loss of a boyfriend who was neither rich nor connected.

Blake had been careful to betray no sign of his coming departure, but Brandy picked up the scent of *something*, some change, the same way he now sensed a change with Jane. During her weeks of rehearsal, Brandy would sing in the house, and when the song was "Send in the Clowns," she always managed to be standing at the door of whichever room Blake was in, looking at him with doe-eyed sadness when she got to: *I thought that you'd want what I want, sorry, my dear*.

Jesus H. Christ, he suddenly thought, my girlfriend may be dumping me and I'm hearing Sondheim lyrics in my head. I'm probably two-thirds gay already.

He stood quickly, pulling his shirt up over his head while simultaneously kicking his loafers off in two different directions. He unzipped his fly and shucked his jeans, goose bumps already rising on his arms.

In the darkness he was a swiftly moving blur of white briefs as he ran down the wooden stairs and sprinted across the yard. Flexing his knees at the last second, Blake shot into the air, arcing into a perfect dive. When his body knifed into the icy water all thoughts vanished, replaced by sensation.

Joe Roberts wrapped up a telephone interview, as the younger of his aides knocked lightly on the open office door. Joe waved him in to a chair in front of the desk. "...several pieces of legislation. My family and I are still mourning the loss, but we'll work tirelessly to see that his senseless death results in something positive for the people of this great state."

As he listened to the voice on the phone for a long minute, Joe glanced at the aide, held up his hand, and made a yap-yap-yap gesture with his fingers. "I will only confirm that we have taken steps to ensure law enforcement followed every protocol and that nothing was overlooked. I'm being called into a meeting right now, but I'm so glad to have had this opportunity to speak with a representative of such a highly respected publication—" He darted his eyes to the list in front of him, reading the next name without a line through it. "—as *Mother Jones*. I hope we can discuss this again sometime." He hung up and drew a line through the name. "What do you have?"

"New polling stats. People are liking this whole 'tough-on-crime' position. Twelve percent up on recognizability, and an even bigger bump on approval." He handed the file across the desk. "Also, campaign donations are way up. Most of it is average-guy under-a-hundred, but your three contacts in Geneva came through with some *very* impressive checks." The aide added the second file to the first one on the desk, then held up two sheets of paper. "What should I do with the report from our two rent-a-cops?"

"Trash them as they come in; they're of no importance whatsoever."

Joe opened the polling file as his aide left the room with the first weekly report from E&O Investigations. Fifteen seconds later, it had been torn in half and dropped into a recycling bin.

Each time Charlie left his office, to bring in the mail or to get a coffee refill, he passed the room in which his daughter and her partner screened CCTV videos. On his third pass that morning, he stopped and glanced over at the screen they were watching. Charlie looked thoughtful for a moment, then went back to work on his blog. With their backs to the open door, Blake and Maureen never saw him stop.

It was Maureen's turn to go out to pick up lunch, so the two men sat in the kitchen after she left. Blake had gotten to know Charlie a lot better in the past week, and he thought he might be a good sounding board. He already knew Maureen's mother was dead, but it had happened when she was still a little girl, so Blake hoped the subject wouldn't be too touchy. "Can I ask you something?"

"Sure."

"When you met your wife, how did you know she was *the one?"*

"She wasn't."

"Oh." Well, I certainly didn't expect *that,* thought Blake.

"From the look on your face, I'd say your next question is why did I marry her."

"No, it's none of my business. I'm sorry."

"H_2O under the viaduct, Grasshopper. I sold my first sitcom in the mid '80s, a show called *Dewey's View*, so I was twenty-two and making obscene amounts of money. On one episode we needed to cast an under-five who was a total bombshell, and in walks Trish Baylor. Back then I was all about the blonde hair and the big boobs, and Trish was looking for a rich guy who could help her career. A match made in Hollywood."

"Doesn't Hollywood like happy endings?"

"Trust me, we were both happy when it ended. I should have listened to the old Borscht Belt comic who played Dewey's grandfather. He saw me sniffing around Trish and said, 'Charlie, when you go searching for a wife, never use your dick as a compass.' So, Blake, is it your dick or your heart that's aching for the girl?"

Maureen came in with the sushi, so the question went unanswered.

When they were alone after lunch and ready to start the videos again, Blake asked Maureen, "What's an under-five?"

"It's a way for a producer to save money on actors. The union gives a price break if the part is under five lines. Why?"

"No reason. I heard it somewhere and wondered."

The afternoon was another fruitless four-hour search through the videos. When Charlie got back from tennis, he stood unseen again and watched what they were watching. After a minute, he got a suspicious smile on his face, but he didn't interrupt.

The reinterview with Kenny Kentner was scheduled for 11:00 A.M. on Tuesday, and Blake and Maureen were getting ready to leave when Charlie came out of his office. "You two coming back for lunch?"

"We'll probably grab something after we talk to our guy."

"Okay. See you later."

Charlie gave his daughter a quick peck, then headed back to his office. As soon as the car pulled away, though, he went to the monitor setup and started reading labels on the SD cards.

"Oh, I'm *so* sorry. Mr. Kentner had to leave for a meeting."

Blake looked around for a camera. "We're being yanked, right?"

"No, sir. Zeitgeist wants Mr. Kentner to develop a new show for them, so he's very busy right now."

They had driven forty minutes from the hills to Culver City Studios so Blake was pissed. He looked at Maureen. "I liked us better when we carried guns and the public was afraid of us."

On their way to the car, Maureen's cell phone rang and she saw it was Charlie. "O'Brien Fish Hatchery. Can we give you a fingerling?"

"No, but could you give me a call when you're five minutes from the house?

"Sure, what's up?"

"A little surprise."

Blake and Maureen dressed their hot dogs at the condiment counter, then carried them to one of the aluminum tables under the striped awning. "I hate this," he said.

"I thought you loved the dogs here."

"I'm referring to my life, not my lunch."

"Sucks, huh?"

"Well, don't you agree? We're a couple of noncops working on a noncase. Even a weasely A-hole like Kentner knows he doesn't have to show us one bit of respect."

"Oh, get over yourself. We're sacrificial lambs, big whoop. Look at what it did for the widows' fund. Or would you rather be on the phone trying to raise that quarter mil? All we have to do is vamp another few weeks, turn in our little reports, and then go back to the force. Meanwhile, can't you enjoy the extra money and stop being so emo?"

Blake was not about to tell her his gloomy mood was caused by something more than his job situation.

When they turned onto Acacia a half hour later, they saw a tall A-frame ladder in front of the house. Charlie stood at the bottom of the ladder waving at them as they pulled onto the circular drive. By the time Blake and Maureen got out of the car, Charlie had climbed to the top, where they now noticed there was a one-gallon can of paint. They also noticed the ladder wasn't even close to anything that could be painted.

"Hey, Dad, what's—"

"Paint in the hole!" Charlie yelled as he dropped the paint can not five feet from where Blake and Maureen stood. When they realized what was about to happen, they both scrambled from the splash zone. But there was no splash. The can hit the concrete with a thud, sustaining no more injury than a deep denting of the bottom edge that had made initial contact. Charlie hurried down the ladder. "Your girl is a liar and a murderer, and I can prove it."

As Blake gingerly picked up the paint can to examine the nonfatal wound, Charlie continued. "Two years into my showbiz career, the Writers' Guild went out on strike for almost four months, and I took a job in the paint department of that big Lowe's up in Northridge. I saw cans of paint hit the deck from shelving twenty feet high. They don't just pop open so you can leave an incriminating footprint behind."

Blake and Maureen tried to digest this out-of-left-field suggestion, so contrary to all they *thought* they knew about their case.

"Is it possible the lid was loose when she bought it?" asked Blake.

"I doubt it. Even when you get a custom mix, the guy uses a special mallet to pound that lid tighter than a Joan Rivers face-lift."

Maureen turned to Blake. "What do you think?"

"I'm not sure."

"You don't have to take *my* word she's guilty. Come on in and she'll show you herself."

Blake and Maureen exchanged a glance. She shrugged, he put down the paint can, and they followed Charlie. When they got to the workroom, he went to the computer.

Four frozen images appeared in a quad-split of the screen, pictures quite familiar to Blake and Maureen. Clockwise from top left, they showed Ali Garland standing outside the Starbucks with coffee in one hand, paint can in the other. The precise moment caught was the one in which she raised her shoulder to reposition the strap of the purse. Top right was her glancing back in fear, a shot from the jewelry store on Camden. Bottom right, still on Camden but in front of the store two doors north, Ali puts her hand in her purse, presumably to find her gun. Last shot, bottom left, Ali is stopped in front of the parking structure on Bedford, looking inside, body language projecting high-alert fear, and her hand still in her purse. Charlie got up and motioned to the two chairs in front of the monitor. "Sit down and tell me what you see."

They slid into their usual seats and stared at the screens, wondering what they had missed.

"Come on, Maureen. Blake's a civilian so he'll never see it, but you grew up on my stages."

Her eyes darted from image to image. "I don't know what I'm looking for."

Finally, she and Blake turned toward Charlie, who stood behind them.

"Remember that ancient punch-up guy on *The Brothers Gunn*? Benny Birnbaum?"

"World's oldest living comedy writer," Maureen replied, then turned to her partner. "He actually had that on his business card."

"Do you remember what he used to say about actors after he'd had a couple drinks?"

Maureen thought a moment, then got a big smile on her face. When she spoke, it was in the voice of an old Jewish man. "Ohl I want from an actuh is that he should pronounce my woids right and that he should always hit—" Maureen stopped suddenly, then looked back at the computer screen. "Oh, my God!"

"*Boom* shakalaka!" Charlie cheered.

"Uh, Robin to Batman. What's going on?" Blake asked.

Maureen turned toward him, excited.

"She hit her marks in every scene!"

"Meaning?"

"Okay, it's always easier to move an actor than a camera, so directors set up their shots, then design the movement so actors are where the camera can see them. If an actor hits his marks—usually masking tape or colored chalk on the floor—he'll always be in frame." She leaned back, smiling. "Blake, she not only knew where the cameras would be, she knew their framing well enough to stop and pose for them!"

"A-a-a-nd scene!" Charlie said, bowing and sweeping his hands down and to the sides.

Blake and Maureen looked at him with amazement. "How did you figure all this out?" Blake asked.

"Oh, I peeked in every now and then, saw dribs and drabs of what you were looking at. When you got to the paint can, I almost laughed. Worst kind of amateur plotting there is, when the writer comes up with a device to serve his own—or *her* own—needs rather than something organic to the plot."

"Ali needed us to find a footprint at the scene," Maureen said, "so we could compare it to the one from the break-in."

"Only there's nothing on a dry sidewalk in Beverly Hills to take an impression," Charlie said. "The spilled latte would have dried too fast, and by the time you were checking a few hours later, who knows how many people would have already walked on it, obliterating the evidence."

"But nobody steps in wet paint if they can help it," Maureen added.

"Especially if it's surrounded by orange traffic cones."

"How did we *not* see this before?" Blake asked.

"I think I can answer that," Charlie said. "Since the shooting, you've been looking at a script titled 'She's Innocent,' and once you bought that script—which Ali Garland made damn sure you did—all the other stuff fit into the premise. Change the title to 'She's Guilty' and go back and see if you can make all the elements fit *that* premise." Charlie watched each of them consider this new approach. "You two kids have fun," he said, turning to go back to his office.

"We have to call the lieutenant."

"Why?" Blake asked.

"Because now we have new information. The so-called mugger is obviously her accomplice; the shoe prints connect him to her seven months ago; the shifting of the purse on her shoulder now looks like a signal that she was in position for the hit. If Rhee puts enough people on this, it could be wrapped up in a couple weeks."

"I know."

"Then what's the problem?"

Blake hesitated. "I hope you won't take this the wrong way. I'm glad you have the life you do, and I don't envy you for what you have, but I'm a working guy and I need to consider that fifty-thousand-dollar bonus."

"Oh."

Maureen was instantly subdued, which Blake read as her realizing she had not given a thought to the money. He barreled on. "Joe's guy made it clear about that bonus. *We* get the proof Ali planned Dev's death. He knows we can't make an arrest, but I think we have to do all the work right up until that time. Maybe it'll take longer this way, but... Are you okay?"

"What? Yes, I'm fine. And you're right. We have to ride this whale all the way to the dock or Joe Roberts might not even make that second payment to the widows' fund."

"So you're okay about us going it alone?"

"Of course." Then in Max Gunn's whiskey rasp, she added, "Let's throw some gasoline on these briquets and fahr up a match."

Blake smiled. He was starting to feel like himself again. "Where do you want to start?" he asked."

"Office supply store."

Two hours later they were trying to put a corkboard, six feet wide and four feet high, onto its rolling metal frame. On the floor in a plastic bag were pushpins, markers and packs of index cards in white, pink and blue.

The corkboard was exactly like the one Maureen remembered from the writers' room of *The Brothers Gunn.* She had spent much of her childhood watching the neat rows of blue cards slowly fill up with story—one card for each plot point—while the white cards that represented commercial breaks separated the blue ones into more or less even pods. It was an efficient, albeit low-tech, way to look at all the elements at once, keeping an overview that was sometimes lost in the pinpoint minutia belched out by a computer.

By 4:30, the board was covered with neat vertical rows of blank white cards. At the top, three pink ones carried the words: *TITLE: SHE'S GUILTY.* Blake and Maureen stepped back to admire their board.

"What do we know so far?" he asked.

"We know Dev was shot; we know Ali had a break-in; and we know her purse disappeared. Pretty much everything else is speculation. So let's put those three facts on blue cards and position them in our story line."

"The break-in is the first time we can connect Ali to her mystery man, so I say we lead with that." Blake replaced the first white card with a blue one that read *BREAK-IN* while Maureen wrote *DEV SHOT* on a second blue card.

"If she planned this, her goal was killing Dev Roberts, so I think this one should be at the end," she said.

"The purse disappearing comes after that, though, so put it in the last column, but move it up a few cards."

Maureen pinned the *DEV SHOT* card on the board, leaving four blanks after it. Blake wrote *PURSE?* on a third blue card and pinned it immediately following that one, and the two stepped back to look.

"That's still a lot of white cards," Blake observed.

"Then why don't we each choose a line of inquiry. Once we've put up the blue cards for those, we move on to the next two."

"Sure, throw logic at me. First choice?"

"I want to find out how she knew where the cameras were aimed. You?"

"Well, since half her fairy tale is based on the fact that Dev was dressed exactly like her 'assailant,' I'd like to know how she found out ahead of time what he'd be wearing."

They made plans for Wednesday morning. First would be visiting all four businesses whose

CCTV videos supported Ali's story, then they'd nail down Kenny Kentner to find out where the wardrobe leak occurred.

"Hey, it's five o'clock somewhere," Charlie called from the doorway. "Anyone care to join me for a drink?"

In the kitchen, Charlie gathered what he needed to make his nightly martini, while Maureen took a bottle of beer from the fridge and a shot glass out of a cabinet. As Charlie filled the shaker with crushed ice, he watched her pour beer into the shot glass, then hand it to Blake.

"Are we rationing beer?" Charlie asked.

"Oh, Blake can't drink more than a wee little leprechaun."

"Seriously?"

"Sad but true," Blake said. "It's a wonky liver thing all the men in my family have. My mother and sister could drink like fish and have no problem. They don't, but they could."

"So what happens if you have alcohol?"

"I can only go by the one time I tried. I was seventeen and I was triple-dating to the prom. My friend Danny managed to score three six-packs and had them in a cooler in the limo, and before we went in to the dance, each of us chugged two beers, figuring we'd save our last one for a nightcap later."

"I'm sensing an unhappy ending," Charlie said.

"Somewhere in the middle of a Minnesota boy-band version of 'Two Tickets to Paradise,' I threw up all over my date."

"I hope you had the photos taken pre-barf."

"Spent the night in the emergency room,

with my father saying 'I told you so.' "

Charlie's cell phone rang. He answered it, then picked up his martini and left the room to take the call. Maureen took a hit off her bottle as Blake sipped his microbrew. "I feel good. I feel like a detective again," he said.

"Ah, that's just the beer talkin'."

"We're going to nail her. We're going to unravel every twisted strand of her evil plan."

"*And* we're going to get fifty grand each for our efforts," Maureen said.

"I feel filthy rich already."

Maureen took another pull from her beer. "What are you going to do with the money?"

"Well, after the IRS takes their vig, the first eighteen thousand buys a motorized pool cover. No more frozen cojones."

"Worst margarita *ever*. And the rest?"

"Engagement ring." Blake looked almost as surprised to have said it as Maureen was to have heard it.

"How long has *that* been percolating in your head?"

"I have no idea." Blake was telling the truth; he hadn't been consciously considering the idea of proposing to Jane, but as soon as the words were out of his mouth, he *knew*.

They sat quietly for a moment, each lost in their own thoughts. "Blake?"

"Yeah."

"When this is over and we're carrying badges again instead of business cards, maybe we should both put in for new partners."

"Where did that come from? I think we've been working great together."

"I do, too. But you might be better off

working with someone you have more faith in."

"O'Brien, I told the lieutenant your first day on the job how amazing you were at the crime scene. You were a beat cop for what, ten months with LAPD? And you'd only gotten your sergeant's stripes a few weeks earlier, so I wasn't expecting all that much from you, but you rolled out of the car and drew your weapon like you'd been a deet for years. Not to mention you saw right through Ali's lies while I didn't."

He reached over and took her hand, his instincts, for once, pointing him in the right direction. "You're good at this. And I like you. Why would I want another partner?"

Maureen looked down at their hands, slowly withdrawing hers from beneath his. "Because then you wouldn't have to work with someone you think is a spoiled little rich girl who's only *playing* at being a cop."

Stunned, Blake was about to say he had never thought anything like that. And then he remembered what he had said earlier about needing the bonus money when she so obviously didn't. He apologized for his clumsy words, turned down Charlie's invite to stay for dinner, threw back the rest of his teeny-tiny beer, then left for home, upbeat for the first time in weeks.

Ali Garland applied makeup carefully. This morning she would have her first meeting with a potential distributor for *Condom Nation*, her projected indictment of the religious right's stand against providing adequate sex education and actual protection for middle-school and high-school students, a stand she would show resulted in tens of thousands of abortions and unwanted babies every year. And where were those same good Christians when it came to helping those kids whose ignorance and unstoppable hormones got them into trouble? They were blocking access to affordable abortions and pretending all those unwanted babies were someone else's problem, while sticking to the ludicrous premise that sex education and access to protection were not the cure for teen pregnancies, but the cause.

Ali would travel the country interviewing both the politicos and religious leaders who spoke against condom distribution and sex ed, as well as the victims at the grass-roots level, the kids who were aware only of the fix in which they found themselves, not the socio-religious debate raging far above the level of their life-changing problems.

It hadn't been easy coming up with a polarizing social issue Michael Moore didn't already have his mitts on, and although she didn't give a crap about the boo-hoo problems of a bunch of knocked-up teenagers, Ali knew she could ride this to a new career as a serious film producer. Never again would some snotty little casting director tell her she was a smidge older than what the producers were looking for, or take a shot at her acting ability by reminding her that she was "no Maggie Gyllenhaal."

Her brilliant decision to give away Dev's fortune had won her a lot of support in the biz. People were puzzled by her magnanimity, but also strangely fascinated by someone who did what was unthinkable in Hollywood: see money and walk in the other direction.

Quiet financial offers were already coming in to her agent and, if Ali played her cards right, she could get the project funded and keep that million for herself. It was time to go out in public again, to begin raising her profile as a serious filmmaker. Time to shed the dumb ingénue persona that had carried her so far.

Blake walked in carrying *People, Us, The Enquirer, The Star* and *OK!*

"Good Lord," Maureen said, "how much time do you intend to spend in the bathroom today?"

"If Ali thinks nobody's investigating her anymore, maybe she'll relax and make a mistake. So if we DVR the entertainment news programs and read all these, we can keep tabs on her."

"It's a good idea, but we don't have to do so much work. I'll hire a clipping service."

"What's that?"

"You give them any name—an actor, a movie, a TV show—and they search every media reference and send them to you weekly. It used to be all paper, hence the name clipping service, but now it's completely electronic."

Blake put the pile of magazines on a chair in their workroom and noticed an open transcript on the desk. "What have you been reading while I've been following Taylor Swift's love life?"

"Our inital interview with Ali. Do you realize she mentioned the jeans and black hoodie *twice?* Once in reference to the mugger, once about Dev."

"I guess she wanted to connect the dots for us dimwitted cops."

"Exactly. Another thing that's bothering me is those car keys. Why weren't they in the purse that up and disappeared?"

"Pocket maybe? That's where mine are right now."

"Men do pockets, women not so much. And do you remember that key ring? It had a big stupid troll doll on it with a long tuft of hair. Maybe if she had been wearing cargo pants, or a jacket with big pockets, but she was wearing *yoga* pants. Even if she could have crammed the thing in one of those tiny pockets, she couldn't have done a Downward Dachshund with a plastic troll jabbing into her hip."

Blake thought about what she had said. "All right, Ali needed to give us her keys so we could find her parking receipt and start confirming that timeline."

"And if those keys were on her person, instead of in her purse, it means she knew the purse was going, as Max Gunn would say, *hasta la pizza, baby.*"

"Let's put the purse next on the agenda after the CCTV cameras and the wardrobe leak."

"Sure, one of your people came in a week before the shooting. Said he was matching the private sector closed-circuit systems with the police traffic cameras. Something about making a master grid."

"Did he want to see your coverage?" Blake asked.

"Yes. I brought him in here and he asked me to have an employee step outside. Then he watched the monitor and jotted some notes on a clipboard. He couldn't have been here more than five or ten minutes. Very official, very polite."

The four monitors were in the manager's office. Three of them showed the interior of the small, exclusive jewelry store, but Maureen focused on the fourth screen, the one showing the now-familiar patch of sidewalk out front.

"Do you remember what he looked like?" asked Blake.

"Not as tall as you, but tall. Sandy blond hair, a little longer than I thought most cops would wear it."

"He told you he was with the police department?"

"Well, I don't recall that he *said* it, but that's certainly the impression he gave."

"Any facial hair or other distinguishing characteristics?"

"Only his glasses. The frames were that plastic that's supposed to look like tortoise shell but never quite does."

The stories they heard from the parking garage and the other two businesses were reruns of the one from the jewelry store manager, and as they were about to leave Beverly Hills to visit some of Kenny Kentner's employees at his Culver City office, Maureen suggested they talk to someone at the yoga studio. "I mean, since it's right here, it'll save us a trip back."

"Sure."

"And what do you want to bet it was Ali who suggested painting the studio?"

But it hadn't been Ali. The instructor for the early morning class was very sure it had been another one of the women who had first brought up painting the studio. Maureen and Blake didn't spend a lot of time puzzling over this small glitch, but took the woman's name and phone number for a later follow-up.

Their next stop was the wardrobe service Kenny Kentner used for *Yanked.*

"Coming!"

They heard the shouted response to their knock, and a moment later a harried-looking woman of about forty-five jerked open the door marked Wardrobe. She had a pile of red dresses draped over her arm.

"Okay, I've got all the dresses, but UPS didn't bring the dirndls yet. I'll track them and get them to the stage as soon as they're in."

She dumped the armload of dresses on a surprised Maureen, then crossed back to a rack of clothes. "Mr. James is going to *have* to find time for a final fitting, so if you could motivate his ass to get down here, I'd be grateful. How many elves are there again?"

"Uh, would you by any chance be Sandra Bodner?" Blake asked.

She turned and saw the bewildered looks on the faces of the two people at the door. "Oh, crud. You're not from *The Travis James Country Christmas Special,* are you?"

"No. We're detectives following up on the Dev Roberts shooting last month."

"I'm so sorry," she said, grabbing the load of dresses from Maureen. "I'm trying to service five different shows, so it gets a little crazy."

"This will only take a minute. I'm Blake Ervansky and this is my partner, Maureen O'Brien. We read the statement you gave Det. Willis right after the incident, and we're trying to learn if there's any way the information about Dev's wardrobe could have been leaked in advance of that morning."

"I don't think so."

"How many employees do you have?" Maureen asked.

"Oh, sweetie, don't I *wish* I could afford employees. But it's just me, myself and I. Back when there were only three networks, you could make a good living at this because everybody had a budget for wardrobe. Nowadays, there's a couple hundred pissant little cable outlets, and all their shows want an Oscar-winner look on an Oscar Meyer budget. I run like a gerbil on a wheel to stay out of the red."

"And are you the only one with a key?" Blake asked.

"Hell, yes. Half of what's in here is on loan from department stores. I lose it, I buy it."

"Did Mr. Kentner ever talk to you about Dev's wardrobe?" asked Maureen.

"His Highness doesn't mingle with the serfs."

Blake mulled this over for a moment. "So you and Dev were the only ones who knew about the jeans and black hoodie?"

"Us and that prissy little assistant he sent over to make sure I'd gotten the *correct* four-hundred-dollar jeans and two-hundred-dollar designer hoodie. I had to call upstairs to get the extra expense okayed. And those movie star types *always* figure on keeping the clothes."

"Do you remember his assistant's name?" Blake asked.

"It was Chip or Chick or something like that. Flitty guy, very rainbow flag."

Maureen hung up the phone. "Sam Klein says the only assistant Dev ever had is a woman named Lily Sims."

"So we can surmise rainbow flag guy was the same person as the CCTV inspector."

"*And* the mugger *and* the guy who broke into her house."

"Who the heck is he?" Blake asked.

"If Ali planned all this, she took a big risk. Everything had to go perfectly for her to look innocent, and I don't believe she would trust a hired hand."

"Boyfriend? Relative?" Blake looked at the several blue cards with MM—for mystery man—on them, each card representing one small beat of what they were both beginning to view as a story. "Let's focus on him all day tomorrow; figure out who he is."

"Okay, but we'll have to push our meeting with the lady from Ali's yoga class to Friday."

"We should also talk to that assistant. Maybe Dev told her what he would be wearing and she let it slip out to the wrong person."

They spent their last working hour on Wednesday making a list of people they wanted to speak with, leads they needed to follow and research they had to do. Blake realized he'd gotten used to having a larger support team. Now he had no Keesha, no Libby, no uniforms, not even a Willis to pick up some of the slack. And he had always thought Lt. Rhee's job was the easiest one in the house, telling people where to be and what to do. Now that he was "management," Blake had a new respect for Rhee. What the lieutenant did every day with multiple cases and dozens of people, Blake was struggling to organize on one case with one other person.

Relieved when Charlie announced cocktail

hour, Blake asked for a Pepsi after they gathered in the kitchen.

"I noticed you've worked out a few more of your story points," Charlie said, straining his gin Slurpee into a Riedel martini glass.

"Mostly guesses," Blake said.

"But probably closer to the truth than the *facts* we knew when Ali was innocent," Maureen added.

"Let's pitch on one of your guesses. It'll make me feel like I'm back doing *The Brothers Gunn*.

Blake looked at Maureen. "The purse?"

"Definitely."

"Okay," Blake said, "you already know her purse disappeared. We originally thought it was stolen, maybe by some jerk in the crowd taking advantage of the confusion."

"What changed your mind?"

"Ali needed us to have her car keys to set up a timeline for her alibi as fast as possible," Maureen said. "They weren't in her purse—the most logical place—so she must have known it was going to disappear."

"What we can't figure out is why. I mean, she would have been stupid to carry anything incriminating in it, just in case her accomplice couldn't manage to grab it."

Charlie sipped his martini thoughtfully. "What if the incriminating evidence wasn't *in* the purse? What if the purse itself could have given away the game?"

"How?" Maureen asked.

They all went back to the workroom, and Maureen pulled up the Starbucks video. They watched the quick tussle several times.

"Everything about this scene screams amateurish plotting," Charlie observed. "Paint can, footprint, woman in jep."

Blake glanced at Maureen, who mouthed the word "jeopardy." He nodded his thanks.

"There it is," Charlie said, sitting up and backing the video to the spot before the mugger appeared. Then he slowly advanced the images. "Maureen, look at her right arm."

"Okay. The latte's in her hand, and her elbow looks like it's holding the purse against her side."

"Right. Now look at her earlier when she approaches the Starbucks door." He pulled up the second image. "See how she's holding her purse, with her right hand around the strap?"

"Yeah, that's the same way I carry a shoulder bag. Along with almost every other woman in the world."

"Why?"

"*Why?* It keeps the strap from slipping off your shoulder and I guess it feels more natural than letting your arm dangle over the purse."

"You agree?" Charlie asked Blake.

"Don't ask me. I'm straight."

"Maureen, would you mind getting one of your shoulder bags? Something with a strap roughly this length?"

She raised her shoulders and eyebrows as she looked at Blake, communicating that she had no idea, either. "Sure." When she left the room, Charlie turned away from the screen and faced Blake.

"Would you and your girlfriend care to join us for Thanksgiving? It'll help Maureen out a lot. We always have a bunch of guests, and if you two come she won't be the only one at the table who isn't drunk, divorced, depressed, a TV writer or some combination of those four."

"I'll talk to Jane about it this weekend. Thanks."

"Tell her it's basically an Irish wake with a side of turkey."

"How's this?" Maureen said, walking into the room with a purse over her shoulder. She carried it the same way Ali had carried hers walking into Starbucks, with her hand holding onto the forward strap just above the body of the purse. She did the Vanna White sweep with her other hand, as if presenting a Miata that was up for grabs in the lightning round.

"Okay, Blake, try to get the purse away from her."

"What?"

"Make like hoodie boy, snatch her bag."

Blake shrugged, then lunged at Maureen, grabbing for the strap. She side-stepped him, turning so the purse was protected.

"God, you are the worst actors I've ever seen, and I wrote two episodes of *Saved by the Bell*. Go on; get the bag."

The struggle turned serious, and Blake yanked violently on the strap while Maureen held onto the bag, trying to stay on her feet.

"Cut!" Charlie yelled. "Okay, why didn't the strap break?"

"Because it's an Yves St. Laurent made with double-stitched leather."

"And that one," Charlie said, pointing at the screen, "was made of what? Papier-mâché?"

Blake and Maureen looked at the screen and Blake said, "The strap was rigged to break.

Maybe to make the incident look more real."

"I'm betting it was cut almost all the way through, then held together with tape," Charlie said. "Her hand covered the damage on the way in, also making sure it didn't come apart before the big dramatic moment."

"But on the way *out*, both hands were full, so she couldn't hold it up except by pressing it against her side with her elbow," Blake said. He turned to Maureen. "What do you think?"

"I don't know if she killed Dev Roberts or not, but if she deliberately defaced an Etienne Volanté, I hope she gets a lethal injection."

On Thursday, while they waited for Libby to send them enhanced images of the purse strap, Blake and Maureen tried to figure out Mystery Man's identity.

Ali had seemingly dated dozens of men since her break-up with Dev Roberts, mostly low-level industry players—agents, casting directors, entertainment lawyers—but only two fit the description of MM. The pair of candidates who appeared tall enough and fit enough were eliminated quickly. One, the head of a special-effects company, had been showing off his latest CG innovations at a Tokyo geekfest the week of the shooting. The second had been pulling a court-mandated stint in rehab at the time.

They moved on to check out relatives, but here, too, they came up dry. An online search of Garland's fan site revealed her parents had been killed in a car accident when she was sixteen, and her last year of high school had been spent in foster care.

They watched an old TV interview from a

local entertainment program featuring Hollywood newbies. More than a year before Ali was featured in *Don't Kill Me on Monday*, she landed two smaller roles, one on the soap opera *Days of Our Lives* and the second in a lesser-known Scorsese film. During the interview, she spoke of her parents' death with the same tears and trembling she had displayed in the interview room the day of the shooting. She then went on to express her gratitude to the foster parents who had taken her in.

Maureen jotted down the names of the foster parents, phoned CPS to verify they were part of the foster care program, got their number, and called them directly. Mrs. Wojcek confirmed that Ali had been with them for fourteen months and she still sent a Christmas card every year.

"Unless she began setting up her alibi ten years ago, Ali doesn't have a father *or* brother who could have helped her," Maureen told Blake.

The enhanced images they had requested from Libby began spitting out of the printer at that moment, so Blake picked up the first one and scrutinized it. "Doesn't look like the strap was doctored." He handed it to Maureen while he retrieved the following sheet. "Yep, it's another dead end." Blake handed her the second image. Maureen looked from one print to the other, then got an idea.

"Maybe not. Pull up the video showing her about to enter Starbucks."

Blake sat at the computer and keyed back to the image on the screen. "Here?"

"Yes." Maureen looked from the screen to the two pages she held, then smiled. "Well, she is one wascally wabbit. Look on the screen. See that tiny glint on the side of the purse? That's the signature 14 karat-gold Volanté clasp."

Blake squinted at the barely perceptible V-shaped bright spot. "Okay, got it."

"Now," she said, handing him one of the enhanced images. "Look at her coming out."

Blake looked closely at the print. "No logo. She turned the purse around, didn't she?"

"She knew where the camera was; she had a latte in her hand, so she couldn't cover the break; and she didn't want some police tech spotting proof she staged her own mugging. She *had* to turn the purse around and use her elbow to hold it so the strap wouldn't separate before her big scene."

Blake pulled the rest of the pages from the printer and examined each one for a moment before passing it to Maureen. About eight pages in, he stopped at one and looked closely before quickly flipping through the next several pages.

"Check it out," he said, handing one of the pages to his partner and pointing to a spot on it. "As he reaches out to grab the strap, his sleeve pulls back slightly. Mystery Man has a tattoo."

She looked at the page and then at Blake. "Are we the worst two cops who ever lived? How did we not see all this before?"

"We were investigating a shooting, not a mugging. So all this was incidental to the bigger picture. Plus, the guy is as generically dressed as possible and he knows to keep his face down. We would never have found him even if we *had* been following up on a purse snatching."

"You think we can up-res the tattoo?"

"I'll call Libby."

An hour later they walked through the

door of Inkerzink, a large tattoo parlor on the seedier end of Hollywood Boulevard. The walls and the three tattoo artists were all colorfully and intricately decorated. "Like walking into a Buckcherry concert," Maureen observed.

The only artist who wasn't working on a customer walked over to them. "May I help you?" the young woman asked. She had foaming tsunami waves blue-and-whiting up the sides of her neck, their crests meeting the large gold hoops dangling from her ears. Blake could not help but notice through her clingy tank top that her ears weren't the only things pierced and hooped. He handed her the enhanced print of Mystery Man's arm.

"Yes. We're wondering if you can tell us anything about this tat."

She glanced at it, then looked up at Blake. "You mean other than that the pixels are so far apart I can't tell if it's Gwen Stefani or George Stephanopoulos?"

"That's what we were afraid of," he said, reaching for the page. The girl, however, pulled it back.

"Hey, because I can't see *what* it is doesn't mean I can't give you some information about it. You cops?"

"Private investigators," Maureen replied, showing her a business card. "But we're working closely with the police on a possible homicide."

"So, what does your trained inker's eye see in this over-enlarged blur that my partner and I don't?" Blake asked.

The girl examined the image again. "This is a dude, right?"

"Yes," Blake said.

"Well, the ink's on the wrong side of his arm." She held the paper close enough to her chest that Blake had to reach out to it. As soon as his sleeve pulled back, the girl took his forearm in her free hand. Once he took the page from her, she brought her other hand up and stroked two fingers lightly along the inside of his wrist. "See how smooth? Perfect dermal canvas for a single tattoo. But over here," she purred, turning Blake's wrist and brushing the flip side, "we've got all this manly nap. I can shave it and ink in your girlfriend's face, but pretty soon she's gonna look like Willie from Duck Dynasty."

"I see guys with full sleeves all the time," Maureen said, giving Blake a chance to retrieve his arm. "What do they do about the hair?"

"We shave it or Nair it to do the art, but if he's really into sleeves and full body, he isn't going to sweat the fuzz."

"Other than the odd placement, is there any more you can tell us?" Blake asked.

"Sorry, no. But why don't *you* come back tonight? Alone." She dropped her eyes to Blake's crotch, then lifted them again to meet his. "I specialize in taint paint."

Blake colored as he realized what she was suggesting. Maureen rescued him by linking her arm through his and smiling sweetly at him.

"I've been wondering what to get you for Christmas." She then turned to the tattoo girl and asked, "Do you do gift certificates?"

The girl now turned her hungry eyes on Maureen, smiling suggestively. "Chica, there isn't much I *don't* do."

Back at the house, they tried to fit the tattoo into their story.

"Considering how hard Ali tried to make the struggle look real and yet not provide any clues, why didn't she have Mystery Man cover his tattoo with makeup?" Blake asked.

"Maybe she *wanted* us to see it."

"That would explain the placement. The inside of his arm was out of camera shot. So maybe it's yet another runaround to throw off the police if they decided to look for the guy."

"Still, it's risky."

"Only if it's real," Blake said. "What if like everything else visible from that camera, the tattoo is only part of an alibi construct?"

"A decal? Or stick-on?"

"A little soap and water and the cops are looking for the wrong guy forever."

Lily Sims folded clothes half-heartedly and packed them in her suitcase. Boxes were stacked against the living room wall, taped and labeled for the movers, who would be there on Monday. The decision to leave LA had not been as difficult as she thought it would be. In the end, what had she ever gotten from this city except a slap in the face and a lot of money? It was time to take the money and walk.

Sharing the same property with Brianna was unthinkable, even though a note had told her she could stay indefinitely at the same "sallery." Another gift from Ali, Lily assumed. Sam Klein had been sweet to offer her a job and, if Lily had been able to picture him as even long shot husband material, she might have said yes.

With her savings and the money from

Dev's will, Lily could pay cash for a luxury condo back in Coeur d'Alene and have enough left to live comfortably for many years. Years in which she could gradually get the stink of Hollywood off her and decide what to do with the rest of her life. Maybe she would write a tell-all book, give the public a peek inside the glitter-sprayed septic tank that is show business.

Lily wondered when she had become so cynical. Was it when she finally realized Dev would never love her? When she overheard that awful nickname? Or when Dev started screwing around on his pregnant girlfriend? All those were certainly bricks in the wall, but the ugly and threatening betrayal by Ali is what finally made her understand she didn't belong here.

A glance at her watch told her the two detectives who had called yesterday would arrive any minute. Lily was prepared. No one would trip her up or cause her to reveal her inadvertent role in Dev's death.

She had rehearsed her story a number of times, and was sure she could deliver it without blushing, stammering or implicating herself in any way. She had to if she wanted to be able to move back to Idaho with nothing hanging over her head. She didn't dare point a finger at Ali, but she could throw Buddy under the bus.

Suitcases were being packed at Joe Roberts' home, too, though less efficiently. Ellen had drunk twice her normal breakfast vodka, needing that third and fourth screwdriver to give bravado the feeling of bravery, if only to herself. No amount of alcohol could have girded her for a final confrontation with Joe, but the orange juice double-down gave her enough gumption to make her escape. By the time her husband came home tonight, Ellen would be changing planes at JFK on her way to a new life, albeit a short one.

Through the years she had lost her youth, her looks, her dignity, her children. And now her health. She refused to allow her last few months on Earth—the doctor had predicted as many as ten—to provide fodder for the Joe Roberts spin machine. The fabric of lies woven around Dev's death had provided Joe with a mantle of grieving fatherhood. It had springboarded his anticrime platform, a platform that might be compelling enough to land him in the U.S. Senate. The investigation he pretended to be conducting with his hired cops provided nothing more than the constant picking at a scab, assurance the wound wouldn't heal.

Let's see his advisors put a positive spin on a nasty divorce, she thought. Maybe she wouldn't live to see the final decree, but she could fully enjoy making him pay for all his sins while she drank vodka tonics on a balcony overlooking Lake Como in Italy.

When the maid knocked softly and told her the car had arrived, Ellen let her close the last bag and carry it out. She went to the small escritoire where she had tried and failed the night before to find the perfect words for her exit. They came to her now, and she pulled out one creamy white sheet of her personal stationery. No salutation, no signature. Only the words: *You know why.*

Satisfied, she crossed to the bed and propped the page against a pillow. She slipped off her wedding band and engagement ring, dropping them onto the silk duvet and, with one more glance around her luxurious prison cell, Ellen walked out of Joe's life and into her own.

It was a divorce lawyer's wet dream and Sam Klein could not believe his luck. When Ellen Roberts had walked in yesterday morning, he assumed she was there as Dev's mother. He had put on a serious face, preparing to console her if she were grieving or enlighten her if she had come to question the will.

When she said she wanted him to handle her divorce, Sam was about to decline, his most recent money-losing marital fiasco still fresh in his mind. But then she had placed an accordion file on his desk and invited him to glance at the first few pages.

The mealy-mouthed wives of wealthy men were often contractually shackled in a divorce. Hubby insured she kept her yap shut about any dirt by penalizing her financially if she talked. Most of those women, Sam knew, were so damn anxious to hop on the gravy train they didn't care what they had to sign up front. It was only later, when they wanted to draw blood, that Sam or some other attorney had to explain the price tag of verbal revenge. That's why there are so many "amicable" divorces among the super-rich.

The only weapon a woman like that has is a passive-aggressive prolonging of the process. Tying up his assets in divorce limbo so he can't make some bold business move or investment venture he had planned on. Keeping even hostile interaction going until the mistress waiting in the wings loses patience and begins nagging him to wrap it up, already starting to sound a lot like the wife he had dumped for her. If a lawyer had the stomach for the process, billable hours multiplied like drunken hamsters.

As Sam had glanced over the first few pages of the file, he realized he was holding the Holy Grail. He looked at the woman across the desk from him with new interest. Unless he was mistaken, Ellen Roberts was already half in the bag and it wasn't even lunch time. But she was crystal clear in explaining what she wanted from him—the biggest, messiest and most public divorce battle possible. She offered him double his rate, and promised a fat bonus if he could bring it home within six months. Assuming she was throwing out big promises of money that technically belonged with joint assets, Sam had at first demurred. She knew what caused the reluctance, so she assured him she didn't have to tap community property to pay the cover. When her mother died two years earlier, Ellen had become the sole inheritor of the Carmichael family money.

Sam had agreed to handle the divorce, pending his reading of the entire file. After she left, he began scanning what was, in essence, an insurance policy written over a thirty-year marriage. It contained proof of every unethical, illegal, morally reprehensible thing her husband had ever done. If the contents of the file were made public, Joe Roberts would be savaged by everyone from the IRS to the California Attorney General, and from the SEC to a surprisingly large number of illegitimate children.

This was the kind of dream leverage a lawyer could use to take away every dime a man had ever made in return for the wife's silence.

Ellen Roberts, however, did not want or need money. And she was done with staying silent.

At 9:00 o'clock on Friday morning, Sam called Ellen and agreed to be her hatchet man. His bank account was then fattened significantly by a wire transfer before 10:00 A.M.

Ellen had given him three instructions: wait till Monday to begin strafing her husband's political ambitions; draw up a will dividing the Carmichael fortune between Ellen's daughter Susannah and her unborn grandchild; and make sure Joe Roberts never got within a mile of that money. The divorce had no downside for Sam, and the will put a big juicy cherry right on top.

The three interviews had taken up much of the day, and Blake found himself on the front end of Friday afternoon traffic as he and Maureen headed east on Sunset.

The morning had begun in Santa Monica, where they spoke with Yvonne Snell, the woman who first suggested painting the yoga studio, at least according to the instructor. Mrs. Snell confirmed she had been the one to bring it up, but when pressed, finally told them the idea had been Ali Garland's. The two had met for lunch about ten days before the shooting, and Ali had shown her a book that analyzed the emotions evoked by different colors. They both agreed a soothing blue-green on one of the yoga studio walls would make the environment more relaxing, but Ali had been reluctant to front the idea herself. She had not wanted to be seen as a pushy celebrity trying to get her own way, and was grateful when Yvonne Snell offered to throw the idea out in their next class.

Their second stop had been Dev Roberts' house, where they spoke to Lily Sims, the former assistant. She had been very straightforward in all her answers, hesitating only when Maureen asked her who might have leaked the wardrobe information. Ms. Sims had appeared reluctant to speculate about one of Dev's oldest friends, but she eventually told them Buddy Jensen had sat in on the planning session with Dev and Kenny Kentner. She was certain Buddy would never be so irresponsible as to give away the surprise, but Blake and Maureen weren't so sure. They asked for Buddy's new address and were told about the Venice Beach apartment where he was crashing.

Buddy had turned out to be an almost incoherent pothead who answered a question one way, then two minutes later answered the same question another way. Most of the time, though, he seemed to be answering questions they hadn't even asked. Questions like *why are giraffes?* Or *what is the sound of purple?*

They had come away from that interview with two things: the belief Buddy could easily have leaked the wardrobe details, and a bit of a contact high.

Blake's phone rang as he was stopped at the light at Doheny. "Hi, Janie. Chinese sounds perfect. Get me chicken chow mein and pork fried rice." He paused to listen to a question. "We still have a report to write, but I should be there by six at the latest. Me, too. Bye."

"Since when do you eat chow mein? Every time we have Chinese, you get lobster Cantonese and spareribs."

"Yeah, well, when I'm the one paying, I get what I like. When Jane's buying, I try to be more fiscally conservative."

"You make *her* pay for the take-out?" she asked incredulously. "El cheapo boyfriendo."

"Don't get me started. Jane's very touchy about taking advantage. You'll see. If we come for turkey day, she'll want to bring something."

"No need. We're having the whole dinner made at Trends. All we do is pick it up."

"Good luck convincing her of that when she calls you."

They had no trouble knocking out a three-page report for Joe Roberts. Everything was circumstantial, but all the arrows pointed in one direction, and the two were confident they would eventually bring Dev's killer to justice.

Maureen proofed the e-mail one last time before hitting send. Blake checked his watch. "5:15. No one's going to read that till Monday, but what do you bet we get a call when they do?"

"I won't take that action, because I agree. Roberts should be thrilled to see a potential payoff to all his anticrime breast-beating."

No congratulatory call came on Monday. Their report didn't even make it to the recycling bin this time. The young aide who arrived early to sort communications to be passed on to Joe hit delete when he read the subject. And by noon Joe Roberts had much bigger problems to worry about than his phony murder investigation.

Monday wasn't a total loss, though. That night Ali Garland made her first mistake.

"Wait'll you see what I have," Blake said, rushing in as soon as Maureen opened the door. "DVD player, stat!"

"And good morning to you, too," Maureen said to nobody. Blake had disappeared into the living room, and when she followed him she saw he was already setting up the DVD to play the disc he popped out of a plastic sleeve.

"Ali went to a premiere party last night."

"On a Monday?"

"Not a *real* movie. It was a documentary about polar bears. But the guy who produced it is apparently an investor in that condom project Ali's going to do. Anyway, take a look."

Blake advanced the DVD until Ali was helped out of a limousine by her date. "Look at her purse," he said, stopping the action as Ali waved to the small crowd.

"That's the Volanté."

"I remembered you said there was a waiting list, so I called the store to see if Ali had somehow cut in line and bought another one. Turns out she *never* bought one."

Maureen looked back at the TV screen. "A knockoff? No way. Those red carpet sharks *always* know the real from the fake. No actress would risk the humiliation of being exposed."

"I said she never *bought* one, but she does own one. Turns out Dev Roberts bought the bag for her for Christmas last year. By the way, Beyoncé took delivery three weeks ago, so there's only one Black-Eyed Pea standing between you and your own Volanté."

"Ali must have used a knockoff the day she killed Dev. That explains why she didn't mind cutting the strap. She also knew it was never going to make it to yoga class where some real housewives of Beverly Hills might have spotted the fake."

"Plus, shooting a man point blank in the face can really divert attention away from your counterfeit bag," Blake said.

"And she knew the CCTV pictures would be too grainy to show the bag wasn't the real deal. Blake, we have to prove she purchased a Volanté knockoff. That's a slam-dunk link to her planning the murder."

"Already on it. Libby's sending me the names of all businesses currently under investigation for selling high-end fakes."

Blake hardly recognized Maureen when she emerged from the back of the house twenty minutes later, but he had seen the type. Usually entering or leaving Saks or Neiman's. Her hair was in a smooth chignon, exposing gold button earrings that plainly advertised she was too wealthy to have to prove it with diamonds. She looked every inch the pampered trophy wife, right down to the perfect French manicure. She waggled her fingers in front of Blake's face. "Cool, n'est-ce pas? They're stick-ons. I keep them around for emergencies."

"See, that's the difference between Venus and Mars," Blake said, grabbing his car keys. "In a man's world, nothing about the fingernails would ever be considered an emergency unless bamboo was involved."

It wasn't until Maureen went into the third place that she scored. Like the previous two stores, this was small, quiet and lined with display shelves showcasing handbags in the one-to-five-hundred-dollar range. The proprietor here was a fiftyish man of Middle-Eastern descent, who smiled and nodded as Maureen entered, too savvy to approach her and hustle a sale. He was an expert on wealthy women, so he understood they always wanted to browse first, if only to let you know by their clothes, jewelry and attitude they have more now than you ever will.

He watched as the beautiful redhead walked slowly along the shelves, sometimes picking up a purse and examining it briefly before putting it back. Probably wondering if it would go with some new couture outfit she had just bought in Milan. She looked at one gray leather messenger bag for a long time before carrying it over to him.

"This is very nice," she said in an accent he thought might belong to Texas. Oil money. That boded well. And the bag she held was tagged at four hundred.

"A new designer. Not so well-known yet in America, but they are crazy for his shoes and bags in Europe." She would now pretend to recognize the designer, not wanting to appear to be behind the fashion curve.

"Yes, now that you mention it, I think I saw something quite like this in a shop on the Champs-Elysées." Her drawl was spot-on and she knew it. All she had to do was Max Gunn minus the whiskey baritone.

Maureen held out the bag, examining it at arm's length, cocking her head and *mm-hmm*ing. He now knew he had the sale. Another minute and she'd plunk down her platinum card.

But then she surprised him. She glanced around subtly to make sure no one else was in the shop, set the gray bag on the counter, and leaned in toward him. "Actually, what I am looking for doesn't seem to be on your shelves."

"And what is it you are interested in?"

"Well," she said with a smile, "a very good friend told me I might be able to buy an Etienne Volanté here."

Instantly he went on guard. It was not unheard of for the police to use decoys, although they were usually easy to spot, middle-class working girls who thought all they had to do was put on expensive clothes to look like they were wealthy. If this one was a decoy, she was the best he'd ever seen. Even her perfume whispered trust fund. Still, it was a risk. "Sadly, madame, the Volantés are sold only in the designer's own store. A humble merchant, such as I, is denied the privilege of providing a beautiful item like that to discerning ladies such as yourself."

He smiled ingratiatingly. If she wasn't a cop, maybe he could still sell her the gray, which she had picked up again. She examined the bag and, without raising her eyes to his, laughed softly to herself. "Well, darn it, then I must be wrong. But I was so *sure* my friend said this was the place."

He understood her message. She would have what she wanted or she would leave without buying anything. "Might I be so bold as to ask the name of your friend?"

Gotcha! Maureen knew all she had to do was to remain coy and charming. Now that they were in a negotiation, she put the gray bag on the counter and smiled at him. "Well, I *could* tell you, but then I'd have to kill you." She waited a perfectly timed beat, then added, "On Monday."

His broad smile told her she had scored. "Ah! Madame should have said immediately. Miss Garland buys here quite often." He locked the door and went into the back.

"What took you so long?" Blake asked, as Maureen got into the car with a large silver shopping bag. "Did he make the thing while you waited?"

"Even with the right bait, it takes a while to hook a fish. And let's don't forget to put in for fifteen-hundred dollars in petty cash."

"Cripes, that much for a fake?"

"Hey, that's only thirty-three cents on the dollar. And it's a very good fake."

Calls that afternoon confirmed what they already suspected. Ali had never reported her credit cards lost, nor had she applied for a new driver's license. More blue cards went up on the storyboard, but without Mystery Man's identity, they still couldn't tell the whole story.

Charlie ducked in to say they should turn on the TV. When they did, they found out why they hadn't gotten a call from Joe Roberts congratulating them on their progress.

California's Attorney General was opening an investigation into violations allegedly committed by Roberts during his two terms as Governor. Joe angrily dismissed the allegations as politically motivated smears and said he looked forward to disproving the scurrilous lies when hearings began.

Blake had much on his mind as he drove home. The case was finally pulling together and he allowed himself to believe that fifty-thousand-dollar bonus was not so much a fantasy as a solid possibility. He had not thought beyond a pool cover and an engagement ring, but he had spent a lot of time weighing those two. The cover was a no-brainer. To be able to swim year-round without owing his soul to the power company would be heaven.

The idea of the engagement ring, begun as an unconscious blurt-out, had taken shape in his mind during the last couple days, slowly becoming as real a goal as the pool cover. He loved Jane. And nothing she had ever done contradicted the fact that she loved him. He had based his insecurity on what she had *not* done. When would she do laundry, buy groceries, have time to herself, if not on Sunday afternoon? How could he not have been satisfied when the rest of their time together was always close to perfect?

Tomorrow night she would come over and they'd have four days, spending Thanksgiving with the O'Briens, then leaving Friday morning for the drive to Carmel. One of Charlie's buddies owned a small hotel right on the ocean and had given Blake what he called his "unemployed writer's discount." The room looked beautiful online and would cost him about the same as a cut-rate motel. And when Blake had assured Jane they could leave early enough on Sunday for her to have her afternoon, she said they didn't need to rush back. She was looking forward to a lazy Sunday brunch, after which they could meander down the coast toward home.

She had actually used that word, *home,* referring to his house, and in prior relationships that might have been a red flag for Blake. This time it felt like a confirmation. He wished he could afford a ring right now.

Joe Roberts did not give thanks on Thanksgiving. He was furious. Wasn't it typical of Ellen to pull a stunt like this right when he needed to present the public with a settled, solid, trustworthy image? Could she possibly have gotten early word of the Attorney General's investigation and decided to duck out before the flak? He doubted it. Worse charges had been leveled against him during his career, and she had always weathered the storms with her Jimmy Choos, her Manolo Blahniks and copious amounts of alcohol. In fact, she'd worn her vodka goggles so long he wondered if she ever noticed anything at all.

Oh, he had found her easily enough; she hadn't even tried to cover her tracks. At least she hadn't spoken to the press, and at least *those* jackals didn't know she had flown. He would set aside the issue of his wife for now and spend the four-day media lull developing a plan less of defense than attack. Joe already had people looking into the Attorney General's past. Any small scrap would suffice to deflect. Make the guy look like old clean-up-the-whores Spitzer when his own call girl action was exposed. In Joe's experience, it was the biggest do-gooders who had the nastiest skeletons closeted.

Still, from what his legal team had told him, the AG had some damning evidence, stuff that could only have come from the inside. Joe and his aides were going over old lists of staffers, right down to the State House pages. Low-level people wouldn't have been privy to any of that information, but even peons had eyes and ears.

Ali Garland had much to give thanks for that day. The unexpected and delicious charges against Joe Roberts ensured that the only person still questioning her innocence would be turning his attention to proving his own. She knew the jerk had never seriously believed he could pin anything on her, but she'd had enough talks with Dev about his father to know the old man would try to make political capital out of an overcooked steak at a restaurant if he could.

Now, with Joe out of the way, full funding in place for *Condom Nation*, and Christmas in Vail to look forward to, Ali felt she was home free and on the right track.

She would always believe she had been cheated out of an acting career, that Dev had lucked into roles which made him a star while she continued to be offered the same role again and again until she was too old to play it. Over the hill at twenty-seven. Even NFL players had careers longer than an ingénue.

If Hollywood wouldn't let her segue from dewy ingénue to leading lady and, ultimately, to Streep-like *grande dame*, she'd prove herself as a producer. That's where the real power was. She had already noticed the male executives were now as likely to talk grosses with her at dinner as to stare at her breasts.

Yes, Ali had much to give thanks for.

For Jane it was the strangest and most memorable Thanksgiving of her life. As a child she had looked forward to the holiday, knowing they would all have enough to eat. Surrounded by cherished family and the rare bounty of food, Jane had always felt truly grateful. She and her brothers and sister ate slowly and somberly, trying to show respect for the people and forces that had provided for them.

Her first Thanksgiving away from her parents had been with Blake last year. They had been dating only a few months, so the meal had felt slightly forced, slightly awkward. Neither of them had yet said I love you to the other, so when they sat down to what is, in essence, the most familial meal of the year, things suddenly felt *too* intimate.

Thanksgiving with the O'Briens was a boisterous celebration, the two monstrously large roasted turkeys with all the trimmings the only traditional part of the day. Besides Charlie and Maureen, Jane had met Sol, Bernie, Sheldon, Larry, Marty and Jock, although she never quite figured out which man was attached to which name. Except for Marty. At seventy-four he was the youngest, and the others referred to him as "the kid."

They were all old writers. Sol had given Charlie a job on a summer variety show when Charlie was a teenager selling one-liners to Jimmie Walker. Their material was as old as they were, but with a fresh young audience like Jane, they could trot out the vintage jokes and still get laughs.

Through the meal they were crude, funny and nonstop. Three of them did a whole routine to show off for her at one point, forty years of doing the same bit having honed it to perfection.

Jane listened sympathetically as Jock said, "I have a terrible problem. Every morning I wake up at 7:00, I try to urinate and I can't." Then Sol said. "*That's* a problem? Every morning *I* wake up at 7:00, try to defecate and I can't." "You two don't know what a problem *is*," Sheldon complained. "Every morning at 7:00 I urinate *and* I defecate." "So what's the problem?" Jock asked. "I don't wake up until 7:30."

Cranberry sauce had shot out of Jane's mouth with her laugh, and she went red with embarrassment until she realized the old men were acting like they'd been paid a compliment.

Sometime during dinner, the man across from Jane—Larry?—had stood and raised his glass. "I'd like to propose," he said, then stopped. One of the others jumped in. "Your Alzheimers is showing. You left off *a toast*." "Hey, who says I'm proposing a toast? I'm proposing to this knockout blonde sitting across from me." He looked directly at Jane and said, "Forgive me for not remembering your name, doll, but if you'll marry me, you can have the same deal all my ex-wives got. New car, new wardrobe, a piece of my residuals, and you only have to stick around for eighteen months." "As old as you are," one of the others yelled, "she might not even have to do *that* much time!"

The Beano jokes and sexual innuendo flew for more than two hours before their age and various infirmities began to slow them down. Rather than admit they were worn out and needed to go home, they turned the necessity of leaving into bustling social lives they had briefly abandoned to give Charlie the pleasure of their company.

Sheldon, said, "I hate to leave early, but my girlfriend gets *so* horny when I'm gone more than a couple hours."

"Is that your imaginary girlfriend, Shel? The only one you can satisfy with your imaginary erections?"

"Oh, look who's talking. Wasting all that Viagra on your own right hand."

"Hey, my girl is a lingerie model."

"Depends don't count as lingerie."

In the kitchen, Jane saw why there were two huge turkeys. Maureen was making up care packages, each one large enough to feed someone for days. Jane was glad she had brought such a big tray of mashed sweet potatoes and could contribute to the take-homes. "All of them seem like really sweet guys."

"They are," Maureen said. "And each year there's one or two fewer of them at the table."

"Well, it's nice of your dad to do this."

"Yeah, Charlie considers himself one of the lucky ones. Most of my 'honorary uncles' wound up with nothing after thirty or so years in TV. Eighty-hour weeks meant giving up their lives, their wives and their children."

"That's so sad."

"Price of admission, and I don't think any of them would go back and do it differently. They loved you, though. Normally they do that bit with shorter, punchier words than urinate and defecate."

"Oh. *Oh.*"

"So, what do you think about Blake being a temporary P.I.?"

"He was pretty unhappy about it at first, but now I think he's having fun."

"That's because we're finally making progress on this case."

"Well, I'm glad he gets to work with someone as nice as you."

They carried out all the doggy bags as Charlie helped each man into the limo he had hired to pick them up and take them back to their tiny apartments and rented rooms. Blake collapsed a walker, then handed it in, along with two canes and a rolling oxygen tank. Before they pulled out, Marty—the kid—rolled down his window and called out to Charlie. "Mind if we keep the stretch a few hours? We'd like to hit a couple strip joints."

"Sure," Charlie said, checking his watch. "If you hurry you can still make the early bird special at Lola's Bump-n-Grind. Lap dance and CPR, twenty bucks."

The window closed on cackling laughter, and the car pulled out of the driveway.

For Blake, Thanksgiving had been a great day. An hour after the writers left, he and his partner knew the identity of Ali's mystery man.

It had started with the four of them sprawled around the living room, Charlie vowing he would never eat again and Jane saying her stomach hurt. Not from overeating, but from laughing so hard during the meal. Maureen shared the story of her seventh birthday, when Charlie had been dealing with some actor's meltdown on the set and couldn't get away. The "uncles" had picked her up in a limousine and taken her to Disneyland, where they vowed they would "tear Mickey a new one."

"I had no idea what that meant. I only knew I was going to the big D. Looking back, I feel sorry for all the park employees. During Country Bear Jamboree, Sol kept saying things like 'A bear wouldn't say that' and 'This isn't how a chipmunk would do it.' Then Sheldon and Marty started yelling out lines that were much funnier than what anyone had ever written for the people on stage in the furry suits."

"I hope the boys didn't gross you out,"

Charlie said to Jane.

"No, I'm used to dealing with poopy pants, projectile vomit and loads of green snot."

"And that's when she's with me," Blake said, patting out a quick rim shot on the arm of his chair and waiting for a laugh that didn't come.

"Don't give up your day job," Charlie said.

Blake and Maureen started talking about the case, many details of which Jane had never heard. She knew he was working on the Dev Roberts shooting, if only unofficially, but they hadn't really discussed it.

"You know when that video leaked out the day of the shooting?" Jane said. "I noticed Ali Garland's face looked *exactly* the same as it did in *Don't Kill Me on Monday* when she stabbed the third ax murderer."

"That's because she was acting both times," Maureen said.

"Yeah, anytime she opens her mouth and says something," Blake added, "you can't go wrong assuming the exact opposite."

Maureen nodded, then looked thoughtful. She and Blake locked eyes and got to the same place at the same time. "The TV interview," Blake said. The two of them scrambled to their feet and raced out of the room.

"Was it something I said?" asked Charlie.

Taking him literally, Jane responded, "I don't think so."

Once they started with the supposition that Ali had been lying in that old TV interview when she spoke tearfully about her parents' death in a car accident, finding their man was easy. No live person was available because of the holiday, but since computers never clock out, Blake used their police access code to worm his way into the systems with the information they sought. "You told me something that very first day," he said. "About not believing she was even telling the truth about her own name."

"But I was wrong. I checked her last five tax returns."

"The IRS allows you to file under your professional name, as long as you declare all earnings. So maybe you were right after all."

Ten minutes later they knew the social security number under which Ali filed her taxes had originally been issued to Alice Rose Garcia. She had begun filing under the name Garland when she was seventeen and getting her first acting jobs. And Garland was the name she had used when she joined the Screen Actors Guild.

As soon as they knew her real name, they searched again for family. No Garcias had died in a car crash before Ali went into foster care, but a William N. Garcia had been sentenced to life without parole for the murder of his second wife. His *two* children had gone into the system. Their names were Alice Rose and William Tomas.

Mrs. Wojcek was not happy to be called on Thanksgiving, but Maureen didn't care. She laid out what they already knew, and implied there would be legal consequences if the woman lied to the police again.

"Okay, okay. I don't want to get in any trouble. I have five kids right now that need me."

"Let's start with the obvious. Was Alice Rose Garcia ever even in care with you?"

"Yes, of course. Right after her horrible father was arrested for killing her stepmother."

"What about her brother, Tomas?"

"No. I had too many. She was older and could help out with the little ones and the babies. But Tommy was only nine or ten. He was sent somewhere else and it broke Ali's heart."

"Why didn't you tell me her real last name when I spoke with you before?"

"Would you want to keep the name of a murderer? Forty-two times he stabbed her, high on PCP. And with those two children sleeping under the same roof. Besides, Ali was already getting small acting parts. She wanted a new name for her new life."

"And the car crash was part of her new history?"

"Yes. Will I be arrested?"

"Probably not. But you might have to testify in court."

"Did she really do it? Did she kill that man on purpose?"

"That's what we're trying to find out. Do you remember the name of the family that took Tommy?"

"They don't tell you where the sisters and brothers go, so it makes it hard on the children. You have to understand, Ali and Tommy had no family, only each other."

"One more thing before you go back to your Thanksgiving, Mrs. Wojcek. Do you keep in touch with Ali?"

"Not for years. Only Christmas cards."

"Until this is resolved, you need to keep it that way."

The State of California had never issued a

driver's license to a William Tomas Garcia in the right age range, so they started checking colleges and trade schools.

In the kitchen, Jane washed and Charlie dried the items that were too big or too delicate to go in the dishwasher. Jane had so obviously needed to feel useful that Charlie hadn't had the heart to tell her someone would be in tomorrow morning to do the clean-up. He would call Mrs. Taylor later and tell her to take a paid day off.

"I've never met anybody famous before today," Jane said, rinsing and handing over the first of many wine glasses.

"Well, in another time, every one of those guys was a real heavyweight."

"I was talking about you."

"Oh, me," Charlie said dismissively.

"Blake said he used to watch your show every week. You must be so proud to have created something like that."

"I was proud of creating *The Badge*."

Jane looked confused. "I thought it was called *The Brothers Gunn*."

"Before that was *The Badge*." He stared out the kitchen window and continued to dry the already dry glass in his hand. "I was a sitcom guy who got lucky and sold a gritty cop drama. It went on midseason, the critics creamed over it, and I got my first Emmy nomination."

"I'm sorry. I never heard of *The Badge*."

"You're not alone. It was cancelled after the initial thirteen episodes."

"But why?"

"Who knows? It was opposite *Murder, She Wrote* when that show was number four in the Nielsens, so it didn't really get *sampled*, as the suits like to say."

"But still, *The Brothers Gunn* made a lot of people happy. And I'm guessing that's the show that bought this house."

"It did indeed. Although one could wish to be remembered for something other than being the first producer to get the word poontang on in primetime."

He could see Jane was searching for some other angle to snap him out of his mood. "Oh, don't pay any attention to me. I'm a lucky man, and I've had tee many martoonies today." He used the damp dishtowel to create a squeak from the wine glass and was rewarded with a smile.

As Jane wiped down the countertops and Charlie made a pot of coffee, Blake and Maureen came back.

"We found him! We know who Mystery Man is," Maureen called out as she entered. She looked around at the clean kitchen and then at Charlie. "Didn't you tell her—"

"Not to bother?" interrupted Charlie. "Of course. But Jane wanted to save you and me from having to clean up later."

Maureen got the message. Jane's background didn't include maids and gardeners who kept her world tidy and beautiful.

"Focus, people!" cried Blake. "We have our first break."

"So who is he?" Charlie asked.

"Ali's half-brother. A theater arts major at Pepperdine," Blake replied.

"Are you two going to bring him in for questioning?"

"We can't, Dad. We're not cops anymore."

"And we don't want to tip off either one of

them that they're still being looked at."

"So Monday morning when school's back in session, we're going to run a little sting op on Tommy Garcia."

"The problem is that he may have seen Maureen and me at the crime scene or on TV the night of the shooting. We need somebody else to front the sting."

Blake and Maureen turned to Jane and smiled.

"Me?" she squeaked.

Their two-day getaway in Carmel was relaxing and fun, with Jane only saying fifty or a hundred times she wasn't cut out for the job they were asking her to do. Blake reassured her all she would have to do is sit at a table and hand out cash.

"But he helped a murderer. What if he suspects and tries to kill me?"

"You'll be in a crowded school cafeteria. Maureen and I will be across the room. And if he so much as looks cross-eyed at *my* girl," Blake growled in a tough-guy voice, "I will be all over him like scabs on a leper."

"You make me feel so safe. *And* a little creeped out. But it's nice being a detective's moll."

"I think molls belong to gangsters. And the 1930's. Private eyes have dames."

When she left for her apartment Sunday evening, Jane promised she would do her best when they needed her.

That first Monday in December was a big day for everybody.

Ali Garland (nee Garcia) began meeting with prospective directors for *Condom Nation.*

Attorney Sam Klein lobbed the second grenade from the arsenal his client had so sagely stockpiled over her three-decade marriage.

Joe Roberts was notified by the head of the Securities and Exchange Commission that he was being investigated for insider trading.

Kenny Kentner sold Zeitgeist a new show featuring reenactments of the deaths of rock stars, actors and other public figures. According to *Variety*, February 10th would be the premiere date of *Dying With the Stars.*

And Glendale Feet issued a massive recall of its shoes. At least the e-mail sent to Tommy Garcia *said* it was a massive recall. It also said a company rep would be in the main cafeteria at 2:00 P.M. the following Saturday to hand out one thousand dollars in cash in exchange for the return of their defective shoes. "He might not still have them," Maureen said, sending a recall notice to exactly one computer.

"Maybe not. But if he does, I don't think a college kid is going to walk away from that kind of money."

"I wish we had more sophisticated software so we would know if and when he opens that e-mail."

"Hey, the worst that happens is we make a trip out to Malibu for nothing on Saturday. In the meantime, we need to get a photo of him and try to figure out where he and Ali meet."

At 9:00 P.M. Tomas "Tommy" Garcia returned to his dorm room after four hours of rehearsal. Friday would be the opener for the ten-day run of *The Tempest,* and he was playing

Trinculo. He had wanted the part of Caliban because it offered the chance to show off a wider dramatic range, but he would make the best of the jester role. Tommy knew he could breathe life into the part by giving it a bit of a Jack Sparrow twist, but the director kept squelching his makeup and wardrobe ideas as "too faggy." If that guy only knew, Tommy thought, how good an actor I really am.

When he checked his e-mails, he saw one from Glendale Feet: *Shoe recall pays cash!* Intrigued, he opened the file. The company was offering a thousand bucks for the return of defective product. He went to his closet and pulled out one of the shoes he had told his sister he destroyed. He compared the model number to the one on the screen and found a match.

A thousand dollars! He couldn't believe his luck. Ali paid for tuition and books and gave him an allowance, but it's hard going to a rich kid's school without having a rich kid's money. That's why he had kept the stupid shoes in the first place; he needed them. Now, reading about some chemical in the material that caused rashes, inflammation and maybe toe cancer, he was happy to dump them. Even happier to get paid for it. Tommy read on to find out where and when he could turn in the shoes.

Blake stepped back and looked at the sconces flanking the medicine cabinet. He had measured carefully, but as he had learned from his experience with the Snowflake White toilet, it was easy to be off a little. The level said they were even, so he began tightening all the screws.

Three weeks until Christmas and Blake

was already thinking about gifts, a record early start for him. One call to Omaha Steaks would take care of his parents, his brother and his grandfather. No matter how old you were in Blake's family, your teeth could handle a good steak. His little sister would get the usual hundred-dollar check. He knew he had to get at least token gifts for Charlie and Maureen, but what do you buy for people with that kind of money? A T-bone from Nebraska wasn't going to cut it for a guy who probably had Kobe beef flown in from Japan.

Blake and Artie would exchange their usual gag gifts, but he suspected Maureen would have less use for a Whoopie cushion or fake dog poop than he and his former partner did. He would ask Jane for ideas.

Jane. Blake wanted to make this her best Christmas ever, but he wasn't sure how yet. He had already ordered a five-year subscription to *Ladybug* so she wouldn't have to keep checking out copies from the school library. His thinking was that nothing says I want to keep you around like a long-term periodical commitment.

Carefully unwrapping the tissue protecting the face plate of the first sconce, Blake fitted the curved glass into the slender metal trough. Once it was seated firmly, he screwed in the hundred-watt bulb and flipped on the wall switch. Nice and bright. He turned off the light, then began unwrapping the second face plate.

Blake had done a little detective work in Carmel while Jane was in the shower: he read labels. Never again would he make the mistake he had made with Brandy, buying her a sexy black dress in a size ten. When he held it up in the store, it had *seemed* about right, and Blake figured she could always exchange it for a different size. When she opened it on Christmas morning, she had shrieked, "A *ten?* Are you kidding me? I'm a size *two*, Blake. A two!"

He would buy Jane a nice blazer in size six. Something designery, but not so expensive she'd feel like a ho. He might need Maureen's input on this one.

After screwing in the bulb for the second sconce, and flipping the switch to make sure the light worked, he began gathering his tools and the packing material from the afternoon's work.

I need one more thing for Jane, Blake thought. It doesn't have to be expensive, but it needs to be romantic. The old standbys, perfume or a gold bracelet, fell short of the mark. They were about as nonspecific as the drawer full of brass razors he had received from girlfriends over the years. For the first time, he wondered if the women's happy responses to his little bottles of Joy or L'Air du Temps had been as canned and practiced as his had been when he opened his gift and found yet another brass razor with the initials B.A.E. engraved on the handle.

Please God, don't let Jane give me a razor, he thought. Last year, gifts had not been much of an issue. They were exclusive by then, but it was still early in the relationship. Since she was going back east for ten days, they had decided each one of them would take the other out to some new little restaurant for a meal as their Christmas gift. Dinner for under fifty dollars, and extra points for romantic. Blake had gone Moroccan, where they sat on pillows and ate b'stilla with their fingers. Jane had found a mom and pop Italian place that had upped its amore quotient by installing a private booth. It was more like a large cabinet with a table inside, but Jane had shut the doors and made out with him between courses.

Blake looked around the now-completed bathroom, knowing it would add much more than its cost to the value of his house. One reason he had been able to score such a deal when buying the place was few people wanted a three-bedroom home with only one bathroom. Four months ago, this had been a large utility closet, but now, with the help of a plumber, an electrician and a glazier, it was a bright and airy asset to his home equity. Eventually, he would vacuum up all the sawdust and buy a shower curtain and towels, but for now he was satisfied.

The next job would be the Harvest Gold shag carpeting in the living room, some decades-old idea of edgy style. He had pulled up a piece of the rug from one corner and knew there was hardwood flooring underneath, waiting to be restored. He would start that in January.

For now he had three other goals: nail a murderer, win that bonus and get back on the police force where he belonged.

Further digging turned up a DMV photo of Tommy Garcia. They hadn't found it Thanksgiving Day because California issues a separate license for motorcycles, and that information was in a database they hadn't explored. The photo was four years old and had the usual flat-faced distortion found in all driver's license pictures, but they showed it to Jane anyway.

Although the photo was next to useless, at

least they now knew Tommy was six feet tall and had brown eyes and dark brown hair. He did not need corrective lenses.

During Saturday's drive to Pepperdine, Jane nervously fingered the small metal box Blake had picked up that morning from Staples. She knew it contained ten one-hundred-dollar bills—more money than she had ever held at one time—and the responsibility weighed heavily on her. "What if I hand over the money to the wrong person?"

"Only one person believes there's a recall. One or two might come up and ask about your sign," Blake said, "but Tommy Garcia will be carrying the shoes, maybe in a bag or small box."

"Be careful not to touch them. If they're not bagged, have him put them on the table and Blake and I will bag them."

They had no authority to be on campus, so they picked up Pepperdine brochures and carried them as conspicuously as they could, hoping to pass for prospective students while they walked toward the cafeteria.

"What if he asks me my name?"

"Make something up," Maureen said.

"Okay." Jane thought for a second. "How about Penelope Kadoodlepeeper?"

"He's not a kindergartener," Blake said. "And he's not going to ask your name."

"But if he does," Maureen added, "go with Mary Smith."

"Mary Smith. Got it. Should I be wearing a wire?"

Blake stopped, forcing Maureen and Jane to do the same. He stepped off the sidewalk and onto the grass, moving out of the flow of students, putting both hands on Jane's shoulders, then trying to reassure her.

"Listen to me. If there was even a remote possibility of danger, I wouldn't ask you to do this. Maureen can't do it because Tommy may have seen her before. All you have to do is give him the cash and get those shoes for us." He gave her a quick hug and the three moved on toward the cafeteria.

Two o'clock found Jane at a table near the main entrance of The Waves Café, the metal box and a short stack of forms in front of her. The discreet sign reading Glendale Feet was perched in front of her like a desktop name plaque.

Across the room, Blake and Maureen sat at a table with cafeteria trays in front of them. Maureen pulled out her cell phone and took a few test shots of Jane. She and Blake were determined to leave with a good-enough picture of Tommy Garcia to show the wardrobe mistress and the four CCTV people.

A couple of false starts later—a pretty young blonde is bound to be chatted up—a red-haired kid with a pathetic excuse for a goatee entered, spotted the sign, then approached Jane and put a paper bag on the table.

"Who is *that*?" Blake asked.

"I don't know, but we've got his picture," Maureen said, checking her cell phone screen.

They watched as Jane stood and shook the kid's hand. As soon as she did, they saw he was much too short to be Tommy Garcia.

"How tall is Jane?"

"Five-seven."

"Then that guy can't be more than five eight or nine."

Jane checked inside the bag, then pushed the fake release form across for the kid to sign. Once he did, they exchanged words. Then she slid a second form over and the kid wrote on that one, too. Jane carefully counted out the ten bills and handed them to him. They exchanged a few more words, then the kid turned and left.

While Blake and Maureen waited for the guy to clear the door, Jane got up from her seat and crossed to a free-standing notice board. The front faced away from Blake and Maureen, so they couldn't see what she pulled off the board. By the time they got to her table, she was back, picking up her metal box and her sign.

As Blake checked the bag and Maureen picked up the releases, Jane spoke breathlessly. "Okay, that wasn't him, but he had the shoes. I stood up so you could see he was too short to be the right guy, but when you didn't rush over, I gave him the money."

"Relax, you did great," Blake said, giving her a quick hug. "Who was he?"

"Tommy's roommate."

"Stuart Mason," Maureen read from the release.

"Yes. When I saw the name wasn't right, I asked him if he was the *actual* owner of the shoes. He said they belonged to his roommate, so I asked him to print the name of the owner on another release form."

"Tommy Garcia," Maureen said, reading from the second sheet of paper.

"Well, at least we have the shoes. We'll find another way to get a recent photo."

"Oh, I got you a photo," Jane said, flipping over a glossy 5x7 head shot of a good-looking young man about nineteen or twenty.

"How?" Maureen asked.

"Tommy couldn't bring the shoes himself because he's in a play, and the matinee performance is on right now."

Jane pointed to the free-standing notice board, which Blake saw was a promo poster for Shakespeare's *The Tempest,* with glossies of all the student actors. The missing photo by Tommy Garcia's name was the one in Blake's hand. He turned back to Jane, impressed.

"Nice work, Kadoodlepeeper."

Monday, Blake dropped off the shoes at the BHPD, where Libby Johnson said she'd have them tested as soon as possible.

That afternoon, Joe Roberts learned the IRS was coming after him for income tax evasion, and they apparently had the documentation to make it stick.

Sam Klein continued to pull together the disparate elements of what was to be the fourth and final bomb dropped on Roberts before his missus told the world—through her attorney, of course—that his reprehensible behaviour left her no choice but to file for divorce. Not all the little bastards were willing to go after their biological father, but Sam had convinced enough of them with the promise of a fat payoff that he now had a miniature class-action lawsuit of illegitimate children.

Things were shaping up for an interesting Christmas.

While they waited for the forensics report, Blake and Maureen started replacing all the remaining white cards on their storyboard with blue ones. Every one of the CCTV people said Tommy was their guy. His hair had been longer and lighter—wig?—and he'd worn glasses, but they all said they would testify he was the "inspector" who had come around the week before the shooting.

They drove to Culver City where Sandra Bodner stepped away from the little person she was fitting for an elf costume and took the pins out of her mouth long enough to confirm that the man in the photo was Dev Roberts' "assistant."

They met with Dev's manager, who knew nothing about any contract between his dead client and Ali Garland. He speculated they'd been lied to, as Dev couldn't stand Ali and would never have done business with her.

They learned Tommy Garcia had missed all three of his morning classes the Friday of the shooting.

When Blake and Maureen decided to look at all the CCTV videos again, they skipped the sections they had already viewed and worked backwards. Most of the SD cards captured thirty days of images before they started to rewrite, so there was plenty to watch. It paid off when they saw a man in a hooded sweatshirt walk Ali's path at 10:00 P.M. on Thursday, nine hours before the shooting.

The hooded man wasn't the only pedestrian in Beverly Hills that night, but he *was* the only one who kneeled to tie his shoe four times, each time in the exact spot where Ali would stop the next morning to put on her show of fear and innocence. The two detectives searched, but the chalk marks—if they had been put there by the hooded man—were long gone.

They watched Ali leave the big parking structure on Bedford five mornings a week, not dressed nearly as well as she was the morning of the shooting. She went to Starbucks, effectively establishing her routine and making herself familiar to the regulars, but each day when she rounded the corner and was out of sight, she dropped her venti cup in a trash can, skinny latte unsipped. "Makes sense," Maureen said. "Who drinks twenty ounces of coffee before a one-hour exercise class?"

A reinterview with the young barista confirmed that, although he had said she was a regular the day of the incident, Ali had only started coming into the coffee shop two-and-a-half weeks earlier.

By the time the forensics report came back with an exact match between the paint on the sidewalk and the tiny flecks of paint in the treads of the shoes, Blake and Maureen had a full storyboard of blue cards. They knew it was time to go to Lt. Rhee with what they had.

Friday, a little more than a week before Christmas, Blake and Maureen were in Rhee's office telling their story, an alternate script to Ali's professionally produced one. Their police liaison, Libby Johnson, was also present.

It took thirty minutes to lay everything out, and when they were done they looked at the lieutenant expectantly, waiting for him to say he would send out two teams to arrest the homicidal brother-and-sister act. Instead, Rhee looked at the photographs and reports spread across his desk, then leaned back in his chair and sighed. "What you have here is exactly nothing," he said, stunning Blake and his partner.

Blake found his voice first. "She did it. She killed him with premeditation."

"It certainly appears that way."

"And we can prove it."

"See, that's where we disagree, Ervansky. There's a whole lot of circumstantial here," Rhee said, sweeping his hand over the evidence piled on his desk. "But not a shred of proof."

"What about the paint on the shoe?" Maureen asked.

"Doesn't connect to our homicide. All it proves is somebody wearing them tried—and failed—to snatch her purse a few minutes before the shooting. You can't even say for sure Tommy Garcia ever had possession of the shoes. If it came right down to nuts and bolts, it would be the brother's word against his roommate's. So unless you paid in marked bills that can be traced to Garcia, the shoes are a dead end."

"We could always send them out for DNA testing," Blake replied.

"Say we do and they come back positive. All we could charge the kid with is an attempted purse grab and breaking into his sister's house. If the two of them planned this whole thing, do you really think she'll press charges?"

"What about the purse?" Maureen asked. "We can prove she bought a faux Volanté to use in the murder."

"It isn't a crime to buy a designer knock-off, Sergeant. Well it *is,* but you know what I mean. Ali will claim she carried the fake for everyday stuff like grocery shopping and yoga to save wear and tear on the real deal between red carpet appearances."

"Okay, maybe it's mostly circumstantial evidence," Blake said, indicating the desktop, "but people have been convicted on the basis of less than what we have here."

"True. And if this were a virgin case, I might be willing to go for it. But this old whore's already been screwed, blued and tattooed by the grand jury *and* the public. The DA is not going to risk having his head handed to him twice on the same shooting."

Blake slumped, his height creating a considerable curve of disappointment in the chair. "So we let her get away with it?"

Lt. Rhee leaned forward, clasped hands on top of the desk. "Is Joe Roberts still paying you every week?"

"Yes," Blake said. "Apparently the wheels of bureaucratic machinery continue to turn regardless of what's happening to the bureaucrat himself."

"So keep on this and come back when you can prove she did it. Operative word, *prove*."

Blake and Maureen followed Libby into the break room.

"Don't kid yourselves. He's blown away by the work you've done. And so am I."

"If that's how he acts when he's impressed," said Maureen, "I'd hate to catch him on a blasé day."

"Look, Rhee told me about the money on the line for the Fallen Officer Fund the day you went on leave. It was a pipe dream then, but now he knows it's possible. Officially, he can't put any people on a closed case, so everything depends on how good you two really are."

"Jesus, Libby, we've busted our asses on

this," Blake said.

"So go back and bust them a little more."

Blake and Maureen decided to quit early. All they were doing anyway was staring at their storyboard, trying to figure out how they'd been outsmarted by an actress with a *CUL8R* license plate and a troll doll key chain.

"I'm going to hit some stores this weekend and wrap up the last of my shopping," Maureen said. "You?"

"Mine's all phoned in and ordered, except for Jane."

"Christmas is a week from Sunday and you don't have a gift for the woman you're hoping to spend your life with? And men wonder why so many women turn lesbo."

"Actually, I *don't* wonder about that, and I already have two nice presents for her. But I think I need something else. Bigger, splashier."

"What do you have so far?"

"A magazine subscription and a jacket." Maureen arched an eyebrow and looked at him. Blake wilted. "Okay, when you put it that way, it isn't great. But if I spend too much she'll give it back."

"Then you have to get creative."

"Oh, hell; I'm dead."

"Think. I mean, you two practically live together. What does she like?"

"Five-year-old kids. But Target was all sold out. Come on, you have to help me."

"Nope. Because I can tell you one thing a woman does *not* want in a gift from a man. And that's another woman's fingerprints all over it."

Jane was off work for two weeks and would be staying with Blake the whole time. He was happy to have an opportunity to show her what bliss it would be to share a home with him permanently, but he was having trouble shaking his feeling of failure on the Roberts murder.

When he got home late Friday, Jane was already there and she had brought food from Blake's favorite Thai place. She listened to him sympathetically while he groused about the case, and later on in bed she graciously acquiesced to his more-selfish-than-usual lovemaking.

As Jane's breathing deepened and slowed, he lay awake thinking: wow, I really sold myself as husband material tonight. Whining about work, forgetting to thank her for dinner, and rounding out the evening by using her like a prostitute. And would it have killed me to pick up some flowers on my way home?

When he finally drifted off to sleep, he was thinking it didn't really matter if he got that bonus. He wasn't sure the nicest engagement ring in the world could compensate for his shortcomings as a man.

Ali met Tommy in the hidden grotto of the Lake Shrine at 3:00 on Sunday. He stood as soon as she entered. "Did you see it?" he asked.

"Last night. You were incredible!"

"The staggering wasn't over the top?"

"Hey, Trinculo's drunk; you've got to sell it. The guy playing Stephano wasn't half as good as you were." Tommy beamed in the shower of compliments. "Okay, I have our tickets. You fly out of LAX next Saturday afternoon, and I'm on a late-morning flight out of Burbank. We'll have

Christmas eve in Vail." She pulled the e-mail confirmation out of her purse, not noticing his sudden look of disappointment.

"We're not flying together?"

"Tommy, we still have to be careful. But it's only for a little while longer." He took the confirmation, and Ali wrapped both her hands around his free one. "How were finals?"

"I think I did all right. How's *Condom Nation* coming along?"

"I have a commitment from a pretty good director, but he has a limited window between two bigger projects, so I've got to be ready to go in April."

"And I'll still get to work on it?"

"Of course. The last day of class you'll be on a plane to wherever I'm shooting." Ali stroked his face, and he nestled his cheek into her palm. "I promise."

"Did you see the news this morning?" Maureen asked, as Blake came through the door on Monday.

"The Joe Roberts rainbow coalition?"

"If the oldest is twenty-nine, the guy had to be hound-dogging around on his honeymoon." As they went to the kitchen for coffee, Maureen asked, "And speaking of clueless men, you come up with something for Jane yet?"

His grimace answered her question. "She was out all yesterday afternoon, so I know she must have been buying my gift."

"Hey, cheer up. You have literally days to come up with something spectacular."

His look said two words and they were not *hi there.* "Where's Charlie?"

"Early golf game. And I think that's all the small talk we have time for, so let's go see where we are on this."

They stared at their story board most of the morning. In blue index cards, it told the tale of a murder they couldn't prove.

"What time is it?" Blake asked, hoping they could break for lunch.

"A quarter past we're jacked."

"What do we do? Call Joe's guy and tell him our reports were all blowing smoke?"

"I'm beginning to think no one over there bothers to read those things."

"With all the charges he's facing right now, Roberts might not even care anymore if we can prove anything."

"Yeah," sighed Maureen.

"Yeah," sighed Blake. They stared at the board a bit longer. "Still," he finally said, "she *did* commit murder."

"Be-yotch."

They heard the front door close, and a minute later Charlie came into the workroom. "You kids having fun?"

"No," Maureen said. "We're having to face the fact that we suck as detectives."

He looked at their board. "You're terrific detectives. That's a good, solid murder plot."

"But we couldn't sell it," Blake said.

"Been there. Why not?"

"Somebody already sold them a similar story."

"Ah, you mean the one where the actress is innocent."

"Correct," said Maureen.

"And *your* plot has her as the murderer."

"Again, correct."

Charlie studied the board. "All you need to do is punch up the ending."

"What?" Blake asked.

"You're a little blah at the finish line. I mean, everything's leading right up to Ali's the killer, but it doesn't have any edge, any shock."

"Dad," Maureen said patiently, "may I remind you this is a real crime? It isn't a script and we can't rewrite the ending."

"Oh, bullshit." Charlie grabbed a marker and scribbled something on a blue card. He then picked it up, along with a pushpin, and tacked it onto the board at the end of the last column. As he stepped aside and slapped his hand against the newly pinned card, he said, "Now, *that's* an ending! And I guarantee it'll sell your script."

Charlie walked out of the room, leaving Blake and Maureen to stare at the two words he had written on the last card: *ALI CONFESSES*.

It was the kick in the butt they needed, and by the end of the afternoon they knew how to prove Ali Garland was guilty of murder.

Charlie was mixing his martini when they burst into the kitchen. Maureen threw her arms around him and hugged him hard.

"Whoa! It's supposed to be shaken, not squeezed."

"Dad, we love you."

"Really? I figured you two weren't even speaking to me."

"Why?" Blake asked.

"People *hate* to be rewritten."

"No, you gave us the perfect ending. Blake and I are going with it."

"Yeah, Ali handed us her own script the first day, and she's been directing the show ever since. If we can't nail her the official way, we're going to do it *her* way."

"But we're going to need your help, Dad."

"Sure. What can I do?"

Blake slapped a hand down on Charlie's shoulder and gave him what is known in show business as a big shit-eating grin. "Charlie, old pal, how'd you like to produce another show?"

Charlie spent Tuesday morning on the phone, calling in chits and contacting the people who could help them pull this off. He was well-liked in the business and, as most places would be shut down until January second, he easily found luxury office space to borrow and a vacant studio on the Paramount lot. Charlie's favorite prop guy, Eddie Chang —long since retired—was thrilled to go back into action, especially knowing the thank-you would be accompanied by several bottles of Glenlivet. Ten seasons of *The Brothers Gunn*, Eddie remembered, and Charlie O'Brien had always done right by the little guys.

Blake invited Libby to lunch, where he and Maureen told her the plan. Part one would roll out on Friday, two days before Christmas, and did not involve the police.

Part two was trickier, with two teams in different places and a window of opportunity of less than twenty-four hours, during which time it was imperative that brother and sister have no contact. Blake would call Libby on Monday to tell her if they were still a go, and if they were, Libby would pick up Tommy Garcia on Tuesday and bring him in for questioning about the break-in last April.

When Blake and Maureen got back to the house, Charlie was at the computer. "I have one small SNAFU," he said. "Because it'll be the day before Christmas eve, I can't find anyone to play my assistant. Can you get me a young female cop for Friday?"

"No," Blake replied. "We can't have them involved before we're ready to make an arrest. We don't want a lawyer calling it entrapment."

"Well, Maureen can't do it; Ali's seen her. So who?"

"You know, Blake," Maureen said, "that Kadoodlepeeper wasn't half bad on the gig at Pepperdine."

Blake decided not to tell Jane she'd be doing covert ops again, preferring to let Charlie ease her into the idea. Jane already knew they were having dinner and exchanging gifts at the O'Brien house the next night, and Blake rationalized it would mean one less day for her to worry about it.

On Wednesday Charlie wrapped up the writing he had to do for their little charade, Jane baked mini banana breads, Maureen phoned in a big dinner order for delivery at six, and Blake desperately tried to come up with an idea for Jane's special gift. He had already considered and dismissed having a star named after her, new tires for the Honda, a makeover, Fruit-of-the-Month Club and a puppy.

Jane loved the Chilean sea bass with sesame ginger sauce, but mistook the wasabi for a dollop of guacamole. As her mouth caught fire, she automatically reached for her water glass, but Maureen realized what had happened and grabbed a handful of pickled ginger. "Antidote!" she said, thrusting the damp, pink wad at Jane.

The poor girl shoved the whole thing in her mouth, instantly extinguishing the fire, but leaving her eyes streaming and limp ginger slices hanging from her lips. Maureen said she didn't have to swallow, so Jane leaned forward and let the whole mess drop out onto her plate.

Blake hooked a thumb at her and looked at Charlie. "I can't take her anywhere."

Jane punched him in the shoulder as she dabbed at her watering eyes. "You people need to put up a sign if you're going to dump industrial waste on a girl's plate."

After dinner, they gathered in the living room for presents. Jane gave the O'Briens a dozen little banana breads, individually wrapped and ready for the freezer. Blake gave Charlie a bottle of Cadenhead's Old Raj gin, and Charlie gave Blake the complete ten-season DVD set of *The Brothers Gunn.* Blake had gone with his instincts and gotten a gag gift for Maureen, a policewoman Barbie, with handcuffs, a gun and hair exactly her color. He was nervous when he saw the expensive-looking little box she handed him, but laughed with the others when he pulled out a pewter beer stein only three inches tall.

"For those hot summer nights when you want to chug down an ounce-and-a-half of cold brew," she said.

Charlie reached under the tree and pulled out one last gift. "Here's something for Jane from Santa." He winked when he handed her the gift. "He always comes here a couple days early, me being famous and all."

Jane darted a worried look at Blake. She hadn't expected them to give her anything.

"Open it! You're killing us," Maureen said.

Jane carefully untied the bow and pulled the paper from around the framed photograph. She looked puzzled. "What is it?"

"Satellite photo of Cobalt, West Virginia," Charlie said.

Jane stared at the picture for a moment, then put her hand to her mouth in shock. With her other hand, she reached to touch a spot on the glass. "That's my mama and daddy's house," she said, her voice breaking. Nobody moved or said anything to end the moment. Finally, Jane put her arm around Maureen. "Thank you, Maureen." Then she got up and hugged Charlie. "Thank you, Charlie. This is the best present I ever got and I'll treasure it forever."

"Who's for coffee and banana bread?" Maureen asked.

"I'll help," Jane said, standing.

When they left, Blake turned to Charlie. "Like the pressure wasn't bad enough already."

"No gift yet?"

"I'm down to considering a puppy."

"Yikes," Charlie said.

"I know. So, are you ready for tomorrow?"

"Well, I'm ready to bait the hook."

"Think we'll catch her?"

Charlie leaned back in his chair, smiling. "I'm using *really* good bait."

At 10:30 A.M. Thursday, Blake and his partner sat quietly as Charlie picked up the phone and baited their hook. When he hung up, he nodded to Maureen and she hit send on the computer. A few minutes after that, an agent named Rudy Claytor downloaded three pages of the nonexistent movie script *So Many Heathers.*

Ali sat at her kitchen table, trying to pull things together for *Condom Nation.* Fucking unions. It wasn't only the money, it was all the rules you had to follow. Number of hours worked before a break. Length of lunches and breaks. She pushed aside the IATSE package and went back to the budget she was attempting to write. Every time she thought she had it worked out, she'd realize something else needed to go in it. Fucking investors. Turns out they don't give you the checks until they see paperwork proving you know what to do, how to do it and how much it's going to cost.

Producing always sounds so important, she thought, but what it comes down to is kissing ass and counting beans. She had considered hiring some old line-producer to take care of the petty details and calling herself the executive producer, but two of her investors had already demanded that title as a quid pro quo for their financial participation.

She got up to pour a cup of coffee, more to distract herself from the tedious paperwork than from any need or desire for more caffeine. As she reached for a clean cup, the phone rang. "Hello?"

"Ali, Rudy Claytor."

"Hey, Rudy, what's up?" She was in no mood to talk to the man she blamed for fumbling the ball on her acting career.

"Something I've been working on for a while came through a minute ago. You ever hear of Charles O'Brien?"

"The blogger?"

"Nah, different guy. Anyway, he used to be big in television, *Dewey's View, The Badge, The Brothers Gunn.* A lot of it was before your time, but trust me, he was a major player."

"Can you get to the point, Rudy? I'm up to my eyeballs here."

"Bottom line, he does features now and I've been hawking you to him for six months. He finally wants to read you for a lead."

"What's the budget?"

"Thirty-five million." That O'Brien guy had actually said twenty-five, but Rudy wanted to sweeten the pie to get her interested. This broad was earning him zip with her rubbers project, but if he could get her an acting gig, he could start ten percenting her again.

Ali's mind raced. Thirty-five is a major film. *Monday* had shot for seven hundred and fifty thou, and *Tuesday* was only a million two. How much of that thirty-five could her hack agent get for her? If it was a bona fide lead, could she demand a million? Or should she ensure landing the part by laying back and getting less up front? Maybe take some net points and pretend she didn't know she'd never see a dime?

"Rudy, is this a cattle call?"

"No, I swear. I've got him sold on you, babe. If you aren't interested, of course, he'll move on and do a call. I have sides."

"Send them to me and I'll get back to you."

A few minutes later, she printed out the sides and a cover page. The movie was called *So Many Heathers,* and the sides showed a scene between Heather and her mother. It was gut-wrenching, confrontational stuff, the kind of scene an actress could make a splash with. Like Dev had done in the final scene of *Lamb to the Slaughter*. What the critics had all yammered on about was that Private Jesse Marino had no words in the scene. His eyes and body language were his only tools. He'd had a lucky break with that. Maybe now she was holding her own luck in her hands. She made the call.

"Rudy Claytor, agent extraordinaire," he answered.

"When and where?"

Blake glanced at his watch. Almost noon. "What's taking so long?"

"It's a game," Charlie said. "He doesn't want to look too eager; wants me to think I'm one of a dozen guys throwing scripts at his client. So, even assuming he reached her immediately and she wants to go for it, Rudy will take his sweet time letting me know."

"But why? Doesn't he want her to get the job? Isn't that how he makes his money?"

"Oh, he's *creaming* for her to get the job. But he's trying to position himself for a more profitable negotiation, so he's walking a fine line between teasing me and losing me. It'll be after lunch but before five."

"I'll order pizza," Maureen said.

Ali went online to check out Charles O'Brien. Rudy was right. He had been a player, but only in television, so the whole thing might be bogus. Hollywood was crawling with wannabe movie people.

She looked at the sides again. At the top of all three pages something was blacked out. The sides must have been scanned and sent. If they had been computer-generated, anything O'Brien didn't want her to see would have been deleted, not covered over.

Checking again, she saw the blacked-out area was maybe an inch and a quarter wide and was followed by an ampersand and O'Brien's name. Was there a partner? Or a money man? And why didn't O'Brien want her to know who it was? Curiouser and curiouser.

She looked at the cover page. In the corner where the production company name should be, there was another blacked-out area. The words *Charles Michael O'Brien Productions, Inc.* topped a smaller-type line that read "in association with." And underneath it, another blackout. Not everything had been covered, though, when the marker had swiped across the line. She could see a comma and the word "Inc." Right before the comma, she could just make out a "K" followed by an "S". Why was O'Brien being so coy about his business partner?

Blake picked at a piece of pepperoni from the cold pizza. "Maybe she won't go for it."

"She'll go for it," Charlie said.

"How can you be sure?"

"Because I put her character's name in the title, and actors need to believe it's all about *them*. Also, the character is five years younger than the age she claims on her website, so it's probably eight years younger than her real age."

"Charlie knows what he's doing, Blake." Maureen then growled in Max Gunn's gravelly drawl, "This ain't our first rodeo, dipstick."

"That's my little girl," Charlie said.

The phone rang at exactly three o'clock. Charlie checked the screen, then handed the phone to Maureen. "It's him."

"O'Brien Productions. How may I direct your call?" she said in the breathy, chipper voice of a front desk person. "Certainly, sir. And may I tell him who's calling?" She listened, hit hold, then passed the phone to Charlie.

Blake waited. And waited. "Aren't you going to talk to him?"

"Not for another few seconds. Mandatory rudeness is part of the negotiations tango."

Maureen gave Blake a sympathetic look and whispered, "Patience."

At last, Charlie sang out "show time" and answered. "Rudy, sorry. Fucking Brad Pitt, once he starts yapping about those African orphans, you can't get him off the phone. Tell me you have good news for me, buddy." Charlie listened, giving Blake and Maureen a thumbs-up. "Yeah? Great! Look, I owe you, man. After the holidays let's do sushi. I'm sure you've got some other clients I should look at for future deals. I'll text you the 411 on the Heathers meeting ASAP. Ciao, buddy." He hung up and beamed. "It's on."

"When do you need Jane tomorrow?"

"I'll pick her up at 8:30. That'll give us an hour to drive there, a half hour to set up, and plenty of time to rehearse."

"We'll wait for your okay before we call Det. Johnson to set up Tuesday's arrest."

Blake stood. "All right then, I'm going to shove off."

"No, stay," Maureen said too quickly.

"Yes," Charlie added, "let's bask in our success."

"Shouldn't we celebrate our success *after* we succeed?"

"Come on, I'll take us all down to Los Lobos for margaritas."

Blake checked his watch. "At ten after three?"

"Isn't it ten after five *somewhere*?" asked Charlie, a touch of desperation in his voice.

Blake looked from Maureen to her father, not sure why they were acting so weird. "I'll see you both tomorrow."

As soon as the front door closed behind him, Maureen made a dive for Charlie's phone. "We tried," she said as she made the call.

"Jane? It's Maureen. My dad and I did everything short of tying him to a chair, but he's on his way."

At Blake's house, Jane hung up. There goes plan A, she thought. She had really liked plan A. It had her wearing the silky peignoir set she had splurged on, and standing in the dark on Blake's deck with candles surrounding both his Christmas present and the ice bucket—well, the saucepan—containing two chilled flutes and a bottle of ginger ale.

Plan B was not nearly as romantic, but a glance out the window confirmed it wouldn't be full dark for more than an hour. She picked up the matches, the masking tape and a box of baby animal cutouts.

At 3:35 Blake nosed his car in next to Jane's Honda. It was still early enough to take a short, brisk swim before the sun went down and the temperature plummeted. Maybe he could talk Jane into a dip and some afternoon delight. Tomorrow morning when she's with Charlie, I will absolutely, positively come up with a gift for her, Blake thought.

Approaching the house and pulling out his keys, Blake noticed something stuck at eye level on the front door. He saw it was a cutout baby goat wearing a red ribbon. In block letters, the sign it was attached to said, "Can you find the little kitten? Ask the baby birdies."

Blake took down the sign and carried it inside. Above the small table where he always dropped his keys, there was another one. A nest full of baby bluebirds on a sign reading, "Where is the little kitten? Ask the puppy."

The Beagle pup directed him to the pony, which sent him on to the bunny, each animal wondering where the kitten was, and each sign taking him closer to his bedroom. On the bedroom door, a baby elephant asked, "Oh, where is the little kitten? Maybe the duckies know." Wondering what animal would query him next, Blake turned the knob and opened the door.

He stepped into the room and his breath caught, paper animals fluttering down from his open hand. Jane lay on the bed, smiling at him seductively, her blonde hair spread out on the pillow. She was naked except for the paper kitten curled up on a bed of dark blonde pubic hair and the duckling over each nipple. Blake began unbuttoning his shirt. "I may be a dumb-as-a-bag-of-rocks detective, ma'am, but the symbolism of that kitten is not lost on me. The duckies, though? Not a clue."

"You're so right," Jane murmured. "Lose

the quackers." With that she reached up and removed the web-footed pasties. "Better?"

Blake moaned, yanking at his belt and fumbling with his zipper. Jane watched him strip down, only pulling away the paper kitten at the last second before he hurtled onto the bed.

Afterwards, they propped themselves up on the pillows and leaned against each other. "You have a *peee*culiar idea of foreplay, Miss—what did you say your name was again?"

"It's a game I came up with for my class."

Blake sat up straighter and looked at her. "I hope to God they don't get the same payoff."

"No," she said, curling in closer to him. "If they find the kitten, they get sparkly badges that say 'winner.'"

Blake tightened his arm around her. "Badges? I don't need no stinking badges."

"That's too bad. I'm pretty sure I put one on your neck."

"Branded. I'll be the laughingstock of the boys' locker room."

Jane saw it was getting dark and hoped her Dollar Store candles would burn the four promised hours. "Due to circumstances beyond my control, I have to give you your Christmas gift early, so if you want to take a shower, I'll go set up the surprise."

"That wasn't it?"

"*That* was the warm-up act."

While Blake showered, Jane slipped into the pink peignoir set, put the champagne glasses and ginger ale on the table out on the deck, then lit the two candles. The ones below were still flickering, visible now in the darkness. When

Blake came through the sliding glass doors, he took the glass she handed him and clinked it against hers. “Merry Christmas, Janie-boo.”

They each had a sip, then she took him by the hand and led him to the railing, where he looked down on dozens of flickering candles. They formed a large rectangle, a frame of stars surrounding the pool. It took him a moment to realize something was wrong: the little flames weren’t reflecting on the surface of the water. “No,” he whispered in shock, before tearing down the stairs and running across the yard.

Jane remained at the railing, a glowy Juliette looking down from her balcony as Romeo kneeled and touched the pool cover. This can’t be, Blake thought, closer to tears than he’d been since the Vikings lost the NFC championship to the Rams in ’99. He looked up at her. “How?”

Jane raised her glass and called down to him, “Merry Christmas, Sugarpop.”

“Oy vey!”

“I know. It’s even motorized.”

Blake and Maureen looked down at the covered pool thirty minutes after Charlie had picked up Jane. Maureen had driven over in response to Blake’s frantic call.

“Did she win the lottery?”

“No. But a couple months ago she told me about this autistic kid in her class. Anyway, six weeks into the school year, Jaden’s parents noticed so much improvement that they offered Jane money to spend Sunday afternoons working with their son.”

“And you didn’t know about that?”

“No, I thought she was—well, it doesn’t

matter what I thought. The point is that her first Sunday there, she learned Jaden's dad owns the largest pool construction company in the San Fernando Valley."

"And she did a barter."

"Exactly. She's working every Sunday this school year except Thanksgiving, Christmas and Easter. This cover is worth almost twenty grand. What the hell am I going to do?"

"You are truly screwed, my friend, because this represents planning and months of work, and you cannot make that happen this late in the game."

"I know. I told her I couldn't give her her big gift until Christmas eve, but that's tomorrow night. Should I go out and charge a diamond necklace or something?"

"No. Shut off your man brain and let's think like a girl." Blake looked on helplessly as she paced the deck. Suddenly Maureen stopped. "Where's your bathroom?"

"End of the hall, through my bedroom."

"No, the new one you've been working on."

"Uh, there isn't even toilet paper in that one yet."

"Take me to it, now."

He led Maureen to the new bath, then started to walk away to give her some privacy.

"Where are you going? Get in here."

Blake came back to the open door as she flipped the switch for the sconces. Maureen flinched at the stab of bright light, then turned the switch back off. "Yowza, were you planning to do brain surgery in here?"

"Trash my wattage choice later, but help me now. Please."

"Okay. Charlie said they'd be finished by noon. I'll call him and have him take Jane out for a long lunch. That should give us time."

"To do what?"

"To turn this into her very own private spa and sanctuary."

"I'm going to give her a bathroom?" Blake asked skeptically.

"I know men only see it as a place to shit, shower and shave, but it's different for a woman. Think about it. Jane grew up with four brothers and sisters. That's seven people sharing one bathroom. And what's her living situation now?"

"She shares a three-bedroom one-bath with two flight attendants. Actually, four, but there's never more than two there at a time."

"Five women, one bathroom. Even when she comes here, she has to share your macho black pissoir."

"Okay, I'm liking this more and more. How do we do it?"

"You clean, I shop. Now, how much do you want to spend?"

"Whatever you need to."

"*Never* say that to a rich man's daughter. Seriously, I need a budget."

"Will three hundred cover it?"

Maureen slowly looked around the blank bathroom, calculating. "Can you go to four?"

"Yes."

"Five hundred it is. Now, what's Jane's favorite color?"

"Oh, crap."

Eighty-five-year-old former prop master Eddie Chang met Charlie and Jane at the suite of offices Charlie had commandeered for the day. Eddie's three helpers, ranging from sixty-four to seventy-eight, took pictures of everything, then began their thirty-minute transformation.

Jane watched with amazement as Eddie gave her the old hairy eyeball, then riffled a stack of photos till he found the one he wanted. He slipped it into a frame and stood it on the reception desk that would be Jane's today.

She saw it was a picture of two fair-haired adults and a little blonde girl holding a doll. The frame had the words "Love Means Family" on it, and a stranger would assume the blonde girl was Jane as a child.

In and Out baskets were put on her desk, and into the Out basket went a thick, 10x13 envelope addressed to Stephen Spielberg at DreamWorks, Inc.

A stack of scripts with blue covers was placed alongside "Jane's" computer. The title was *So Many Heathers* and the DreamWorks name was on the front next to O'Brien Productions. When no one was looking, Jane opened a script, but all the pages were blank.

An ornate bronze plaque was stuck over the nameplate on the outside door. Jane watched, fascinated, as it was attached with double-sided tape, the large brass screw heads merely dummies.

The inner office was also undergoing a change. The law school diploma and civic awards were taken down and replaced with framed pictures of Charlie with everyone from Bono to Barack Obama. He stood in shirt sleeves next to George Clooney in one, Habitat for Humanity houses all around. He and George Lucas were in tuxes at the Oscars in another, and Lucas was leaning in and speaking intimately into Charlie's ear. Charlie shook his head when Eddie held up one showing a younger Charlie dining with Pope John Paul II. There was only so much bullshit even an actress would buy.

Issues of *The Hollywood Reporter* and *Variety* were scattered on the coffee table, along with *The Robb Report* and a recent *Departures*. Two Emmy statues and a Peabody Award went on a shelf, and a scattering of pink While-You-Were-Out slips covered one side of the desk.

Charlie gave Eddie money to take his helpers out to breakfast, where they would wait for the call to come back and reverse everything. After they left, Charlie turned to Jane, "I slipped a twenty to the guard downstairs at the desk, so he'll call and warn us when she's on her way up. You've seen one of her slasher films, right?"

"Yes."

"Good. What's the first one called?"

"Don't Kill Me on Monday."

"Can you tell me something about it? I need a scene where she's not trying to kill anybody and she's not being chased."

Jane thought. "Well, there *was* this scene after her boyfriend was murdered where she sat crying in a rocking chair with his cat on her lap."

"That's perfect. What was her character's name?"

"Jillian."

"And the cat, what color was it?"

"Gray."

"All right. Now here's what you're going to do..."

Certainly a prestige address, Ali decided, as she rode up in the elevator. When the doors slid open, she stepped out onto the neutral Berber and saw the discreet sign with office listings straight ahead. The arrow for O'Brien Productions directed her to the right, and she walked down the deserted hallway.

She didn't allow herself to believe this would be her big chance. Her last chance. She had learned the hard way that on a very good day, show business was ninety-nine percent heartbreaking disappointment. And on a bad day? You don't want to know.

Ali felt she'd had plenty of bad days, and that if the world were fair, *she* would have been the star, not Dev. This meeting was probably nothing more than a glad-handing exercise, but tomorrow she would get on a plane to Vail, and she and Tommy would have nine days together. She would come back refreshed and get *Condom Nation* rolling. If acting wouldn't make her a player, maybe producing would.

She opened the door on the typical bored, corn-fed-blonde receptionist. As soon as the girl heard the door opening, she ditched the emery board she had been using on her nails and sat up straighter. As if *that's* going to make you appear more qualified for your job, Ali thought. "Good morning. I'm here to see Mr. O'Brien."

"May I tell him your name?"

Bitch. You know my name as well as I do. Sleeping with the boss, are you? Pissed he hasn't put you in a movie? Ali had seen Blondie's type a hundred times. She smiled. "Ali Garland."

Not only had Blondie mastered the art of looking unimpressed—so essential for a would-be starlet—she actually smirked as she got up, knocked lightly on the inner office door, and then disappeared inside. As soon as the door closed, Ali scanned the desktop, looking for clues.

She spotted the stack of scripts on the other side of Blondie's computer, easily read the large title and, by leaning slightly, saw the name of O'Brien's partner. Holy shit! This was for real. And there, in the outgoing mail tray, was a large envelope addressed to DreamWorks. *That's* the name that was blacked-out on the sides, she thought.

She quickly stepped back from the desk, heart pounding, pretending to study a framed print in the seating area. I have to make this work. If I have to get on my knees and service this O'Brien guy, I have to get this part. Steven Spielberg! Finally, I get a shot at the bigs.

"Mr. O'Brien will see you now."

Ali smiled at Blondie as she passed her, thinking: *you are the first to go if I get this.*

He stood up when she entered, a courtly gesture that did not go unnoticed.

"Mr. O'Brien," she said, giving him her hand and a five-hundred-watt smile.

"Charlie, please. Have a seat."

She did, placing her handbag on the floor and the sides on his desk. He reached over for the sides and balled them up. "You don't have to read; I already know how good you are." He tossed the crumpled pages in the trash.

This is a surprise, she thought. He isn't going to make me grovel? Good-looking man, too. Late forties, I'm guessing, but in great shape. I've done worse guys for smaller parts.

"Ali, let me start by saying I've been a fan

of yours since *Don't Kill Me on Monday*. We both know it was a formulaic screamy-teen, kill-flick, am I right? But I'm a guy who believes a quality stone sparkles even in a cheap setting. And you, my dear, sparkled in that movie."

"That's very sweet of you to say."

Charlie laughed. "You think I'm blowing smoke, don't you?" He leaned forward, elbows on the desk. "The scene where Jillian sits in the rocker, stroking that gray cat? Without a word, you showed her grief over her boyfriend's—what was his name again?"

"Jimmy," she said, amazed he recalled *her* character's name from nine years ago.

"Jimmy, right. Over his death. It was so obvious you were going to protect his cat because you were eaten up with guilt about not being able to protect Jimmy. You were way too subtle for the acne set, but my heart was in my throat when I saw it."

He leaned back again, as if remembering the scene. So this is what respect feels like, Ali thought. She had put her soul into the scene, and that shit director had edited it down from two minutes to forty seconds. Even then, he did cutaways to a pair of muddy feet creeping down the hall toward her room and another to the shadow of a man holding an ax. She had felt dissed and unappreciated, and had always wondered if anyone in the audience really got it. She saw Charlie shake himself out of his reverie. "Point being, Ali, I know you can play the hell out of this part."

"I'm flattered by your confidence in me."

"She's modest, too," he said, throwing his arms wide and telling the ceiling. "I *love* her!"

Ali rewarded him with a big smile. He returned it, then put a serious look on his face, indicating that the shmoozing portion of the program was over and business had officially begun. "Let me lay all my cards on the table. I want you for this role. My partner, however, isn't a hundred percent on board. He's giving me a lot of leeway, but the final call is his."

"Okay, I understand," she said, nodding while her brain raced: *what flaming hoops do I have to jump through to get on a Spielberg film? And where are the hoops?*

"He knows I'm meeting with you, and he wants a recommendation from me when we're finished. But I've got two major problems to solve before I can cleanly sell you."

"What can I do to help you, Charlie?" Oh, please God, don't let this slip through my fingers.

"First thing is money. I got a pretty good budget here, and—this doesn't leave the room—I could go high as one and a half million for you." Ali started to speak, but Charlie held up a hand to stop her. "Now, I have never spoken to your agent before yesterday—"

Fucking Rudy. Lying rat bastard.

"—but if he's the kind of guy who's going to ask for ten mil, hoping to screw me down to five, you and I need to shake hands and quit now. Maybe catch each other on another film."

Ali's mouth was dry. A million and a half without even fighting for it? "Charlie, I really want to do this movie with you. And contrary to what Rudy Claytor thinks, *he* works for *me*. So I will personally inform him that if he jerks you around, I will find new representation."

Again, he addressed the ceiling. "My God,

she's even got a business head on her shoulders."

Ali tried to make her laugh as humble and appreciative as possible.

"Okay, one more hurdle, but it's a biggie."

"At this point, I think you and I can work out *any* problem, Charlie."

"I hope we can. *So Many Heathers* tells the story of a young woman with multiple personalities. Five distinct personas and one of them is a serial killer. Her mother suspects, and there's a bunch of cat-and-mouse psychological games going on between them. Now I don't want to sound like an asshole, but from a producer's standpoint, your recent, uh, legal situation translates to major box office with you in this role. But if it's too sensitive and emotional an issue for you to take on a part like this right now, I'll understand."

Are you fucking *kidding* me? Bring Dev Roberts here and I'll kill him all over again. Multiple personalities? This is Oscar bait, *Rain Man* turf. Ali knew she had to play it cool to reel him in. Chastened by the shooting, but strong enough to let the experience bring verisimilitude to the role of Heather. Looking down at her lap, she said softly, "Charlie, I feel instinctively I can trust you."

"You can," Charlie replied, giving the two words enough sincerity to launch a new religion.

"Then I won't lie to you. I *was* devastated by what happened, but I've been working with a therapist who has made me see I can't blame myself for what was, in essence, a tragic accident."

Charlie knitted his brow and toyed with a pen on the desk. "Are you *sure* you've processed enough to handle the sliming you're going to get from certain press sources? I mean, if I go out on a limb for you on this, I need to know I'm not going to get dorked in the heinie."

Brave face. Brimming eyes, but no teary spillover. Deep breath. Sell it. "I promise you, Charlie, I will *not* let you down."

They locked eyes, and she could tell he was touched by her moving facsimile of honesty and raw emotion. It would be a nice change to work with such a decent man. When he smiled, she knew she had overcome his final hesitation.

"All right, then, let's do this." He slapped his hand on the desk and got up to open the door. "Penny? Get him on the phone." He closed the door and returned to his desk. A moment later, the phone rang. "Steve? Charlie. Listen, she just left and I'm sold." He winked at Ali and put his finger to his lips. "Yeah, I ran the money thing by her and I think she's strong enough to keep her agent in line." He listened for a few beats, giving her an encouraging thumbs-up. "Sure. When are you leaving? So, what's good for you?" Charlie listened again. "Done, buddy. I'll see you then." He hung up and looked at Ali. "We're almost there, babe."

As she drove out of the underground parking garage, Ali wondered how Tommy would take the news. His heart was set on Christmas in Vail, spending time with her, but a screen test for Steven Spielberg didn't come along every day. Tommy wanted to be an actor, he'd understand. In many ways he was still a kid, naive enough to believe the jobs would be waiting for him when he was ready. Pepperdine University was not exactly the school of hard knocks. It was time he grew up a little, started facing reality.

After Eddie Chang and his eldercrew put the office suite back exactly as it had been three hours earlier, Charlie left the keys at the guard desk and invited his partner out for lunch. His choice was an out of the way Beverly Hills bistro where Jane was guaranteed to spot at least a few celebrities, and where Charlie knew the service was excruciatingly slow.

By 1:00 P.M. Blake and Maureen had finished their episode of *Pimp My Bathroom* and they stepped back to admire their handiwork. The stark white necessity had morphed into a lilac-and-pink luxury with deep purple accents.

For Blake, a shower curtain had always meant a sheet of plastic that kept water from getting all over the floor. Now he knew it could also mean a sheet of plastic *inside* the tub, a coordinating fabric curtain *outside* the tub, and a heavy drape of bold color held to one side by a matching tie-back.

The shelves of the white wicker étagère held, shampoos, lotions, bath gels and a pink robe folded with the terry cloth belt in a neat bow across the lapels. The towels hanging from the racks and stacked on the wicker bench were the heaviest and fluffiest Blake had ever felt, and they matched the plush throw rugs that warmed the floor. Lacy curtains framed the window above several candles in apothecary jars.

"Suck on *that*, Martha Stewart," Blake said, admiring the room. He indicated the small figurine on top of the toilet tank—an adorable porcelain toddler making wee-wee on the grass while his puppy did the same against a tiny tree. "Sweet touch," he said, meaning it.

"It's disgusting and Jane will hate it."

"Then why did you buy it?"

Maureen held up her hands and wiggled her fingers. "To remove my fingerprints. Only a man would think that tacky thing belongs in this perfect bain de toilette."

"Jane has to look at something she hates so I can cover my tracks?"

"Of course not. She'll tell you she loves it, then in a few weeks it'll disappear into a drawer. In five or six months, it'll accidentally fall on the floor and break."

Blake met her hazel-for-today eyes. "Men don't stand a chance, do we?" The sympathetic shake of her head confirmed his epiphany.

"Hello?"

"Tommy, I have incredible news. I am *this* close to being cast as the lead in a Steven Spielberg film."

"Oh my God! Are you serious?"

"Dead. Thirty-five-million-dollar budget and the role of a lifetime. MPD serial killer with mother issues."

"I can't believe it. You actually met him?"

"Well, not yet. The meeting was with his partner, but it'll be locked in as soon as I do a screen test for Spielberg. There's one problem, though. He's leaving to shoot in Dubai next week and he'll be gone for months, so I have to do the screen test at Paramount next Tuesday."

Ali heard nothing from Tommy's end of the call. "Tommy? Are you still there?"

"I'm here," he answered, voice tight.

"We're still going to Vail, but I had to change our flights to Wednesday night. We won't have Christmas there, but we *will* have New Year's eve. That's probably even better. *And* I bought you a five-day ski pass."

"Great," he said flatly.

"Come on, Tommy, don't be like that. For once luck is breaking *my* way. If I do a Spielberg film, everyone will want me, and that means I'll have the juice to get parts for you, too."

"Yippee."

Ali was fed up with his petulance and attitude. If he was too stupid to see the bigger picture, she would enlighten him. "Oh, suck it up, you little shit. I've handed you everything on a silver platter since the day you came out of foster care. A motorcycle, tuition for a first-class university, a very generous allowance. You know what I got when *I* turned eighteen and was kicked out on my ass? Bubkis, that's what. You prance around on a stage in a doublet and tights, totally unaware of what it's like in the *real* world, trying to get a *real* acting job. I fought for everything I ever got, and now I'm going to fight for this movie. So spare me the pissy attitude because you're losing a couple days of your all-expense-paid Colorado trip."

She had never before spoken to him so harshly, and didn't know how he would react. When he finally responded, his voice was small and worried. It was the voice she remembered from the day their father was taken away, the voice that had asked her what was going to happen to them. "I don't have anywhere to go."

"Stay on campus for a few more days."

"I can't. They're shutting it down. Noon

tomorrow all students have to be gone until January third. Can I come to your house?"

Ali hadn't seen any reporters for weeks, but that didn't mean they weren't watching. She was so close to having everything she wanted, and she wouldn't risk losing it, even for her own brother. "We can't do that, Tommy. Paparazzi are watching my every move."

"Then what'll I do?"

"You hang tight. I'm going to arrange a hotel room for you, close enough to LAX that you won't have far to drive next Wednesday."

"I have to spend Christmas in a hotel?"

Ali wanted to scream. Could he for once in his life think about *her* needs? She calmed herself. What she had to do was settle him down so she could focus on her screen test. "Why don't I come by tomorrow night and we'll exchange presents and order all the stuff you love from room service. How does that sound?"

"Okay, I guess."

"Good. I'll text you the name of the hotel."

They all met back at the O'Brien house late in the afternoon to compare notes. At 5:30, Maureen slipped out of the room to shower and get ready for a date while Charlie and Jane relived their adventure for Blake's benefit. "And you're sure she bought it?" he asked.

"Oh, she bought it," Jane volunteered.

"What's great," Charlie said, "is that she thinks *I* think she still doesn't know who my mysterious partner is. She even noticed that the script on my desk was face down."

"What do you do next Tuesday? You can't exactly deliver Steven Spielberg to the stage."

"Of course I can. With the same kind of truthiness Ali used when she conjured up a burglar and a mugger. You and Maureen have to let me know by noon Monday what exactly you need Ali to say. I promised to send her the test scene by 5:00, and I'll need a couple hours to write it."

"We'll get on it first thing Monday," Blake said. He turned to Jane. "You ready to go?"

"Let me get my leftovers from the fridge."

As soon as Jane exited to the kitchen, Charlie turned to Blake. "I'm assuming the long lunch had a purpose?"

"Yes. And mission accomplished. Thanks for the help."

Maureen walked into the room wearing the hottest outfit Blake had ever seen on her. From the floor up, she was sky-high heels, patterned black stockings, pencil skirt, tight silver tank and the strangest jacket he had ever seen. It was jet black with long sleeves that belled at the wrists. Three sets of leather straps on either side smartly nipped the waist, giving her even more of an hourglass than she normally had. A thin chain hung between each pair of the big, military-looking silver buttons that edged the open sides of a black-ruffled tuxedo bib.

"Holy Fishla, mother of cod!" Blake said.

"You never saw a girl in steampunk?"

"I never even *heard* of it. But your date's a lucky guy."

"Interesting," Maureen said, raising an eyebrow. "You automatically assume my date is a man."

Blake glanced helplessly at Charlie, who shrugged. "Don't look at me. I'm not the boss of her. And on a side note, *Fishla*?"

"Jane doesn't use profanity so she makes up her own. Sometimes one sticks to my brain."

Jane came back into the room carrying a large aluminum foil swan. As she took in Maureen's ensemble, she said, "Wow, Maureen. You are *rockin'* the steampunk."

Blake turned from one woman to the other. "Who *are* you two?"

Christmas eve. Ali drove south on the 405. On the seat beside her was a large wrapped box containing a pair of Tecnica Dragon 120's, the ski boots Tommy wanted. She hoped those, along with a five-hundred-dollar prepaid VISA gift card, would calm him down, keep him level and out of her hair until after the screen test.

She had spent the whole day tracking down and booking the makeup artist who had done her for that Scorsese film several years back. For double his normal rate, he would be at her house next Tuesday at 4:30 A.M. She had calls in to three hair stylists, and the one who responded first would get the job.

On Monday she would buy an outfit, but nothing that made her look too eager. Something simple and elegant. It would be the day after Christmas, but the places where Ali shopped were unlikely to have bargain hunters pawing through piles of blue-light specials.

Then she would spend Monday evening memorizing the scene. She decided no matter how many pages it was, she would be off book on Tuesday. Steven Spielberg would *not* see her glancing down at the page for her next line.

"Keep 'em closed. Keep 'em closed."

Jane's eyes were squeezed shut as Blake piloted her down the hall. When they got to the closed door of the second bathroom, he positioned her facing it, then reached around and pushed it open. "Okay, peepers up."

There was a sharp intake of breath as Jane looked into the candlelit room.

"Go on in, it's all yours."

Jane stepped through the doorway into the most beautiful bathroom she had ever seen. Her hand reached out tentatively to touch a hanging bath towel in her favorite color, pink.

Blake watched her nervously. He had expected her to love it, to throw her arms around him and thank him, but as she slowly turned she only looked at everything. Judas priest, could Maureen have been wrong? Jane's turn finally took her around to face Blake. She still hadn't said a word, and now there were tears in her eyes. "Merry Christmas?" he asked hesitantly.

Jane stepped close putting her arms around his waist, the side of her face pressing against his chest. "All these months, you've been working on this for *me*?"

"Yes," he said, remembering Maureen's admonition that this was *not* the time for total honesty. "Do you like your new boudoir?"

"I think a boudoir is a bedroom."

"Do you like your new bathoir?"

"I love it muchly."

He put his face down into the top of her hair, breathing in the familiar rosemary scent. "Move in with me," Blake murmured. When she didn't answer immediately, he thought maybe he'd said it too softly.

"That sounded more like an order than a request," she finally replied, but he could hear the smile in her voice.

"The price you pay for being a private eye's dame."

"So, would a yes commit me to a country song kind of life? Being stepped on, lied to, cheated on and treated like dirt?"

Without letting her go, he pulled back far enough to look into her eyes as she tilted her face up to him. "I swear," Blake said in his most sincere voice. "I will never, *ever* step on you."

It took Blake and Maureen only an hour on Monday to come up with everything they thought it would take to convince Tommy Garcia his sister had double-crossed him.

Charlie knocked out the seven-page scene, neatly folding their requests into the moment Heather's therapist begins to realize what his client has done and confronts her, triggering a mad roller-coaster ride through all five of her personalities. This would allow the character to go from a kittenish attempt at seducing her therapist to a screaming rationalization of her murderous rampage and finally, to a calculated placing of blame on her mother.

Charlie handed the pages to Blake and Maureen for approval. "While you read it, think Glenn Beck in drag and you'll have a pretty good idea of the histrionics we'll wind up with."

"How will you edit with only one camera?" Maureen asked her father.

"Oh, Mr. Spielberg is going to ask for a second take. I'll position the camera differently so I can cut between the two."

"Is that how you'll get rid of all this other stuff and leave us with what we need?" Blake asked.

"You'll be amazed what can be done in post-production," Charlie said.

Entering stage twenty-six, Ali felt deep in her soul that the next hour would change her life forever. She had worked the scene last night so many times and so many different ways that any adjustments they asked for would be ready to roll out flawlessly.

The cavernous interior was nearly dark, except for the table where the reading would be. She saw Charlie talking to a stagehand. She also noticed Blondie making a phone call by a jumble of director's chairs. The stupid bimbo had not had the brains to hide the chair with Spielberg's name embroidered on the canvas back.

Blake hung up the phone and turned to Libby. "That was Jane. Ali's at the studio."

"Then let's go pick him up," she said.

Charlie saw Ali and waved her over. "Good morning. You all set?"

"Yes. And Charlie? The scene is brilliant. Really, some of the best writing I've ever seen."

"Aw shucks, you make an old wordsmith blush."

She rewarded him with a tinkling laugh. You could almost gag on the phoniness in the air. Charlie told her his partner was due any minute, then asked his assistant to collect cell phones from everybody. As Ali fished hers out of her purse, Charlie leaned toward her and spoke in a low voice. "He's a wonderful guy, my partner, but—this doesn't leave the room—a cell phone rings while he's working and he goes apeshit." Blondie brought the basket over, so Charlie and Ali dropped their phones in the pile, each taking a stretchy ID band for later matching.

There was a commotion at one of the outside doors and Ali could see a small group of men silhouetted against the bright morning light. Once the door closed behind them, they blended into the darkness at the edges of the vast studio. "I guess it's show time," Charlie said softly to Ali.

While Charlie gave quiet orders to the skeleton crew, Ali watched the cadre of men in the shadows move toward the stairs leading up to the booth. A moment later she saw the dark glass of the booth window lighten from the glow of a low-wattage bulb. She saw movement, but couldn't make out anyone's features.

In the deserted street outside the studio door, Jane went through Ali's phone numbers and texts, then slipped the cell into her pocket.

***"Closed?"* Blake couldn't believe it.**

"Nothing but security guards," Libby said.

"Are they sure he isn't in his dorm room?"

"Electricity's shut off, water's off and they swept for stowaways this morning."

Blake turned to his partner. "Now what?"

"Call Jane. Maybe something on Ali's cell will give us a lead."

Ali sat down at the reading table while Charlie got the cameraman in place, then looked at the small screen. He stepped away from the camera with a concerned look on his face. After a moment, he called to one of the crew guys. “Hey, Eddie? Would you roll a white flat behind Ms. Garland? We need a bounce-back so her hair doesn’t disappear in the dark.” He grinned at Ali and winked. “Just because it’s only a reading doesn’t mean you can’t look gorgeous.”

Ali was impressed that Charlie took even the smallest detail seriously. Since she didn’t turn around, she never saw the flat rolling in behind her. If she had, Ali would have been surprised to note it was covered with wanted posters, shift notices and a sign-up sheet for a police department softball team. She glanced up again at the window behind which Steven Spielberg waited to see her performance, still unable to make out more than shadows.

“Okay,” Charlie shouted. “Quiet on the set, please!”

Libby and her partner Jim picked up Tommy Garcia without incident at the Airport Marriott. When they told him he was being held in conjunction with a home invasion, he smiled and allowed himself to be cuffed. Maureen and Blake followed the car back to the station where they would observe the first interview with Tommy, the fake one.

When Ali finished the scene there was applause from the half-dozen crew guys—per Charlie’s earlier instructions. Charlie, who had read the part of the off-camera therapist, gave Ali an impressed smile. “Well, the crew loved it. Let me go see what my partner thought.”

Before Charlie crossed to the stairs, he

nodded at Eddie Chang, who immediately flipped the board behind Ali. When she stood to stretch and look around, there was only a blank white half-flat a few feet behind her chair. Ali spotted the blonde assistant nearby. "Oh, miss. Could I get some bottled water, please? No bubbles."

The girl stared daggers before flouncing off to fetch, and Ali savored her power position. She could barely make out a tall silhouette in the booth. Probably Charlie. God, what I'd give to be a fly on *that* wall, she thought.

After an unnecessarily long time, Blondie brought the chilled bottle of Solé and Ali took a small sip. She hadn't really needed water, but it was so much fun to order servants around. A few minutes later, Charlie clambered down the stairs and crossed to her. "Okay, he really liked it."

"Charlie, I'm a professional," she said, laying a reassuring hand on is arm. "If you've got notes, you don't have to sugar coat them."

"Jesus, I wish *all* the actors I worked with were as smart as you are. Yes, there are a few little things he'd like you to try."

Blake and Libby looked through the one-way glass at the lanky kid in the interview room, as Maureen went through the plastic bin that held the contents of Tommy's pockets.

"You know, in my career I've played good cop and I've played bad cop," said Libby, "but this will be my first time playing dumb cop."

Blake grinned. "Ask yourself how Willis would do it."

"You give him too much grief, Ervansky. Yes, he's a dick, but he's also a decent detective."

"I'll take your word for it."

Libby went into the interview room, and Blake turned to Maureen, who was looking at Tommy's cell phone. "Anything?"

"One number comes up a lot, but it isn't Ali's home phone or her cell."

"Okay, go get someone to run it and I'll stay here and observe. And would you mind sending Ortiz back here?"

"Sure."

Inside the interview room, Libby flipped open a folder and studied the contents. Tommy sprawled in his chair, all cocky body language with a smile to match. "So, am I under arrest?"

"Not at the moment. But I might hold you for twenty-four hours while we decide if that's going to happen."

"Or not," he replied.

"Or not." She closed the file and put a serious look on her face. "Where were you the night of April eighth this year?"

"Nine months ago? Are you kidding?"

"So you don't remember where you were?"

"Probably playing beer pong with some friends. You'd have to check my Day Planner."

"Oh, I will. Who's Stuart Mason?"

"My roommate."

"Hmm," she said, staring steadily at him.

Did she really think he was going to be intimidated by her bald head and information anyone could get for the price of a phone call? Ali was right; cops are basically stupid. Uh-oh, now she was giving him a wolfish grin. Could she really have something? He tensed.

"Mr. Garcia, would it interest you to know that I have teams searching your hotel room *and* your dorm room as we speak?" Libby leaned in threateningly. “When I find those Glendales, I’m going to nail your smug ass to the wall.”

Tommy relaxed. Oh, this was delicious. “What are Glendales?” he asked innocently.

“Don’t fuck with me, little boy. You know exactly what they are. Those kicks are going to have paint in the tread that will match the paint spilled in an attempted purse snatching. And that will link you via footprints to two crimes, a failed mugging and the break-in at the home of Ali Garland.”

“Who?”

“Very famous actress.”

“Never heard of her.”

Outside the interview room, Officer Ortiz approached Blake. “You wanted to see me?”

“Yes. When I tell you to, go in there and whisper something to Det. Johnson. It doesn’t matter what you say, only make sure that kid doesn’t hear you.”

Ortiz nodded, and Blake saw Maureen heading toward them.

“That number’s not assigned. Probably a prepaid burner. But we have a bigger issue.”

“What?”

She handed him a sheet of paper. “This was folded up in his wallet. E-mail confirmation of a flight to Vail tomorrow. And yes, I checked. Ali’s not booked on that plane.”

“But I’ll bet she’s on *some* flight.”

“Keesha’s running down all the airlines. If they’re planning a family getaway tomorrow, we’re shafted.”

“Then I guess your dad’s going to have to come up with a reason for her to cancel.”

“I’ll call Jane.”

She got out her cell and stepped away to make the call. Blake nodded to Ortiz.

Tommy watched as a cute young Latina in uniform entered and crossed to his interrogator. She whispered in the bald woman's ear, then nodded when asked if she was absolutely certain. Baldy cursed under her breath.

Sweet. She just found out her search teams hadn't found the shoes. Tommy knew there was nothing to link him to either "crime" in his hotel or dorm. The only thing that might give the police a reason to look at him as anything other than a harmless college boy was in the lockbox on his bike. And that was still in the underground parking lot of the Airport Marriott.

When they finished the second take, Blondie came over to whisper in Charlie's ear, and Ali saw him glance up at the booth.

"I have to run upstairs for a minute," he said, then left with the blonde in tow.

Ali watched them go upstairs, praying nothing was wrong.

Charlie and Jane stepped into the booth, where five men were playing poker. "You guys doing okay?"

"Yeah," the dealer said. "And thanks for the sandwiches and beer."

"I'll extend your compliments to craft services." Charlie turned to Jane. "What's up?"

"Maureen called and we have a problem."

Tommy watched the bald cop pretend to be studying the file in front of her. She's got nothing, he thought.

"What would you say if I told you your

roommate remembers seeing you wearing a pair of Glendale Feet tennis shoes?"

"I'd say Stuart is either misremembering or lying."

"And if I put you in a lineup and bring in Ali Garland, are you *sure* she isn't going to ID you as the scumbag who broke into her house and later mugged her?"

"I didn't do either one of those things, so knock yourself out."

"I wasn't asking for permission, and I *am* going to go call Ms. Garland and put you in a lineup," Libby said, standing up.

Tommy almost laughed. She was one tick shy of giving him the old Clint Eastwood fave: "Are you feeling lucky, punk?" Well, Dirty Mary can spin her wheels all she wants.

As soon as Libby closed the door behind her, she looked at Blake and Maureen. "Christ, it's hard to play this dumb."

"But you're doing a very convincing job," Blake said. When Libby glared, he hastily back-tracked, "Uh, you know what I mean."

Charlie came down the stairs, calling out, "That's a wrap. Everybody can go home."

Ali watched, wondering if Spielberg had loved it or hated it. Charlie crossed to her while his assistant held the basket of cell phones so each crew member could grab his or hers on the way out. The booth window went dark and, a moment later, the group that had been inside left as mysteriously as they had arrived. Charlie sat across from her and when she looked at him inquisitively he shook his head and indicated the door. Oh shit, Ali thought, he's waiting for everyone to clear out. This is bad.

The last one to leave was an old Asian guy pushing the rolling half-flat. When the door closed behind him, Ali and Charlie were alone, except for the assistant waiting by the door.

"You got it!" Charlie shouted.

"I did?" She breathed a sigh of relief. "He liked me?"

"No. He fucking *loved* you!"

She reached across the table and took both Charlie's hands in her own. "Thank you, Charlie. Thank you so much."

"I'm nothing more than the middleman. Your talent got you the job."

"Do I get to know who the job is with?"

"You do, and I'm sorry to have been so mysterioso. His call, not mine. How'd you like to be the lead in a Steven Spielberg film?"

Ali faked a charming gasp. "No way!"

"Way. My company has a three-picture deal with DreamWorks, and *you* are now the star of my first one."

"I can't tell you how grateful I am that you went to bat for me on this."

"We'll pencil in a lunch so we can tell each other how great we are, but right now, let's get down to the nitty gritty."

"Of course."

"Business Affairs is closed until after the first, so you won't have the official offer until next week. Steve told me to open with a million, so tell your shark he can counter with two, and we'll settle in the middle. Deal?"

"Absolutely."

"But there's even better news. Steve's postponing his Dubai departure until Sunday so he can have you over to his house Friday night for dinner and a get-to-know-you session. It'll be Steve, his wife, me, my lady and you. And, of course, you're welcome to bring a date." He turned toward Jane at the door. "Penny? Can we get our phones?"

Ali's mind raced as Blondie walked across the stage. Do I dare bring Tommy to Spielberg's house? Would that be enough of a payoff for him to let go of the trip to Vail?

Charlie reached into the basket, pulling out the phone with the stretchy band that matched the one he pulled off his wrist. There was only one phone left in the basket as Blondie held it out to Ali.

"That isn't mine."

"Are you sure?" Jane asked. "It matches your wristband."

"I'm *very* sure," Ali said, knowing this was Blondie's revenge for the bottle of water. *God*, this bitch is going to pay when we start shooting.

"Aw, hell. Somebody must've grabbed the wrong one," Charlie said. "I'll call the guys who were working today and find out who has it. It'll be messengered to your house ASAP."

Everybody was on the move. Eddie Chang's white van tooled along Santa Monica Boulevard heading west, its destination the Beverly Hills Police station. Charlie and Jane took the Pass Avenue exit off the 134 on their way to an editing facility in Burbank. Maureen drove east on Sunset, bound for the 101 North. She and Blake would meet Charlie and Jane at the edit bay.

Ali's black BMW cornered sharply as she

negotiated the last turn before her Beverly Hills home. She needed to get to her land line quickly.

"Ribby Johnson?"

Libby looked up from her desk and into the face of a tiny, ancient Asian man. "Are you Mr. Chang?"

"Yes. My van oussigh. You wan come get you plops?"

Tommy's phone started ringing, and Blake checked the screen. "Incoming from Ali's home phone. Jane must've grabbed her cell."

The ringer stopped as the call went to voicemail. "Tommy. Call me at my home phone as soon as you get this. I have to talk to you about the trip to Vail. Love you."

Blake and Jane sat in the back of the edit bay, watching Charlie and a man called Horst turn Ali's scene reading into a raging, crazy indictment of her mother as a killer.

Maureen had seen her father do this a hundred times, but she could tell Blake and Jane were fascinated. She had been leaning against the back wall, but now she flopped down onto the couch next to Jane.

"Okay," she said quietly. "See how my dad's making the edits right on the word every time she says *mother* or *mommy*?"

"Yes," Jane whispered.

"That's gotta be killing Horst. You never, *ever* do that."

"So why's Charlie doing it now?"

"Because when we change those words to *brother* and *Tommy*, there'll be a mismatch between the lip movement and the sound. The edits will keep Tommy from noticing."

"Wow."

"You could never get away with this on a *real* show, but a police interview video should look like it was shot by an amateur."

Ali called her investors to tell them *Condom Nation* had been shelved. She left a message on the director's agent's assistant's voicemail that an offer would not be coming. She cleared her table of the union bullshit, budget bullshit, and all the standard showbiz *bullshit* bullshit. She never wanted to produce anyway, so let Michael Moore have this one.

Tommy still hadn't called her back by 4:00 o'clock. Probably seeing a movie or out spending that five hundred dollars.

She had three days to decide what to wear for dinner at Steven Spielberg's house.

The first person Blake saw when they entered the small looping studio was a beautiful woman reading a book. When she looked up, she smiled warmly at Charlie.

"Hi, Honey," Charlie said.

"Charlie." Her voice was rich and warm, and as she laid aside her book and gracefully rose from the chair, Blake guessed she was somewhere in her mid-forties. But her taut and slender body would have made a twenty-five year old proud. The jeans appeared sprayed on, and her hair fell to her shoulders in a lush, silvering cascade. Her eyes stayed on Charlie as he crossed to her, and though their embrace was short, it conveyed the idea of former lovers a lot more clearly than co-workers.

"Guys, this is Honey Reese, and you've heard her voice a thousand times without realizing it."

Honey introduced herself to everyone in Cher's contralto.

"Gosh," Jane said. "You sound exactly like Cher."

"Honey's the best. Her lips have done more celebrities than Lindsay Lohan's."

"And he's been telling that joke so long," Honey said to Jane, "that the first time I heard it, he referenced Linda Lovelace."

The board man played the scene several times until Honey had the voice down pat. Blake and Jane watched intently, as *mommy* became *Tommy*, *mother* became *brother*, and *she* and *her* became *he* and *him*. When Honey was finished, she and Charlie exchanged low-toned goodbyes at the door. As soon as she was gone, Maureen grinned at her father. "So, Dad, you and Honey?"

Blake and Jane also waited for his embarrassed answer. But Charlie's response was thoughtful and amused. "I had forgotten how smokin' hot Honey is." He turned toward Jane. "Kadoodlepeeper, make a note for me to call her next week. Okay, Blake, you're up."

Blake had never done an interview where the answers were pre-recorded. Charlie worked with him until his questions were looped in, the board man layered ambient stage sound under the video, and the four watched the finished product all the way through. It was perfect, and Blake, Jane and Maureen applauded. Charlie bowed, picked up an empty vase from the coffee table, and held it to his chest. "I'd like to thank the police academy for this award..."

Charlie and Jane hung around the station long enough for him to "dress the set." The half-flat of wanted posters and athletics sign-up notices was rolled into an interview room and parked against the wall. Libby handed him the copy of *The Hollywood Reporter* Eddie Chang had delivered. "Here's one of your 'plops'."

"Oh, jeez, did Eddie pull that crap on you? He speaks better English than I do. But he gets his jollies winding people up."

Charlie put *The Reporter* on the table next to the closed laptop that would soon air the world premiere of Ali's performance.

"What about her cell phone?" Jane asked.

Blake checked his watch. "Okay, it's 5:30 now and we'll start on Tommy by 6:00. Say, 7:00 o'clock you can release it back to her, Charlie."

"I have a driver on standby. Now, if you don't mind, I'm taking your girlfriend out to dinner. She's been a better assistant than most of my *real* assistants ever were."

Jane sketched a modest curtsy. "Good luck, you guys. Blake, I'll see you at home later."

Blake gave her a quick hug and a peck on the cheek, the most he was willing to do in front of Libby and Maureen. Once the door had closed behind them, Blake turned to his two co-stars. "I guess it's time to bring Lt. Rhee in on our plan."

The lieutenant was skeptical about the unusual approach, but he finally gave his permission for Blake to lead the second interview with Tommy Garcia. "That's only because he's not the main target. When Garland is brought in tomorrow, Libby and Jimbo do *that* interview by themselves and they follow all the Marquess of Queensberry rules. Agreed?"

"But O'Brien and I have—"

"Agreed?"

Blake sighed. Libby was perfectly capable of wrapping up the loose ends with Ali, but he hated having his mouse snatched away when he and Maureen had so cleverly catted it into a corner. "Agreed."

When Tommy was brought into the interview room—a different one, he noticed—he saw three serious-looking people sitting at the table across from the chair to which he was led by the cute Latina. Baldy to his left, a sort of familiar-looking guy in the middle, and hello there, Miss America, on his right. Where had he seen *her* before? Officer Ortiz uncuffed Tommy and he sat across from his inquisitors while she stepped back into a corner.

"December twenty-seventh, 6:08 P.M.," Libby said mechanically. "Second interview with Tomas, called Tommy, Garcia. Present in the room are Det. Blake Ervansky, Sgt. Maureen O'Brien and Det. Liberty Johnson."

"Good evening, Tommy," Blake said.

Tommy eyed Blake, then looked again at the redhead. Realization dawned, but he kept his face impassive. He wondered why the homicide cops who had tried to nail Ali were sitting in on a failed purse snatching.

"Maybe for you," he said levelly.

"I believe Det. Johnson spoke with you earlier about a break-in and a mugging."

"She did." Tommy turned to Libby with a

smile. "I thought you were gonna call in that actress and put me in a lineup."

"Changed my mind," Libby said.

"A lot of things have changed," Blake said. "We're not interested in trying to connect you to the break-in, now that we know it was staged."

What the hell, Tommy thought, though his face kept its neutral expression.

"Kind of like that little performance you and your sister put on outside the Starbucks." Blake saw uncertainty flicker in Tommy's eyes before his face retook the bland ground. "Yes, we know Ali's your sister. Half-sister if you want to go all hair-splitty. Tell me, you two ever get up north to visit your dad?"

Tommy kept his eyes locked on Blake's, determined to let nothing show. But his mind raced. How much did they know? Now Miss America leaned forward and spoke. "We asked Ali to come in for a lineup and guess what? She overheard one of our guys mention you were in a holding cell. Imagine our surprise when she started singing like a birdie. Sat right where Det. Ervansky is and said you masterminded that whole Dev Roberts shooting."

Tommy leaned back, confident they were on a fishing expedition. In a million years, Ali would never sell him out. "Bull. What time did you bring her in today?"

Libby pretended to check the file. "11:15. We picked her up at her house."

Now he knew for sure they were jerking him around. Ali's screen test was at eleven and she would have left home by 10:30. He relaxed.

"Gosh, Tommy," Blake said, "you look like you don't believe us. I'll bet that's because she told you she was doing a screen test." He smiled at Libby. "With Spielberg, if you can believe it."

Libby chuckled. "Is that the reason she gave for postponing the trip to Vail, Tommy?"

Tommy's heart beat faster as he looked at baldy, then back at the other two. This was some kind of trap, but how did they have so much information? Time to show them he knew they were gaming him. "Yes, Ali's my sister, but so what? And don't waste your cop head games on me. I *know* she had a screen test today. While you were supposedly picking her up at her house, she was already at Paramount."

Blake nodded to Libby, who picked up *The Hollywood Reporter*, opened it, then slid it across to Tommy. Highlighted in neon yellow was an article titled "DreamWorks to Shoot in Czech Republic." Tommy quickly scanned the article, which said Steven Spielberg had left yesterday to begin shooting his newest film. Tommy's eyes darted to the date at the top of the page. The twenty-third, four days ago.

Blake saw the kid trying to contain his panic, so he pressed harder. "Tommy, there was *never* going to be a trip to Vail. She lied to you."

"No," he said, voice beginning to go shaky. "We just postponed it until tomorrow."

"Really?" Blake turned toward Maureen. "Show him."

Maureen pulled out Tommy's phone and handed it to him. "Check your voicemail, dude."

He listened to Ali saying she had to talk to him about Vail.

"You think she's calling to remind you to bring warm underwear?" Maureen asked.

Tommy set the phone down, his mouth

suddenly very dry.

"I think he's beginning to catch on," Blake said to Libby. "All this time she's had him convinced the two of them were scamming *us* when she was actually scamming *him*."

Shut up, shut up, Tommy thought. Give me a minute to think. But Miss America took another run at him.

"Poor Ali. She thought the gun was going to shoot blanks. That she was going to yank the yanksters. She says *you* loaded the gun, Tommy. *You* put the real bullets in it."

They had meant it to sound like an Ali lie, but from the expression on Tommy's face, they knew he *had* been the one to load the gun, a bonus Blake capitalized on. "The remaining rounds in the gun are being tested. Are your fingerprints going to be on those shells?"

Tommy felt himself sweating. How did they know he had loaded the gun unless Ali really *had* told them? What the hell was going on? He saw the bald woman open the laptop and key something in. She then turned it around so he could see the screen. "This was shot a couple hours ago," she said.

Tommy heard the male detective's voice asking questions, then he saw his sister lying her ass off. Making it look like *he* had planned everything, like *she* was the dupe. His eyes darted from the wanted posters and notices behind Ali to the ones behind Blake. He should have felt anger, but all he felt was sadness. The only person in the world he had ever been able to depend on had turned against him and was "acting"—her word for lying—like she was the victim here. He knew she had done it a million times, but always to others, never him. When the piece ended, tears streamed down his face and he slumped in the chair.

"I have to talk to her," he sobbed. "Please let me talk to her."

"She's not here," Maureen volunteered. "We let her go."

"What? Why?"

"She convinced us she was innocent. *And* she gave us everything we need to convict you, so why would we hold her?"

"But it wasn't like that! I'm telling you, it *didn't happen like she said!"*

"Tommy," Blake said, voice gentle now. "Somebody's going to ride the needle for this murder. And right now, that somebody's looking a lot like you."

Ali's phone rang at 7:00. Tommy finally reporting in, she thought, but then she heard Charlie O'Brien's voice. "Ali, your cell is on its way back to you. The guy who took it was half-way to Big Bear when he realized he had the wrong phone. Sorry for the mix-up."

"That's all right. Thank you for tracking it down."

"See you Friday night at Steve's house."

"You bet. Bye, Charlie."

She hung up. Maybe Tommy had been leaving messages on the burner cell. Maybe that's why she hadn't heard from him.

When Tommy finally folded, he folded big. In less than an hour, he had given the police every detail of the crime his sister had planned and executed. The mystery of the six-month time-lapse between the break-in and the murder was cleared up at last.

After Dev had dumped her—and Tommy confirmed it had not been the amicable split the tabloids reported—Ali intended the break-in to be a little stunt to get her name in the papers again. She couldn't get any auditions, and she suspected Dev of poisoning studios against her, so she wanted to try for a bit of public sympathy. Brave girl defending herself against a thug in her own bedroom. Then that whole *Yanked* thing came along, and she saw a way to connect the two events and build a rock-solid alibi.

Blake had everything he needed to convict Ali except proof. Luckily, Tommy's sadness had turned to righteous anger during the gut-spilling, so he was now willing to wear a wire and get his sister to incriminate herself.

Ali tried to tip the guy who handed her the phone, but he declined, saying it had been his pleasure to drop it by. See? I'm already getting the deference due a star. Once the door closed, she checked her phone. Sure enough, there was a text from Tommy. *Out 4 the evening w/friends. Usual place? 2morrow 11 a.m.*

This was perfect. Much better to tell him face to face than over the phone that Vail was off. And it wasn't likely he would throw a hissy fit in a peaceful setting like the Lake Shrine.

Maureen saw the text first—*C U @ 11.* "That's Ali confirming."

"Okay," Blake said to Tommy. "If all goes as planned, we'll have proof against your sister, and you'll get off with a slap on the wrist."

"Someone needs to drive me back to the Marriott in the morning."

Tommy explained that Ali always waited at the same restaurant, watching for his bike to go by and turn onto Sunset. And his bike was in the parking garage at the hotel.

Ali slept like a baby. Her big break had finally arrived. Smoothing Tommy over would entail some work, but taking him to dinner at Spielberg's house ought to do the trick.

Awake in her bed, Maureen thought about the case wrapping up tomorrow, not sure how she felt about it. The freedom of being a private investigator, rather than an official cop, was pretty heady. She had always wanted to be like true-blue cop Danny Gunn, but when Maureen analyzed it, she realized it was P.I. Max Gunn she remembered and quoted all the time.

Blake drifted off listening to the regular sleep-breaths of his holiday housemate, thinking about that bonus and the engagement ring he would buy with it.

Tommy lay awake a long time, tossing and turning on the thin mattress of his cell cot. He thought about what he was going to do in the morning to the one who had always protected him from his father's wrath, the sister who had provided him with his admittedly cushy life. The only person who had always been on his side.

An acting teacher had once told him that love and hate were so close emotionally, any good performer should be able to slide from one to the other effortlessly. Now Tommy knew that was true, not only for acting, but in life. He had crossed from love to hate in a matter of hours, and felt no guilt about tomorrow. Let Ali find out what betrayal felt like.

Tommy knew that detective had lied to him. Slap on the wrist? Not bloody likely. His sister may have planned the murder, but he had been a willing participant every step of the way. If he was honest, he had been an enthusiastic participant, giving panache to the gay assistant, relishing his role as the CCTV inspector. And he had absolutely loved being a badass street punk for a day. If Ali got a lethal injection, he would probably do life without parole.

The intermittent swish-thunk of the wipers was the only sound in the car as they drove through the predawn chill and drizzle to pick up Tommy at the station. Maureen had handed Blake a steaming cup of Jamaican Blue as she slid into the car, careful not to spill hers as she buckled up. Blake had made the sign of the cross and murmured, "Bless you, my child."

Now they rode in silence, sipping their coffee and making good time in traffic thinned by the weather, the time and the holidays.

Finally, Maureen said, "Same as the day this all started."

"How's that?"

"You picked me up at 5:30, and we were supposed to bring in a felon."

"And look how great *that* turned out."

"Maybe no one will get shot in the face today and distract us."

The turn signal's rhythmic click joined the wipers for the few seconds before Blake headed south onto Crescent Heights Boulevard. "We did good work yesterday," he said. "The kid bought the whole package."

"That scrote is so dumb, he spells moron with a B," Maureen growled.

"A little early for Max, isn't it? He's usually still hung over this time of the morning."

"I've been thinking about Max a lot lately. How he left the force, became a P.I."

"Max Gunn didn't *leave* the police force. He was kicked off for boozing, brawling and shtupping the lady witnesses."

"You say those like they're *bad* things."

Blake glanced over, but Maureen stared out the window and took another sip of the Blue.

They waited in the sitting area of the hotel room while Tommy changed into his motorcycle leathers. He was subdued, not reacting as Blake patted him down. "It's nothing personal, Tommy. We don't want any surprises today."

"I understand."

"Any chance your sister will be packing?" Maureen asked.

"No. She hates guns. That's why I had to load hers the night before...*whatever*." After Tommy resnapped his Western-cut leather shirt, slipped on his jacket and picked up his helmet, the three headed for the elevator.

In the Marriott's underground parking garage, Blake pulled the car over to where his partner and Tommy stood next to a shiny red Suzuki V-Strom 1000. "If you try to run, all bets are off," Maureen told Tommy. "You know that, don't you?"

"I'm not going to run," he said quietly. Tommy put on his helmet, then pulled the chain attached to a key in one of the many pockets of the Hell's-Angels-lite jacket he wore. He reached toward the lockbox behind the seat.

"What are you doing?"

"Driving gloves. It's freezing out there."

"Go ahead."

Maureen noticed the Fox decal on the engine cowling, but was pretty sure this poser college-boy biker didn't even know what it stood for. Tommy popped the lockbox lid, reached in and took out a pair of black leather gloves long enough to cover his sleeves and seal out the wind. Tommy straddled the bike, turning over 996 cc's of liquid-cooled engine, while Maureen got back in the car with her partner. "Think he'll make a run for it?" Blake asked, following the bike out of the garage.

"Not a chance. That kid is well and truly squashed, another victim of the Divine Miss G."

Libby, her partner Jim and Det. Willis were with the com van in a restaurant parking lot about a ten-minute drive north of the turnoff to the Lake Shrine. As Blake pulled in after the motorcycle, he noticed someone had slapped a landscaping company logo on the side of the van, the better to make it invisible at its destination.

Jim was the communications expert. He got Tommy wired-up in the van while the four others huddled outside. At least the rain had stopped and the weak winter sun had upped the temperature to fifty.

"So, if I understand this correctly," Willis said, "we pick up a hot young actress, then bring her back to the station so I can drill her."

Three pairs of eyes turned to him with disgust.

"Did I say drill? I meant *grill.*"

They ran a sound check, getting nice, clear audio on the wire. Jim would monitor from the van. The other four would be able to hear what was being said, but would not be able to communicate with each other or with the van.

Libby and Willis took off first to get to the Lake Shrine thirty minutes early: the van was right behind them. At 10:40, Tommy started up the Suzi and rolled out. Blake and Maureen waited another ten minutes.

Libby watched from the dark-tinted window of the van as Tommy's bike pulled onto the gravel lot. Jimbo had parked out of the way at the far end, but she could still see Tommy as he dismounted and pulled the Suzuki back onto its stand. He took off his helmet and hung it on one of the hand grips, then pulled off his gloves. Libby saw him key a lockbox and fumble the gloves inside before putting his hands deep in his pockets and trudging toward the leafy bower that marked the entrance.

Five minutes later, Ali's BMW crunched over the gravel and parked a hundred feet from the bike. As she walked to the entrance, Jim told Blake to come ahead. Two minutes later, Blake and Maureen pulled in alongside the van where Libby and Willis stood waiting.

"There's only one way in and one way out," Blake said softly. "Since you're making the collar, you two take the exit. If Tommy stays on script, his sister will stroll right into your arms. Maureen and I will take the entrance in case the kid screws us and they both try to bolt."

"There are three civilian cars in the lot,"

Libby said, "so there may be other people on the path."

"Show them your badges and ask them to wait in the gift shop for a few minutes."

They entered the closed circular path around the lake, Libby and Willis going in through the exit door, Blake and Maureen taking the entrance.

Ali saw a young couple watching the swans, arms around each other's waist. They were already on the far side of the windmill and would be moving away from it when they started walking again. Across the lake a woman sat on a stone bench in the open foliage. She was in a lotus position, eyes closed, face turned to the anemic sun. A final sweep of the landscape, then Ali descended to the grotto.

Her brother stood as she entered, and she went to him and put her arms around him. "Ali," he breathed, wrapping her in an embrace and putting his face in her hair.

Blake and his partner walked in twenty feet, then stopped where they would wait and listen. He could see Libby and Willis do the same on the opposite side of the lake.

"I need to talk to you about the Vail trip." Ali's voice was low but clear in the earpieces of the five eavesdroppers.

"We're still leaving tonight, aren't we?" Tommy's voice now.

"Sit down, Tommy."

Rustling. Presumably, Tommy had joined his sister on the stone bench in the grotto.

"There isn't going to be a ski trip, but before you say a word, I've got something you're going to like even better. How would you feel about coming with me to Spielberg's house? He invited me to dinner Friday night, and I thought you could be my plus-one."

"Cool." Tommy's voice was flat.

Not much enthusiasm, Ali thought, but at least he isn't having a meltdown.

Lying to my face, Tommy thought, but at least it's the last time.

Not much of a salesman, Blake thought, but at least she doesn't suspect.

"So, we're set? You'll come with me?"

"Sure."

"Very dressy casual, I'd imagine. I'll leave you some cash so you can pick up what you need tomorrow."

"Okay."

"Tommy? What's wrong? You seem distracted."

Come on, kid, Blake silently prayed.

"I've been thinking about Dev and all. I mean about how we killed him."

"Jesus! Keep your voice down."

"Why? There's nobody here."

"Still, we have to be careful."

"Well, you know, this is something I need to talk about. You were out of touch for weeks after you shot him, and I was alone trying to deal with these terrible feelings. I can't tell my friends, I don't have a shrink. If you won't talk to me about this, I don't know *what* I'll do."

Once again, it's all about him, thought Ali. *I'd almost rather deal with a hissy fit than this whining self-doubt.* "Tommy, I'm sorry. With everything that's been happening, I guess I didn't give your feelings enough consideration."

Her voice was smooth, concerned. "Talk to me."

"I guess I'm wondering if there was any other way. I mean, did Dev Roberts really have to die?"

"You can ask that after all he did to me? You have the nerve to sit in judgment? Let me tell you something, bro, I'm not sorry I shot him. And I didn't notice *you* being all squeamish and ambivalent when we were planning the whole thing, either. Dev deserved to die, and I haven't lost a night of sleep over killing him. So you'd better suck it up and do the same."

Blake exchanged a smile with Maureen, breathing a sigh of relief. They had done it. Let Tommy make his goodbyes and they were home free.

"What the hell? Where did you get that?" Ali's voice, louder, afraid.

"Same place we got yours."

"No, Tommy, think about it. You do *not* want to do this."

"Surprisingly, I do."

Gun, Blake thought, Maureen and Libby realizing the same thing. As he took off running toward the windmill, the shot exploded, a boom of thunder that shattered the tranquility of The Lake Shrine, and sent a dozen swans flap-skittering across the surface of the water.

There was a lot of ground to cover, but Blake stretched out his long legs and pumped. He saw Libby doing the same from the other side, gun drawn. It was a race between the solid quadriceps of a point guard and the long, smooth leg muscles of a swimmer.

Tommy came up out of the grotto and turned toward the entrance, where he saw Blake fifty yards away and closing around the curve. Blake was unarmed—he'd kick his own ass about that later—but Tommy's arm was down, the gun dangling from his hand. *I have to barrel into him before he raises it.*

Tommy whirled in the other direction, running only ten or fifteen feet before he realized Baldy was coming at him from the other side, her gun up and aimed.

"DROP IT!" Libby screamed from forty yards out. "DROP YOUR WEAPON!"

Tommy froze, glancing back briefly at Blake—who still raced forward—then turned to Libby and began to raise his gun. No player had ever beaten Liberty J on the fast break, but even she couldn't outrun a bullet, Blake knew. He poured it on, intending to lower his shoulder and slam Tommy to the ground with a smash to the kidneys, fearing all the while he couldn't close the gap in time.

Libby ran on the uneven path, her gun bouncing too much to sight accurately. Blake was closing in behind the kid and if she missed Tommy she might hit Blake. She prayed the same bouncing gait that was throwing off her aim would make her more difficult to hit.

While Tommy brought his weapon up, and Libby and Blake ran on a curved collision course, Maureen and Willis chose routes more suited to their shorter inseams. With his gun drawn, Willis bolted through low foliage in a straight line across the inside of the circle, between the path and the lake. He was shorter and slower than Libby, but he knew as long as he didn't trip over some Krishna-looking garden gnome, his diameter would intersect her circumference before the kid could take his shot.

Maureen took the high road. She couldn't shoot from the path with Blake between her and Tommy, but by scaling the hillside that angled up steeply from the lake, she hoped to be able to fire over Blake's head. And although her left brain accepted that she would have to kill a man to save Blake and Libby, a voice in her right brain—one that sounded a lot like her own four years ago—screamed: *Not again! Not again! Not again!*

A thundering lie claimed all three shots fired simultaneously, but that was only their incredibly tight overlaps creating a confluence of sound as two bullets tore into human targets and the third bit into stone.

If you could have captured the moment with multiple cameras, then edited the videos to analyze the separate actions, this is what you would have seen. First, Willis, launching himself across the path, slamming his body into Libby's right shoulder, then shooting high to miss Blake. Tommy fired while Libby and Willis were both still airborne, Libby flying sideways, slamming into a decorative rock, and Willis, falling from his leap, catching Tommy's bullet in the chest before touchdown.

Feet apart, braced on the sloping hillside, watching Blake crouch as if to get out of her way, Maureen raised her Browning Hi-Power and sent a single 9-millimeter round jetting toward the back of Tommy's neck.

As Blake's left shoulder connected with Tommy's lower back, he felt the hard slam of a bullet above his right temple. By the time Blake had crashed to the ground with Tommy under him, he couldn't see out of his right eye for the blood pouring down the side of his face.

The only one unhurt, Maureen scrambled down the slope, running to the closest injury as he staggered to his feet. "I'm hit," Blake said.

She stopped long enough to swipe her hand across his scalp, clearing blood and hair out of the way to see the wound. "It didn't go in. Check Willis." She crouched over Tommy and put two fingers to his carotid, already knowing from the entry wound and the pool of blood under him that she had put the bullet exactly where she had intended to. A second later, she was up and running toward Libby, who lay sprawled on the ground, unconscious, but still breathing. Maureen turned to Blake. "How's Willis?"

"Christ, it's bad."

She cut over to Blake, dropping to her knees, and immediately ripping open the front of Willis' shirt.

"Oh, shit," Maureen said when she saw bubbles frothing the blood that oozed from the hole in his chest. Glancing around, she saw a tropical-looking plant with giant, shiny, heart-shaped leaves. She dashed to the plant and yanked one of the leaves from a thick stem, shredding her palm on its tiny barbs. Crossing back to Willis, she put the glossy side of the leaf against his chest, sealing the hole. "Press here and hold it tight. His lung's been hit and you need to keep the seal." Blake flattened his hands against the leaf while Maureen darted away, pressing her own hand to her hip to stop the bleeding. Her triage wasn't over yet.

Plunging down into the semidarkness of the grotto, she saw Ali crumpled on the floor.

Maureen dropped to her knees again, but even without great lighting she could see the woman had been gut-shot. From the look of it, Tommy must have pushed the barrel right into her belly before pulling the trigger. Small gasps of air were being taken in by Ali's mouth, but the puffs she labored out were more blood than air.

Maureen heard the distant scream of the ambulance, knowing it wouldn't get there fast enough to save Ali. Attempting to show compassion, she put her uninjured hand on the dying woman's shoulder. Ali opened her eyes, slowly focusing on the face above her. Recognition hardened her features, and she managed to literally spit out her last three words.

"You. Fucking. Bitch."

Her face and body went slack. Maureen, who had once read that hearing was the last of the senses to go when someone died, leaned close to Ali's ear and whispered, "Right back at you, babe."

On her feet again and up out of the grotto, she raced over to Blake. "I'll take over here; you see to Libby." She lifted the leaf for a second and saw blood still bubbled, but no worse than before. She pressed her makeshift seal back against the wound, wincing as her lacerated hand flattened on the leaf, aware that Blake was helping Libby to her feet. Libby's left shoulder was obviously dislocated, and she grimaced as she stood up. Two ambulances screeched into the parking lot and Maureen knew the gurneys would be there in a minute. She took Det. Willis' hand, trying to encourage him to hold on.

"Ali?" Blake called over.

"On her way to hell." She turned back to

Willis, realizing she didn't even know his first name. "Hang in there, guy. The ambos are here." She thought she saw his eyelids flicker. "Can you hear me, Willis? If you can hear me, squeeze my hand."

There was no squeeze, but his lips moved, so Maureen leaned down, putting her ear an inch from his lips.

The words were weak but they were clear. "Put something more interesting in my hand O'Brien, and I'll show you a squeeze."

They could hear the crossing of the sirens somewhere out on Sunset. The outgoing carried Libby and Willis to UCLA Medical, and the incoming were bringing the police. Libby's partner manned the entrance, keeping out the lookie-loos and trying to calm a bunch of less-than-serene bald men in saffron robes. The two bodies lay where they had fallen.

Blake held a sterile compress to the right side of his head as he kneeled and looked at the entrance wound on the back of Tommy's neck. The 9-millimeter slug had cleanly severed the cervical spine—right at C-2, he guessed—then passed through the front of his throat, killing him instantly. Maureen had been sixty feet out and teetering on an incline, so either this was the luckiest shot in history or there were things about his partner he didn't know.

"I thought you turned in your gun when I did," he said.

"I turned in *a* gun."

Definitely things he didn't know about her. He stood, and they tried to do a quick assessment before the place was crawling with

CSI and tied up with yellow ribbon.

"Okay, my round exited his throat in a steep, downward angle, but you hit him at the same time, launching him forward, so the brass is going to be under the body."

"The bullet from Tommy's .38 is still in Willis," Blake said.

"And Willis fired upwards to scare Tommy and avoid hitting you."

"So where did the fourth bullet come from? The one that tagged me?"

"There were only three shots. I'm positive on that," Maureen said.

"Then it had to be the bullet Willis fired."

"Not possible. He aimed sixty degrees up and away from you."

"If it isn't in my skull, it has to be here somewhere."

Careful not to disturb anything, they bent and searched the ground near where Blake had been when he was hit.

"I got something," Maureen called out.

Her gauze-wrapped hand gingerly pushed aside the leafy arm of a low fern, revealing a cylindrical object in the dirt. It was three inches long, a little bigger around than a crayon, and it had a streak of blood running end to end.

"What the hell is *that*?" Blake asked.

Already they could hear the slamming of squad car doors, so they quickly straightened to scan the hillside. The only thing on the landscaped incline was a statue of Jesus fifteen feet up the slope. His right hand rested over His heart, and His left was raised beside His head. The son of God had apparently been captured in the act of reciting the Aramaic pledge of allegiance. Blake and Maureen saw that the middle finger was missing from His upraised hand, sheared off cleanly at the knuckle.

As uniformed officers flooded onto the path near the entrance and surged toward them, Maureen turned to her partner.

“Lightning bolts are *so* last millennium.”

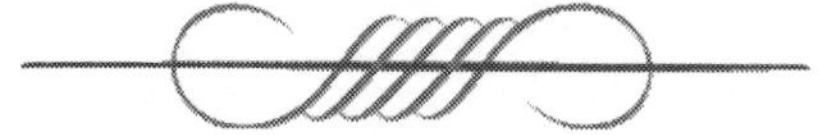

About the Authors

Marsha Lyons and April Kelly were debate team partners at Colonial High School in Orlando and roomies at The University of South Florida, before Marsha went to law school on a mission and April went to Hollywood on a whim.

While Marsha's career includes teaching at the FBI Academy at Quantico, becoming the youngest Assistant U.S. Attorney in Miami, and going into private legal practice, April's began in stand-up comedy, moved into writing on shows such as Mork & Mindy and Webster, then to producing her own shows like Boy Meets World.

Throughout their wildly different professional lives Marsha and April have remained best friends, finally deciding to put their separate talents together to write MURDER IN ONE TAKE, the first novel of their award-winning show-biz crime series.

Marsha is married with children, and April is single with dogs.

MURDER: TAKE TWO

by

April Kelly and Marsha Lyons

What has six legs, black stripes and kills people? A homicidal magician and the biggest tiger in his world-famous show. Murder will be hard to prove, though, because the dead guy never existed, all the evidence seems to have been eaten, and the victim's corpse isn't the only thing that has disappeared.

When Maureen O'Brien suddenly vanishes, P.I. Blake Ervansky learns about her shocking former life, a past he doesn't think he can live with. Then, before he can tell her their partnership is over, a call from a client in hysterics reveals that a recently solved case has come messily unsolved.

Putting aside their own differences, Blake and Maureen circumvent a corrupt sheriff and draw closer to the truth, until Blake winds up in a deadly game of cat-and-mouse in which he's the mouse, and the cat outweighs him by 400 pounds. It's a cage match he won't survive unless the skills Maureen learned in her dark past can neutralize the killer before Blake becomes cat chow.

Please turn the page if you would like to read the opening chapters of MURDER: TAKE TWO.

MURDER: TAKE TWO

Kelly and Lyons return to their distinctive brand of mystery starring the LA-based duo (Maureen O'Brien and Blake Ervansky) who combine traditional investigation with the Hollywood perspective. Darker than its predecessor, this installment doesn't sacrifice the humor or turns of phrase that were the hallmarks of the first. Tight and sharp-witted.

— *Kirkus Reviews*

MURDER: TAKE TWO

Fat, languid drops splatted on the taut skins of the dozen or so umbrellas surrounding the open grave on a gentle slope in a cemetery just a few miles northwest of Los Angeles.

Funny thing about rain. On a sweltering August afternoon in Miami, a half-hour cloudburst feels like a bracing splash of Jean Naté after a steamy shower. A New York City downpour is nature's car wash, sluicing off the top layer of grime on buildings and sidewalks, flushing tons of urban scunge down into the sewers. And anything short of a flood-producing deluge in Kansas is welcome as a layer-down of dust and provider of beverage service for thirsty stalks of corn.

Los Angeles rain is just liquid depression. The parched months of June through October gasp for it but get no relief, proof of the old saying that you can carve a city out of the desert, but you can't carve the desert out of the city. LA rain perversely dumps its payload in December, January and February, honing that suicidal edge ever-present in the shortest, darkest, coldest months of the year.

The late-January funeral of Sol Fein was presided over by an unusual team of clergy: Rabbi Michael Goldberg and Father Daniel Flynn, two men who had not met before that day. Sol had gone peacefully in his sleep, and it was only after his passing the truth came out: he wasn't Jewish; he had been born to Italian-Catholic parents and was christened Gianni Salvatore Fierro ninety-four years earlier.

When Salvatore came back from World

War II and tried to break into radio comedy writing, he found the all-Jewish fraternity closed, so he legally changed his name, then crashed the party when television started looking less like a passing fancy and more like the future.

Sol (nee Sal) had attended a synagogue in Encino the requisite twice a year to keep his ultra-reform Jewish alter-ego believable, but it was at a tiny church in Canoga Park where he did his infrequent communicating with God.

Maureen O'Brien walked over to the large tray of long-stemmed roses as the service officially ended, picking up a red bloom and stepping to the edge of the open grave. Sol had always called her "the daughter of my heart," and began teaching her the mysteries of comedy when she was barely three years old. And so it was with exquisite timing and misdirection that she held out the rose, while pulling something else from inside her coat and dropping it into the rectangular hole.

Both clergymen gasped when the rubber chicken flopped onto the brass-fitted mahogany casket, but a sputter of relieved laughter ran through the crowd of mourners. Maureen stepped back, still holding the red rose, as her father took her place graveside. From under his coat, Charlie O'Brien retrieved a partially inflated Whoopie Cushion. Holding it between his hands, he quickly popped his palms together, birthing a plaintive quack-fart as a salute and farewell to the man who had been his mentor and friend, who had given him his first sitcom job, and who had helped him raise his daughter.

The flabby rubber bladder plopped onto the coffin alongside the limp chicken, bringing another round of chuckles, then an old man's voice piped up from under the canopy of umbrellas. "Sol Fein never met a fart joke he didn't like." This was followed by murmurs of confirmation and a second reedy male voice. "You mean he never met a fart joke he didn't *steal.*"

A-a-and, they're off, thought Charlie. He and Maureen had conspired to lessen the ache of loss for these elderly mourners by sidetracking them into schtick so familiar it was comforting. Even Ethel Rosen, Sol's "younger woman" for the last fifteen years of his life, edged her walker to the side of the grave and addressed the coffin. "I'd throw myself on your casket, Sol, but I can't afford the broken hip."

As the jokes flew fast and hard, the two horrified clergymen withdrew, leaving only two "civilians" at the service, Maureen's business partner, Blake Ervansky, and Blake's fiancée, Jane. They had only met Sol Fein twice, once at Thanksgiving and again at Charlie's New Year's Eve party, but they had been charmed by the still-sharp old man, and were happy to answer Charlie's call for younger, able-bodied people to assist the mourners in and out of the four stretch limousines that now idled a short distance away.

The stand-up routine petered out after a few minutes, standing up being a challenge for most of those present, so Charlie waved at the line of limousines. All four drivers got out in the now-pouring rain to assist Charlie, Maureen, Blake and Jane as they loaded their frail passengers into warm and comfy transportation for the short ride to the restaurant Charlie had bought out for the wake.

In the general confusion of loading up, of putting wet umbrellas into trunks, of trying to collect and properly stow walkers, wheelchairs, and oxygen tanks, no one noticed a fifth limousine as it approached on the narrow cemetery road, stopped briefly alongside the Fein mourners then slowly pulled away.

Blake got Jane tucked into the last limo and shut the door. Charlie and Maureen were assigned the first and second cars, which were just pulling out, so Blake ran to his, the third in line. But just as he reached it, he spotted something on the ground where Maureen's limo had been until a moment ago. He darted ahead and scooped up a cell phone, leaving behind the red rose that had been next to it. Blake dropped the phone into his pocket and splashed back to his ride.

The bustle and confusion of the load-up replayed at the restaurant as the four limos decanted their cargo, so it was another few minutes before Charlie looked around for his daughter. When he didn't see her, he allowed five more minutes for a possible ladies' room stop before approaching Blake.

"Have you seen Maureen?"

"Not since we were loading up."

"Who else rode in the second limo with her?"

Blake remembered lifting up an elderly woman and getting her settled into the car before Maureen told him she could handle the rest. "I know Ethel was there, and a couple other girls whose names I'm not sure of."

"Thanks."

As Charlie crossed to Ethel Rosen, Blake went back to help Jane fill plates at the lavish buffet and deliver them to the tables. Arriving mid-joke, Maureen's father waited patiently until Max Keller got to the punch line.

"—so the crab says to the starfish, 'Hey, I can't get that drunk *every* night!'"

Even those who had heard it before laughed, needing the pressure release to keep their tears at bay. Charlie leaned down to Ethel Rosen. "Hey, Eth, did you see where Maureen went when she got out of your limo?"

"She wasn't in mine."

"But I saw her go around and open the door just as my car was pulling out."

"Oh, the door opened all right, but then it closed, so we figured she was going to ride with someone else."

The sick feeling in Charlie's gut showed plainly on his face, and Ethel laid a fragile, spotted hand on his arm. "Charlie, is everything all right?"

"Yeah, don't worry. I'm sure she's around here somewhere."

He turned away, pulling out his cell phone, then hit speed dial one. He heard the familiar ring—the theme song of his TV show *The Brothers Gunn*—but when he glanced around the room and saw Blake pull a phone out of his pocket and answer it, Charlie's heart sank.

"Hello," Blake said into the phone. No answer, and before he could say anything else, Charlie was next to him.

"That's Maureen's phone," he said.

"I know. She must have dropped it getting into the limo because I found it right after she pulled out."

"She wasn't in the car, Blake."

"Then where is she?"

Charlie seemed about to say something, then abruptly changed tack. "Look, this is really important. Tell me anything you can remember in the moments before you found her phone."

The anxiety in Charlie's voice told Blake what he needed to know about the seriousness of the situation. Charlie was usually the most laid-back, easygoing guy in the world. "Okay, when I left her, she was getting Ethel settled in the second limo. I went back to the last one to give Jane a hand, and when she was loaded up I headed to my own car. I saw Maureen close the right-hand door on hers, then walk around to get in on the other side."

"Did you actually see her get in?"

Blake closed his eyes for a few seconds, trying to bring the picture into focus. "No. But I'm sure I heard the car door open and then close. Your limo was pulling out when I closed the right-hand door on mine. Then Maureen's pulled away while I was running around the back of mine to get in the other side. That's when I saw the cell phone."

"Think hard. What else did you see? Even if it doesn't seem important."

"There was a rose on the ground next to the phone."

Charlie remembered Maureen had held onto her red rose after tossing the rubber chicken into the grave. "Did you see anyone else? Anyone who didn't belong to our party?"

"No. The cemetery was pretty empty because of the rain." Then Blake suddenly remembered. “There *was* another limousine. I mean, not one of ours. It passed very slowly going in the other direction.”

“Did you notice if it stopped?”

“I wasn’t looking. I assume the driver slowed down because the road was narrow and he didn’t want to hit anyone, but I can’t say for sure the car stopped.”

Charlie deflated. “It stopped,” he said to himself.

“What the hell is going on? And where’s Maureen?”

Turning away, Charlie said, “Not here, and not now.”

Maureen did not try to engage either of her captors in conversation. She knew they would have been instructed to say nothing, so she sat—wedged in between their muscled bulks—and waited for the next scene in this stupid little play. She hoped Blake had found her phone; it wouldn’t give Charlie complete peace of mind, but at least he would know she was alive and that she’d be coming back. Eventually.

She glanced to either side. They looked like dumb thugs in dark glasses and cheap suits, but they had made the grab flawlessly, and she knew the kind of skill you needed to snatch someone without an attention-drawing kerfuffle. I guess when your neck is wider than your head, Maureen realized, there are only two choices: defensive linebacker or this.

The limousine stopped smoothly near a parked gray sedan. The driver of the sedan got out, pulled his coat up over his head, then made the short run to the idling limo. As soon as he slid into the seat across from Maureen, he tossed his wet coat aside, reached up to rap his knuckles sharply on the closed privacy panel, and sat back while the limousine pulled away.

The man's thin-lipped smile held no hint of warmth as his eyes locked with Maureen's. "So, how are you?"

"Fuck you and the snake you rode in on."

"Dear me. One would think you're not having a good day."

"You snatched me from a funeral. A *funeral!*"

"What did you expect? You don't return my calls, you ignore my texts."

"That's because I don't want to talk to you."

"Well, in the words of Mick Jagger, you don't always get what you want. Oh, I'm sorry. Is the reference before your time?"

"I know who the Stones are."

"Excellent. Excellent."

She glared at this nightmare from her past, a man she had worked for but whose real name she had never known. His nom de guerre was Lionheart, as unsuitable a handle as possible for such an ambulatory puddle of slime. He hadn't changed much in the four years since she last saw him. The telltale tufts of his latest crop of hair plugs sprouted across his crown, failing to blend into the thinning natural hair with even a glimmer of verisimilitude. The overpowering smell of the breath mints he favored filled the car. "I'd like you to do a small job for me, and then I'll whisk you back home posthaste."

"A job."

"The usual."

"I don't work for you anymore."

"True, true. And I remember what you said to me when you quit. 'Lionheart,' you said, 'my dear, dear friend and respected employer, I really and truly can no longer do the work.'"

"*That's* what you remember me saying?"

"Well, I might be a little bit fuzzy on the endearments, but I'm very sure you said you were unable to continue doing the work. So, imagine my surprise when I read you had killed a man a few days after Christmas." The thin lips stretched into an even bigger nonsmile as he watched her seethe.

"That was a righteous takedown to save a police officer. The man I shot had just murdered his own sister and put a bullet in a detective."

"Compelling reasons. Once again you prove you are willing and able to snuff out a life when the cause is just."

"The answer is no."

He nodded slowly, as if he were lost in his own private thoughts. When he looked into her eyes again, his "smile" was gone. If it had been anyone other than Lionheart, she might have said his eyes were filled with sorrow. Or a shred of humanity.

"Please say yes, Maureen. Don't make me turn over the next card. I promise you I have the winning hand."

"I'm not afraid of you."

"I know that," he said. "You should be, but you never were."

"The answer is still no."

Lionheart sighed. "Okay, here's the flop.

Let me tell you a story about Charlie O'Brien."

Maureen felt as though she had taken a punch to the gut, and her response was immediate. "If you threaten my father," she said quietly, "I will kill you. Right here, right now, and before your meat puppets even get their earplugs out."

Lionheart was impressed. She had rightly figured out that his "aides" could hear nothing of their conversation, an extra security precaution he had only begun taking recently. He was smart to have chosen her; she was the best of the bunch.

"Maureen, Maureen," he said, shaking his head and putting the smile facsimile back on his face.

"You think I'm joking? As long as I keep my body poised as if we're having a friendly chat, they'll never know I'm about to strike. And when I do, as you well know from the training you put me through, I will kill you in two seconds."

"Then we'll both be dead in three. And just think what that will do to this lovely upholstery. What do you think, fine Corinthian leather?" he asked disingenuously, brushing his hand over the seat next to him.

"Read my middle finger, the answer is no."

"First, let me assure you I do not intend to threaten your father. It's *you* I'll threaten with what I have on *him*."

"It won't work."

"No? All right, if you won't fold, I'll show you the turn card. Once, when your father was younger—but certainly old enough to know better—he was involved in an ugly incident for which the statute of limitations will *never* expire."

"You're bluffing."

"I do not bluff. And if you ever decide you want a peek at the river card, just run the name Rhonda Whiting by your father and watch his face. Spoiler alert. Afterwards your relationship with Charlie will never be the same. Think of it as the Pandora's Box effect."

Lionheart reached into his pocket and pulled out a roll of eucalyptusy-reeking hard candies. He popped a fresh one into his mouth, then extended the roll toward Maureen. "Mint?"

She glared at him, her insides a roiling pit of conflict. Could he really have something on Charlie? And if so, would her continued refusal put her father in danger? Lionheart watched as she weighed her options, detecting the precise moment when she chose to throw herself on the grenade to save her father. Maureen slumped back against the seat. "What's the job?"

Lionheart's smile was genuine this time. Winning made him happy. "Do you like the beach, Maureen? Well, of course you do, you're a California girl. I have a jet fueled and ready to take you to a place of sun and sand. Sadly, though, no ocean."

Ah, hell, Maureen thought. The Middle East. Again.

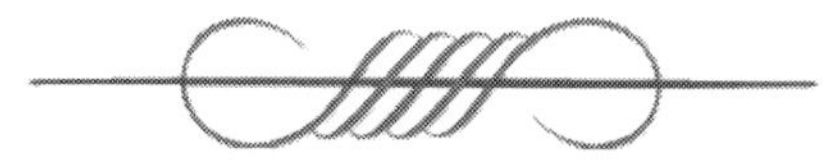

WINGED
by
April Kelly

What if the cavalier decision you made about your child the day she was born had the power to reverberate for more than thirty years, dividing the nation, costing three people their lives, and destroying your family?

Homeless teen Allison Fitzgerald believes the two tiny membranes on her baby's back are not, as the doctors claim, a surgically correctable birth defect, but a pair of wings. And after having a vision of her child flying, she names her Angel.

The "wings" will never flap, fly or lift the child off the ground, but they will engender in Angel a dangerous obsession with flying, an obsession that will one day drive her to attempt the impossible.

A darkly comic contemporary reframing of the Icarus and Daedalus myth, WINGED explores the lengths to which a mother will go to protect her child, and ultimately offers a message of salvation, not just for the family involved, but for all mankind.

Please turn the page if you would like to read the opening chapter of WINGED.

2014 FIRST PLACE WINNER
GENERAL FICTION
Kindle Book Promo/LuckyCinda
International Contest

"Kelly's fast-paced novel takes the reader on a flight of fancy couched in realistic, straightforward and graceful prose that makes the fantastic utterly believable. It's hard to stop reading...fasten your seat belt for an enjoyable flight."

—Kirkus Reviews

"The strong voice speaking from the pages of Winged, by April Kelly, immediately captures both interest and sympathy…with cliffhangers that keep the reader turning pages breathlessly. Winged seizes the imagination because of its unusual premise, but it wins our hearts because it is, after all…the story of the universal need to pursue passions and dreams, often at a high cost."

—Southern Literary Review

WINGED

Smile patronizingly at my naming her Angel, but remember I was only eighteen and my child *was* born with wings. Well, the doctor didn't call them wings. He called them a congenital anomaly and recommended they be surgically removed before we left the hospital.

I had never heard the word anomaly before, and I only recognized three syllables of congenital, the three that had gotten me in trouble nine months earlier when two other twelfth-grade girls and I had crashed a fraternity party where I downed about a dozen drinks that must have been ninety-nine percent wine and only one percent cooler.

The drugs they gave me during the birth—more to shut me up than to ease any pain, I suspect—impaired my ability to detect reactions from either doctor or nurses that would have indicated I had just expelled a freak. The words penetrating my mushy consciousness gave no clue there was a problem: *girl, umbilical, Apgar, turkey sub.* One of the nurses may have been placing her lunch order.

Three hours later I was stitched up, cleaned up, and sitting up when a nurse brought me a pink wrappy thing with a tiny head sticking out one end. Immediately upon off-loading the bundle to me, she gave a tight smile and left. I had just enough time to register the features of the squinched little face before the doctor approached my bed, his own face fixed in a squinch. It looked better on the baby.

Once he had pulled the curtain around my ward bed—broke teenagers who can't even come up with a babydaddy name for the birth certificate don't rate the premium accommodations—the doc began a rambling tale about how some babies are born with webbing between their fingers or toes, and that it was customary to do the simple surgical repairs before they left the hospital.

"So what are you saying? She has duck feet?"

"No, no, no." He seemed panicked by my question. "Her fingers and toes are fine. It's just that she has two very small membranous flaps on her back that we'd like to remove."

"I want to see them."

"I have to discourage that, Miss Fitzgerald. These congenital anomalies are routine for medical personnel, but for a new mother, especially one as young as..."

He might have said more, but I was already freeing my child from the pastel cotton burrito into which she had been stuffed. Once unswaddled, her little arms and legs did a bit of slow-motion waving, and her mouth opened in a gummy yawn, while the doctor held out a clipboard and asked me to sign the consent form.

I gently turned her over to place her on her stomach on my stomach and saw them for the first time: wings.

It wasn't much of an argument. I had only turned eighteen two months earlier, but I knew I was an adult in the eyes—if not the common sense—of the law, and that I had the right to say no to the mutilation of my child. Frustrated, the doctor left and I was finally alone with her.

Still facedown and sleeping on me, her tiny form rode the rise and fall of my belly as I breathed. One arm curved alongside her head, fist extended, and the rhythmic movement combined with the facedown, arm-out position made me think of Superman flying.

I wish I could say I had some warm and maternal feeling for that little stranger, but I didn't. There was a vague sense of obligation to handle her carefully, but no more than when I had held a puppy or a kitten as a child. No, the only feeling I had was a curiosity about her, an interest in this creature created solely by me. Well, by me and some unknown Sigma Tau Gamma.

The doc had been accurate in calling them membranous flaps. Though they matched the cream and pink mottle of her back, they looked more reptilian than human: two tiny triangles of skin which emerged from either side of the small knobs of her upper spine, then curved and hugged her shoulder blades. I gently stroked one with the tip of my index finger, Brailling the info to my brain. Not as soft as I thought they would be, and with the slightest of ridges along the sides, like piping under the skin. When I slipped my fingernail under the edge and lifted the flap, there was a small amount of tensile strength in it, enough to snug it back in place when I took my finger away.

I carefully turned her back over and her arms and legs began that slo-mo dog paddle again. Cradling her against me, I took in the brownish fuzz that capped her head, one piece in front almost long enough for my licked fingertip to paste into a curl. I examined the minuscule diaper, deciding it looked like the one worn by the wetting doll I got for Christmas when I was five.

I leaned over to check out the itty-bitty eyelashes, so we were almost nose to nose when she opened her eyes. We both flinched, and I pulled back far enough to focus. The cliché caught me off guard, that intense rush of love that bonded me to her instantly. That alone would have been a powerful enough experience, albeit shared with virtually every other new mother since the beginning of time. But that was only the first jab of the one-two punch that changed my life forever; the tap that laid me out was looking into her eyes and seeing my own face—twice, tiny—reflected back. Not the face I had then, but my future face, the one that bends over a yellow pad tonight as I sit on this bunk and scribble out my life. Was that future me trying desperately to communicate answers to questions teen me had not yet begun to ask? Before I averted my eyes to break that frightening connection, three powerful thoughts surged into me: one, that this child would save me; two, that I would be willing to give up my own life for her; and three, that I would one day see her fly. All three have come true, but not in a way I could ever have imagined.

A tall, silver-haired priest was the next person to try to persuade me to have my daughter's wings removed. As I was in a Catholic hospital, I was not surprised to see a priest, but from the embarrassed look on Father Paul's face, he *was* surprised to see a female breast. Hey, what could I do? It was snack time for the kidlet, and an open ward doesn't offer a heck of a lot of privacy.

Father Paul was almost too easy a target. When he speculated that my daughter would be teased by her school chums—he actually used that word, chums—when they learned of her secret deformity, I countered by claiming to be reluctant to interfere with God's plan.

"If He created her this way, how can we mere mortals presume to improve on His plan? And she isn't deformed; she has a pair of wings."

"Allison, you can't actually believe they're wings. That defies logic."

"Oh, right. But a pregnant virgin and a dead guy waking up after three days make perfect sense. Sorry, padre, but I'm sticking with the wings theory."

I'm not sure if it was my blasphemy or the sight of my swollen, blue-veined boob as the baby finished brunch and lolled away from it, but the good father stood quickly, scraping his chair back. I'm sure part of him wanted to stay and fight for the soul of a child born to so obviously a lost-cause mother, but I also sensed the larger part of him would be relieved to get back to the terminal patients who welcomed his comforting words. I decided to absolve him of my sins.

"I'm naming her Angel."

Camel's back, meet the straw. Father Paul didn't have much of a poker face and, looking appalled, he choked out a tight blessing, then exited ward left.

I had only said it to be a bitch, but when micro girl burped in her sleep and I looked down at the milk bubble inflating and deflating in the corner of her mouth, I figured Angel was as good a name as any. You don't have to believe in God to believe in angels.

I had three days in the hospital getting to know her, learning how to take care of her basic needs, and wondering where we could go when St. Luke's threw us out. Brian's mom and dad had been amazing, letting me stay at their house when I started looking like I was hiding a basketball under my shirt and my own parents ejected me from their vinyl-sided Eden (with detached garage), but Brian was taking early college entrance and I could hardly ask Mr. and Mrs.

Haywood to let me stay on with the bambina. Nice as they were, I knew half the reason they invited me in the first place was their fervent, long shot hope that Bri was the father. They clung to the belief that being gay was a phase he would snap out of and that Greg was just his study buddy.

Brian came to the hospital the day after Angel was born, carrying a bouquet of daisies for me and a really inappropriate teddy bear in a black leather onesie for her. That was the day he told me he was leaving for Berkeley the following week. We had been good friends since the tenth grade, and his departure would bring me down to zero in the best-buds department, as Heather and Chelsea—my two partners in the great frat party debacle—had been forbidden to have any contact with me since our drunk and disorderly escapade. Most of the rest of my semifriends had pulled back when my pregnancy became obvious, with the few holdouts falling away when the principal told me I could no longer be a Gettysburg Cougar. (Go, silver and blue!) I think it was less that the other kids were judgmental and more that we didn't see each other every day at school anymore. Face it, the foundation for ninety-five percent of all high school friendships is proximity.

I bonded with Angel, ate instant oatmeal and green Jell-O, and resisted two more attempts by the doctor to change my mind about removing the wings. On the fourth morning I was released. I stood on the steps of St. Luke's Hospital without a home, a job, a clue, a high school diploma, a family or friends.

But I had my baby and, thanks to me, she still had her wings.

Jesus, I wish I had listened to that doctor.

APRIL KELLY'S NEXT BOOK

THE LAST FIRST KISS: STORIES SHORT AND TWISTED

will be available January 2015

Made in the USA
Charleston, SC
21 March 2015